BAD
BLOOD
RISING

Best Wishes

Eva Carmichael

BAD
BLOOD
RISING

EVA CARMICHAEL

© Eva Carmichael 2019

British Library Cataloguing in Publication Data. A catalogue record for this book is available from the British Library.

Eva Carmichael asserts the moral right to be identified as the author of this work.

Printed in Great Britain.

ACKNOWLEDGEMENTS

Thank you to Sixth Element Publishing for their expert help and advice in the production of this book. Thank you also to the Novel Writing Group at the Saltburn U3A, The Scriveners Writing Group at Guisborough and my three beta readers, Nicola, Amy and Niall without whose help and encouragement this book would not have been possible.

Last, but by no means least, a big thank you to my husband Derek for supplying copious amounts of tea, coffee (and occasionally wine).

Grateful thanks you all of you.

PART ONE
1990

ONE

Joe parked the car under the streetlamp at the top of a slight incline. This gave him a commanding view of the activity taking place in the road below. Cedar Road was well lit with streetlamps every few yards. During the day it was a busy commercial area with an array of banks and building societies. At night however, Cedar Road took on a more sinister role.

A damp mist filled the air, and a chill wind made the November evening feel bitterly cold. From his vantage point, Joe could see Shirley with her distinctive black curly hair. Perched on a low stone wall and wearing a short skirt and purple fake fur jacket, there was no mistaking her purpose.

A dark blue Ford pulled up at the kerb and Suzie climbed out of the car. Her long thin legs were encased in red plastic knee boots matching her plastic mini skirt. She waved at the occupant of the car as he sped off in the direction of the town. She sauntered over to Shirley and something she said made Shirley laugh out loud.

"The girls look busy tonight, boss," Joe said, addressing the older man sitting next to him. "That's three punters Suzie's had already and it isn't nine o'clock yet."

Karl Maddox, the man in the front passenger seat, ignored Joe as he stared intently at the two women. "I see Paula's not here again. What's that stupid bitch playing at?"

"I'll find out," Joe offered. "I'll ask Shirley, she'll know."

"I'll ask her myself," Karl snapped, winding down the car window. "Shirley, come here a sec," he shouted.

Shirley slipped off the wall and made her way over to the car as quickly as her four inch stiletto heels would permit.

"Hi, boss. You okay?" she beamed, chewing furiously on peppermint gum. She bent slightly to address Karl, her sickly sweet perfume drifting through the open car window.

"Where's Paula? She hasn't been on her patch for a couple of nights."

"Haven't seen her," Shirley answered without conviction. "Not since last Friday."

"Don't fucking lie to me." Karl jumped out of the car. "Where is she?" He grabbed Shirley's hair roughly, pulling her head to one side. "I won't ask you again."

"Canal Street!" She shrieked in pain. "I heard she was in Canal Street, but I haven't seen her, honest."

Karl pushed her away and got back into the car.

"Drive!" he ordered Joe. "When I find that bitch, I'll…"

"Sure, boss," Joe said, starting up the engine.

As the car pulled away, Shirley walked back over to the wall where another girl, Helen, had now arrived.

"What's up with Karl?" Helen asked. "He looks pissed off."

"He's looking for Paula. She hasn't been here for a few nights. I think she's over at Canal Street."

"What, she's gone independent? Karl won't like that. Look what he did to Jenny when she tried to move on."

"Yes, and he'll do the same to you if you don't get your arse in gear and start earning," Shirley said. She moved towards the kerb edge as a red Toyota pulled up.

"Looking for business, love?" she asked in her huskiest voice. "Twenty quid and I'm all yours."

"Yeah, why not?" the driver smirked. "Get in quick."

Shirley climbed into the front seat of the car and the man drove off into the darkness.

Helen walked over to Suzie who was standing at the kerb edge. "What's Paula playing at? She must be crazy to go up Canal Street without a pimp."

"I know nothing," Suzie shrugged. "I see nothing, I hear nothing, and if you take my advice, Helen, you'll do the same."

Before Helen could respond, Suzie was climbing into a light coloured mini.

Left alone on the street, Helen stamped her feet on the ground in an effort to keep warm. Her small denim jacket offered no protection from the chill wind. She lit a cigarette and began to pace up and down when the red Toyota pulled up and Shirley climbed out.

"Bloody hell, girl, that didn't take long," Helen smirked as Shirley walked towards her.

"He just wanted a jerk-off," Shirley grinned. "Easiest twenty quid I'll make tonight." Both women laughed. "I don't suppose Karl's been back?"

"I haven't seen him. I think he's gone to Canal Street looking for Paula."

"Well, let's hope for her sake he doesn't find her. Got a fag?"

"I thought you were giving them up?"

"I was but this bleeding gum's useless."

Helen handed Shirley a cigarette and both women lapsed into silence.

TWO

Canal Street consisted of mostly graffiti-covered derelict buildings. It was a favourite haunt with working girls from Leeds and surrounding areas. Business was brisk as, in the main, the police allowed the girls to work unhindered.

Two women were standing under the only working streetlamp. Joe parked his car behind a white Ford van some twenty yards away.

"I can't see Paula," he said after a few minutes. "It looks like Shirley got it wrong."

"She'll be here," Karl answered, staring into the blackness. "She'll be here, I know she will. We just have to wait."

"What's the big deal with her anyway? Girls are always moving on in this game."

"It's personal. Now shut the fuck up and keep looking."

For ten minutes they sat quietly watching as first one and then the other woman was driven away into the night. Finally a car pulled up underneath the streetlamp and Paula climbed out. She wore a short, tight-fitting black dress and pink woollen jacket. Her jaw-length auburn hair was styled in a neat bob.

"See ya," she grinned, giving a slight wave as the car sped away.

Without hesitation, Karl jumped out of the car. "Stay there," he ordered Joe. "I'll deal with the bitch myself." He ran towards the girl.

Joe could see the fear on Paula's face as she realised it was Karl approaching.

"Keep away from me, you bastard," she screamed, as she turned quickly and began to run up the road.

"Get back here," Karl bellowed. "We've got unfinished business."

He reached out to grab her but Paula was too quick. She ran down the far end of the road towards the canal, her stiletto heels echoing on the cobbles as she ran. As Karl got closer, Paula slipped and fell hard onto her knees. Grabbing her by the hair, Karl pulled her roughly to her feet.

"You little whore," he screamed, punching her hard in the face. "Where is it? What have you done with it?"

"Piss off," she spat, almost hysterically, frantically searching in her bag. "Get your fucking hands off me or you'll be sorry."

Karl brought back his clenched fist and was about to hit her again when, grasping the Stanley knife in her bag, she lashed out at him. Blood poured from the gash on his cheek. He released his grip, yelling in pain. Paula got to her feet and staggered a further ten feet before Karl caught up with her again. Still holding the knife, she attempted to lash out, but this time he was ready for her.

Karl's knife had a six inch blade, a mother of pearl handle and a long history of violence. He grabbed Paula by the hair and drew the sharp blade across her throat in one swift movement. There was a slight gurgling sound, just for a moment, and then silence. He released his grip and Paula's limp body slumped onto the cobbled ground.

"Stupid cow!" he hissed. "I warned you not to try blackmailing me but you wouldn't listen." He didn't hear Joe approaching.

"Everything alright, boss? I…" Joe inhaled deeply at the sight of Paula's limp body. "Christ, Karl, what the fuck have you done?" He bent over her and felt for a pulse. "She's dead. You've killed her."

Karl remained silent, staring at Paula's lifeless body at his feet.

"I'll get the car," Joe said shakily. "You wait here." He disappeared into the darkness and returned with the car a few seconds later. "Bloody hell, are you okay, boss? Your face is bleeding."

"Open the boot," Karl snarled. "Help me get the bitch in the boot. The others will be back any minute."

In a daze, Joe helped Karl lift Paula into the boot of the car.

"Here," Karl said, handing across the knife. "Get rid of this."

Karl got in the car but Joe remained on the pavement motionless.

"Come on, Joe, for Christ's sake, get in the car," Karl urged.

Almost reluctantly, Joe got into the car beside Karl and started the engine.

"Let's get the hell out of here." Karl was breathing heavily. "We have to get rid of her body."

"I can do that later." Joe was thinking straight now. "We have to act normal. The girls are expecting to see us in Cedar Road tonight, and that's where we must be."

"Don't be bloody stupid. We have to get rid of her body, for Christ's sake. What are we going to do about her?"

"I'll deal with Paula later, don't worry. I'll get rid of her and the knife."

They drove for a few minutes in silence.

It was Joe who spoke first. "Karl, I couldn't help hearing what you said to her. What did she do exactly?"

"That bitch had a knife," Karl growled, ignoring Joe's question. "She tried to kill me, the stupid whore!"

"I heard you mention blackmail. What was she blackmailing you with?"

Karl turned angrily to face Joe. "You heard nothing, understand? Nothing. I don't want you to mention this again, ever."

"Okay, boss, it's none of my business." Joe shrugged. "Here, you better take this." He handed Karl a handkerchief. "That cut looks deep. It's going to need a couple of stitches."

"Don't worry, I'll get it fixed," Karl said, dabbing at the cut. He could feel the blood trickling down his cheek and onto his neck. The two lapsed into silence.

It was Joe who spoke first.

"Is this the first time you've killed someone?"

"It's the first time I've killed a woman. The bloody bitch deserved it." He took out a cigarette, lit it and held it to his mouth with a trembling hand.

Twenty minutes later Joe parked the car in Cedar Road in the same spot they'd been a couple of hours earlier. All three women were now sitting on the wall smoking.

"I'll get the money and tell the girls to call it a night. Okay?"

Karl nodded as Joe got out of the car and approached the women.

"Did you find Paula?" Shirley asked, stamping out a cigarette on the ground.

"No, there was no sign of her in Canal Street. We've had a drive round but couldn't find her."

"She's probably gone off with her boyfriend," Shirley grinned. "She said she'd be giving up this game soon and settling down with him. I thought she would have come to say goodbye first though."

"I didn't know Paula had a boyfriend. Who is he?"

"She didn't say," Shirley lied. "She just said he was going to take her away from all this shit."

"Well, let's hope she gets her happy ever after," Joe grinned. "Anyway, it's getting late so hand over your cash and you can all go home to your nice warm beds."

After a few minutes Joe returned to the car and handed Karl the money he'd collected.

"Thanks," Karl said, placing it in his wallet. "Did they mention anything about us being away?"

"No, I told them we couldn't find Paula. Shirley thinks she's done a bunk with some boyfriend."

"Good, let them think that. Now I want you to take me to Danny's Place. I'll see Doc. He'll fix me up."

THREE

Danny's Pool Hall was a large, two-storey red brick building with dark blue double doors to the front. It had once been a public house, then a private cinema for gentlemen and it was now a pool and snooker hall. In reality, it was a front for drug dealing, handling stolen goods and a hideout for people who were of interest to the police. It was owned by Danny Davis who had inherited it from his father a couple of years earlier.

The building stood back from the road with a large area to the front and side designated for parking. A small, private car park was at the rear of the building. It was here that Joe parked the car and watched as Karl climbed the three steps to the private entrance. It was opened immediately by a giant of a man wearing a dark blue suit, the jacket of which pulled tight across his bulky frame. The trousers, bearing a smart razor pleat, were an inch or so too short, revealing bright red socks.

"Mr Karl," he greeted in a thick east European accent, his large doughy face creasing into a broad, welcoming smile.

"Good to see you again, Victor." Karl smiled.

"Your face, Mr Karl, it's bleeding," Victor said with concern.

"Oh it's nothing," Karl said as he dabbed at his cheek with the bloodstained handkerchief. "Is Danny here, Victor? I need his help."

"Sure, the boss is upstairs. I take you."

Karl followed Victor up the steep, narrow staircase. At the top of the stairs was a large metal door. Victor knocked and after a few seconds a peephole at eye level slid open.

"Mr Karl to see Danny," Victor snapped. "Hurry up, fool. Open the door."

Karl could hear bolts being slid back on the other side and it was eventually opened by a surly looking man of about twenty. The young man was just over five foot tall, slim, and with a crop of bright red hair. He was dressed casually in jeans and a sweatshirt.

"There's Mr Karl to see you, boss," Victor beamed, addressing the man lounging on a couch.

Danny Davis was in his mid-forties, short and stocky, with a grey goatee beard and hazel eyes.

"Karl," greeted Danny, walking towards him, arms outstretched. "Long time no see. What the hell's happened to your face? Don't tell me Erica did that?"

"No, it wasn't Erica, just a pissed off punter. Can you sort it, mate?"

"Sure I can. I'm the Doc, remember? Sit down and I'll get my bag."

Karl sat on the brown leather armchair, the only chair that wasn't covered in clutter.

"So, how've you been?" Karl asked. "I haven't seen you since…"

"Since I came out of the nick? I keep a low profile these days, mate. Just the odd job here and there, for old time's sake, if you know what I mean?"

"You were the best there was," Karl said. "Better than those fucking so called doctors they had in there."

"That's because I didn't ask questions," Danny grinned. "The British Army taught me that."

"Well, I'm just grateful that you're still…"

Danny had had his back to Karl as he rummaged through his medic bag. Slowly he turned to face him.

"Sorry, mate, but this is going to sting," he said as he dabbed Karl's face with antiseptic.

"Christ!" Karl shrieked. "That fucking hurts!"

"Don't be such a wuss. That didn't hurt, but this will!" He produced a curved needle and nylon thread. Expertly, he began to stitch the wound on his friend's face, ignoring Karl's profanities.

"There," he said at last. "It's done. You can stop crying now. Tell me, what would the patient prefer, some sweeties or a large malt whisky?"

"Fuck you!" grunted Karl. "Will it scar?"

"Of course it will scar. You've got a deep three inch cut there, mate. What was it, a Stanley knife?"

"It doesn't matter," Karl murmured, carefully examining his reflection in the mirror.

Karl was a little over six foot and in his mid-thirties. His broad forehead and square chin gave him a handsome, if somewhat rugged, appearance. His eyes were brown and his thick dark hair was worn just below the collar. His twice weekly visit to the local boxing gym helped keep his muscular frame taut. He frowned at his image. The wound to his left cheek looked red and swollen with nylon wires sticking out along the sides. It felt hot and sore.

"That fucking bitch," he hissed.

"Here you are," said Danny, handing Karl a large whisky. "You get this down you, mate, and I'll cover it up. You don't want to get an infection."

Karl took the glass and sipped the whisky as Danny taped the gauze dressing over the wound.

"Come back in a few days and I'll take out the stitches."

"Thanks, mate, I really appreciate this," Karl said, draining his glass.

"I hear you've got that darkie running your errands these days, that good looking one."

"You mean Joe?"

"Yeah, that's him. I always thought he had a look of a young Cassius Clay. I fancied a piece of him myself when we were inside. I would have had him too if you hadn't been protecting him. Bloody spoil sport."

"Pervert," Karl hissed mockingly. "Joe's a handy bloke to have around."

"Karl, mate, take my advice. Never trust a darkie."

"Don't tell me you're a racist?"

"No, of course I'm not. I just don't trust darkies, and neither should you." Danny's tone became serious as he poured them both another drink. "Anyway, how's the fragrant Erica these days? I haven't seen her in ages. Got her up the duff yet, or do you need some help in that department?"

"Dirty bastard," Karl grunted. "Erica's as fragrant as ever thank you. And no, she's not up the duff. Bloody miracle if she were, since I've had the snip."

"I would have thought you'd have wanted an offspring, someone to carry on your good name," Danny smirked.

"No thanks. Erica's perfect and she's going to stay perfect. No kid's going to spoil her body. I like her just the way she is."

"You're a lucky man, mate, pulling a classy bird like her."

"Don't tell me you fancy her?" Karl laughed. "Turned a corner, have we?"

"When hell freezes over. No, I just meant it was a surprise when you two got together. I expected you would take a shine to one of the slappers you handle, not the respectable daughter of a schoolteacher."

"Just shows how wrong you can be then, doesn't it? Tarts are just business, Danny, a commodity, that's all. There to make me money. Erica's a lady."

"Sorry, Karl, I didn't mean anything," Danny blustered. "I think she's a lovely girl and you're a good mate. Do you want another drink before you go?"

"No thanks, I'd better get back," Karl said, walking towards the door.

"It's been good to see you again. Don't leave it so long next time."

"I won't. Thanks for your help, Danny. I owe you. Anything you want, mate, just ask."

"Well, it's funny you should say that," Danny grinned. "I've got a proposition you might be interested in."

"What kind of proposition?"

"The kind that can make both of us a lot of money. Interested?"

"You bet I'm interested," Karl smirked. "Who do I have to kill?"

FOUR

David Glendenning drummed his fingers impatiently on the dashboard of his car. It was ten minutes after midnight and there was no sign of her. Canal Street was surprisingly deserted. Usually the working girls were here until the early hours, but not tonight. Too cold, supposed as he turned up the car heater.

"Where the hell is she?" he muttered for the hundredth time that night as he checked his rear view mirror yet again, his handsome face tense with anxiety.

David had inherited his Nordic good looks from his Norwegian mother. With his six foot two frame, blond hair and striking pale blue eyes, he was used to the attention of women. But David chose to turn his back on normal sexual relationships, choosing instead to trawl the city's red light district.

It was on one of these outings in Canal Street that he had first met Paula. That had been eighteen months ago. Paula was a pretty brunette in her early twenties. She was kind and funny and, much to his surprise, intelligent too. Soon they were seeing each other two, even three times a week.

It had come as a shock when, a few months into the relationship, Paula had announced she was pregnant and that he was the father. David had intended ending their relationship then, after all he had a wife and a son at home. He didn't want another family, for Christ's sake. He grimaced as he remembered the terrible arguments he had had with Paula.

"How could you have been so stupid as to get pregnant?" he had demanded, but Paula had stood firm and had refused the abortion David had arranged. It was a relief when she agreed that the child should be adopted.

David climbed out of the vehicle and walked over to the side alley. Sometimes girls would take their punters down there, but there was no sign of Paula. He still felt angry that Paula had gone back to work so quickly after having the child. She had started working for Karl Maddox, a small time pimp. Paula told him that having someone protecting her on the street was much safer than working alone, but then two days ago, without any explanation, she announced she was going back to work in Canal Street as an independent. David had been furious and they'd had a violent argument.

It was then Paula had given her ultimatum.

"Don't be bloody daft," he'd said. "I can't leave my family, my home, my career. You know I love you, Paula, but…"

"In that case," she had sneered, "I'll leave Leeds and you'll never see me again. Is that what you want?"

In the distance David heard the church bells chiming the half hour. Still there was no sign of Paula. He became irritable as he realised that perhaps she had carried out her threat to leave.

The night's silence was broken by the crackling of the car radio.

"Control to all vehicles. Proceed to disturbance outside Bailey's Nightclub. Urgent assistance required."

Automatically David reached for his transmitter.

"Mike Alpha 3 attending," he said as his vehicle roared into life. "ETA five minutes."

"Fuck you, Paula," he hissed through clenched teeth. "Fuck you."

His vehicle sped towards the town centre, its siren wailing, its blue light flashing.

FIVE

It was late when Karl eventually got home. On opening the front door he was surprised to see that Erica was still up. He was even more surprised to see a small suitcase by the side of the couch. As he entered the room she rushed towards him.

"Karl, your face," she said with concern. "What happened?"

"Nothing to worry about," he said reassuringly, kissing her lightly on the lips. "Some irate punter, that's all. What's with the suitcase? Is there something I should know?"

"It's Mary. She telephoned earlier. She's had a fall and wants me to go over to Ireland and stay with her for a few days. You don't mind, do you, Karl?"

"What's up with her bloke looking after her?" he scowled, throwing himself down heavily onto the couch.

"Liam's started a new job working on a building site in Dublin. It's a steady job and Mary doesn't want him to risk losing it by coming home to look after her."

"Why your sister chose to elope with an Irish gypsy is beyond me."

"She loves him," Erica protested, "and Liam thinks the world of Mary."

"I bet they're living in a caravan on a site," Karl said spitefully. "I don't want you going to any gypsy campsite."

"They're not in a caravan. They have a pretty cottage on the coast. Please, Karl," she pleaded, sitting on his lap and stroking his neck. "Please say yes. I'll only be away for a week and…"

"A week? You can't go for a week, I need you here. Three days. If you go at all, you go for three days, no longer."

"But Karl…"

"Take it or leave it, Erica."

"Alright, I'll get the early morning ferry from Liverpool," she sighed. Erica knew from experience it was no use arguing with Karl when he had made his mind up. "Can Joe take me to the port, or should I order a taxi?"

"I'll get Joe to take you. I've got to ring him so I'll tell him to call first thing tomorrow. Now, get me a whisky and then you better get yourself off to bed. You've got an early start tomorrow."

Left alone, Karl sipped his drink slowly, turning over the night's events in his mind. It had come as a shock when Paula had telephoned him a few days earlier demanding money. She had demanded ten thousand pounds be put into her bank account, or else.

"Well, the silly cow won't be telling tales now," he grinned maliciously. "Trying to blackmail me was a very bad mistake."

He picked up the phone and dialled Joe's number. Almost immediately, a familiar voice answered.

"That you, boss?"

"Yeah, just ringing to see how things went tonight."

"Everything went well. You've nothing to worry about."

"Are you sure? I don't want the stupid little cow found."

"Don't worry, nobody will ever find her. I know what I'm doing."

"Of course you do. Sorry, Joe, it's just…"

"How's your face?" Joe asked, changing the subject. "Did Danny sort you out?"

"He put a couple of stitches in. It hurts like hell. Danny said it will leave a scar."

"Too bad," Joe said sympathetically. "Let's hope it doesn't spoil your good looks too much, eh?"

Both men laughed coarsely.

"By the way, there are a couple of things I want you to do for me tomorrow. Erica's going over to Ireland first thing to visit her sister, she's had some sort of accident. Could you take her to Liverpool first thing?"

"Sure boss, no problem. I'll be there at half six."

"Thanks Joe, that's a great help. If I ever get my hands on that bastard judge who took my licence, I'll…"

"Another six months and you'll be back on the road," Joe said lightly. "You said there were two things?"

"Oh yes, I need you to call at Broughton Street and collect the takings. I've got some business with Danny in the morning so I won't be able to go myself."

"No problem. I'll call round to the house as soon as I get back from dropping Erica off at the port. We don't want to put too much temptation Aggie's way, do we? She must have three day's takings by now."

"I don't think we need worry too much about Aggie. She's been working for me too long to try anything like that."

"Okay, boss," Joe yawned. "We'll catch up tomorrow."

Joe put down the receiver and lit a cigarette. He drank the last of the whisky from his glass and took it into the kitchen. He quickly rinsed the glass under the tap, dried it and placed it in the wall cupboard.

"Time for some shut-eye," he murmured, picking up the plastic bag off the drainer. He examined the bag's contents. A knife with a mother of pearl handle bearing Karl's fingerprints and a six inch blade covered in Paula's congealed blood.

"Insurance," he grinned maliciously, as he carried the plastic bag into his bedroom.

SIX

Karl woke with the winter sun streaming into the bedroom. His head ached and his cheek was throbbing. He automatically reached out for Erica and, for a brief moment, was confused to find he was alone in the bed. Looking at the bedside clock he realised that she would have left for Ireland two hours ago. Sulkily, he went through to the kitchen to make coffee. He hated it when Erica wasn't there. This was the last time he would allow her to visit Mary, he decided, even if the silly bitch was dying.

Carrying his coffee cup, he went through to the lounge, a large well-furnished room with the faint smell of lavender. Yes, he admitted begrudgingly, Erica was a good housekeeper. She had been fourteen when they first met. Tall and slim with shoulder-length strawberry blonde hair, sparkling blue eyes, and perfect skin, he remembered how he had stared in disbelief at her uncanny resemblance to someone he had once known.

The telephone rang and he picked up the receiver immediately.

"Morning, Karl," Joe said cheerily. "Just to let you know I saw Erica safely onto the ferry. I'm on my way to Broughton Street now."

"Was Erica okay?"

"She's fine. She said she'd be back in three days. She'll phone me when she knows the time of the return ferry."

"That bloody sister of hers," Karl hissed, "more trouble than she's worth. You get over to Aggie's and collect the money. I'll meet you at Danny's later."

"Okay, boss," Joe grinned. "See you there."

Karl's spirits lifted as he recalled his conversation with Danny Davis the previous night. Danny wanted to sell the Pool Hall and had given him first refusal. Karl had been thinking of opening a club for a while and the old pool hall would be an ideal location. He picked up the telephone and dialled for a taxi.

It was a ten minute journey to Danny's. As usual, he went to the back of the building but before he had the chance to knock, the door was opened by a smiling Victor.

"Mr Karl," he greeted in his usual jovial manner, "boss said you'd be coming round this morning. You're to go straight up."

"Thanks, Victor," Karl said, ascending the steep stairway. The metal door at the top of the staircase was wide open and Karl walked straight into the room he had been in the previous night. Danny was wearing a black and purple silk dressing gown, and was barefoot. He was leaning over a small table with his back to him.

"Good morning, Danny," Karl greeted.

Danny spun round in surprise.

Karl could see the fine white powder below Danny's nose and he gesticulated it was there with his finger.

"Good to see you again, mate," Danny grinned, pushing the powder into his nose. "Just a little something to start the day. Want some?"

"No thanks," Karl grimaced, screwing up his face in disgust. "I never touch the stuff."

"You don't know what you're missing," Danny said as he snorted the remainder of the powder. "Be with you in a sec."

The door at the far side of the room burst open and the young man with red hair that Karl had seen the previous night flounced into the room. He was completely naked. It didn't faze him at all that Danny had a visitor.

"I hope you've saved me some," the boy said peevishly, walking over to Danny.

"Get out!" Danny shouted angrily. "How dare you interrupt when I'm in a meeting."

"Sorry," the boy said, reeling from the rebuke. "I only…"

"Get out," Danny repeated, "and get some bloody kecks on. I don't want you prancing around looking like that."

The boy looked crestfallen as he picked up a pair of grey chinos off the back of a chair.

"Do you want me to make some coffee?" he asked sheepishly.

"Later. Now piss off." Danny waited until the boy had left the room. "Sorry about that. Billy's not housetrained yet. Give me a couple of minutes to get ready, and I'll meet you downstairs for the grand tour."

"No rush, mate," Karl said, making his way towards the stairs. "Erica's gone to visit her sister in Ireland so I'm at a loose end for a few days."

"I'm sure you can find something, or someone to keep you entertained," Danny grinned mischievously.

"No, not interested. Erica's the only one for me."

"Of course she is," Danny smirked sarcastically. "By the way, Karl, I've something to show you that will blow your mind."

"What kind of something?"

"The kind of something that can prove very useful to you in the future, mate. Very useful indeed."

SEVEN

Agatha Jane Benson, or Aggie as she was called by all who knew her, was not a well woman. A combination of poor nutrition as a child, and an abundance of alcohol and cigarettes in later life had left their toll on the fifty year old. Aggie's wispy grey hair fell loosely onto her narrow bony shoulders. Her skin, the consistency of light grey tissue paper, was heavily lined and her pale, watery blue eyes had dark shadows beneath. She had painted her thin lips bright red, more out of habit than any expectation of improving her appearance.

Aggie made her way into the small kitchen, limping painfully, and ran the hot water into a bowl to wash the cups left from the previous day. Then she emptied the kitchen bin and replaced the plastic bag. She'd already changed the sheets on the three beds upstairs with the help of her friend, Frieda, and left clean towels in each room. Frieda had polished the three large mirrors and cleared away the debris left on the bedside tables. All that remained for her to do was to vacuum the carpets.

It was that morning she had received the letter from the hospital informing her that due to a cancellation, she would be able to have her hip replacement operation in one week's time, instead of having to wait the two months she was expecting. She had been in agony with her hip for months and was excited that it was going to be put right at last, but she wasn't relishing telling Karl she would be leaving. She knew that finding someone to take over the running of the house would not be easy at such short notice.

Aggie had worked for Karl at the house in Broughton Street, a three-bedroomed end of terrace property, for nearly four years.

The house was no different from the hundreds of other brothels up and down the country. The sitting room was clean and tidy with a light tan leather couch and two armchairs. A number of adult magazines were scattered on the small table in front of the couch and there was a television in the corner of the room, along with a video recorder. Selections of pornographic videos were on a shelf next to the television.

Aggie loved her job managing the brothel. It was good money and she enjoyed the banter. Six girls worked at the house each day. Three started their shift at noon and worked until six in the evening. A further three girls worked from six until midnight. Each girl paid a shift rent of one hundred pounds and they were free to charge the punters whatever they could get for their services. The girls soon made up their rent and everything they made over that was theirs. Aggie was paid one hundred pounds for the day and Karl got the remaining five hundred pounds. This money was collected every couple of days by either Karl or Joe.

There was a sharp rap on the door and a smiling Joe entered the room. Aggie was pleased to see it was Joe who had come to collect. He was much kinder and understanding than Karl so it would be a lot easier to tell him her news.

"Morning, Aggie," Joe greeted, kissing her lightly on the cheek. "You're looking as ravishing as always."

Aggie blushed. "Good morning to you," she replied. "I thought you'd forgotten about me. Nobody's been to collect for three days."

"Busy, busy, busy," Joe grinned, sitting down in one of the chairs.

Aggie perched on the arm of the couch. "Have you got yourself a young lady yet?"

"No, Aggie, I'm still looking, but you're a hard act to follow."

"I'm serious. You should find yourself a nice young woman and settle down. You're too good for all of this shit."

"I like what I do. Where else would I find myself surrounded by beautiful young women twenty four hours a day?"

Aggie gave a disapproving tut by way of response. "I'll get

the takings and then I need to talk to you about something important," she said, her tone suddenly becoming serious. Slowly she made her way into the kitchen and removed the takings from the safe, handing them to Joe.

"Is everything alright, Aggie?" Joe asked with concern. "You look…"

"It's my hip," she sighed heavily. "It's knackered. I'm in agony with it."

"You poor thing. Why didn't you say? Is there anything I can do?"

"No love, it's down to the doctors. They want me in the hospital next week."

"As early as that?"

"They've had a cancellation so I've been brought forward. I know that it's short notice Joe, but…"

"Don't worry about work, you just get yourself right," Joe said comfortingly.

"The thing is, once I've had my hip done I won't be coming back to work."

"You won't? Why not?"

"I've bought a bungalow in Bournemouth with my cousin, Lucy. It's a lovely little place with a sea view. I'll be moving there once I've had the operation."

Joe had always been fond of Aggie, and he gently put his arm around her shoulder, giving her a slight squeeze. "Well, if you're sure that's what you want to do," he said affectionately. "I hope everything works out for you, Aggie. I really do."

"I'm just worrying who you will get to run this place. I know it's not easy finding someone suitable who knows the business, but…"

"Aggie, love, don't you worry about that, just concentrate on getting better. I'm sure we'll manage, in fact I have someone in mind that fits the bill perfectly."

Aggie hugged Joe tightly, her relief obvious. She had been convinced that leaving so suddenly would cause trouble.

"Want a coffee while you're here?" she asked, smiling.

24

"No thanks. I can't stop. I've got a lot on today," He counted the money given to him by Aggie and placed it in his inside pocket. "Who have we got working?"

"There's Josie, Maria and Cassandra. They're all popular with the punters so it should be a busy day."

"I thought Cassandra was up the duff?"

"Not anymore she isn't." Aggie said.

"What about later? Who's working the late shift?"

"Kathy and Debbie. Paula's supposed to be working but she hasn't turned up for her last couple of shifts. I had to put Claire in."

"Claire? I haven't met her. She doesn't work the streets, does she?"

"No, she's got more sense. She was asking if she could have more shifts in the house but we don't have any spare places unless Paula's packed in."

"I think Paula's moved on," Joe said lightly. "Manchester, so I heard."

"Manchester? She never said. What made her do that?"

"Who knows? Girls move on all the time, Aggie, you know that. Give Claire a place in the house and let's see how she gets on. Okay?"

"Alright, if you say so," Aggie shrugged. "I can't believe Paula would leave without letting me know. She seemed such a nice girl."

"Well, I'd better be off and leave you to it. I'll have a word with your replacement and bring her over to meet you in the next couple of days."

"Okay, Joe. See you soon, and don't forget what I said about finding yourself a nice young lady to settle down with."

"If you only knew, Aggie," Joe smiled to himself as he walked out onto the street. "If you only knew…"

EIGHT

"Where's Billy?" Karl teased as Danny joined him in the snooker hall. "Gone back to bed?"

"Don't be daft. He's doing what he does best, spending my money."

"He's what?"

"He's gone into town shopping. I've told him to buy some gear for Spain."

"So, Billy's your mister right, then?" Karl grinned.

Danny gave him a hard stare. "Let's just say he's my mister right now."

Both men laughed.

"I hope we can do this deal quickly." Danny suddenly became serious. "I'm missing out on the sun and the sea stuck here." He walked over to one of the pool tables and removed two empty beer bottles off the baize. "This place was a private cinema when my old man took it on, did you know that? Dirty old men would sit in the dark watching porn whilst having a wank." His face expressed repulsion. "Dad had the whole place remodelled into the pool hall. He had it up and running in just two months."

The two men were walking through the spacious ground floor. The distinctive aroma of stale tobacco and booze lingered heavily in the air. Twelve pool tables were arranged around the room, each one with a large overhead lighting fixture. To one side of the room was a small bar with four stools to the front. Half a dozen bottles of spirits were behind optics on the back wall, and shelves containing bottled beers and lagers were to the side. Wooden bench seats were fixed to the nicotine stained cream plaster walls and above them were a line of coat hooks. Several small tables and chairs were arranged at the far side of the room.

The wall at this end of the room was panelled from floor to ceiling in a dark wood. Five feet off the ground, a line of open fretwork in a fleur-de-lis pattern ran the full length of the wall. In the centre hung a large framed photograph of three smartly dressed men smiling at the camera. Each was holding a pool cue in one hand and a beer glass in the other. Karl stared at the picture in disbelief. The central figure he recognised immediately as Danny's father, but it was the other two men in the photograph that held Karl's attention.

"Bloody hell!" he cried in disbelief. "That's the Krays. Ronnie and Reggie Kray."

"Yes," Danny beamed with obvious pride. "They were good mates of my old man. They actually came here to meet him once."

"Bloody hell!" Karl repeated. "I never knew that, mate."

"My dad was really proud of this picture. I'll be taking it with me when I leave."

"I thought you said you had no sentimental attachments," Karl smirked.

"I don't, apart from this picture."

"But what if I count it as a fixture and fitting?"

Danny stared at his friend. He was never quite sure when Karl was serious.

"Tell you what I'll do," he said at last. "You buy this place, minus the picture, for the price I've asked and I'll throw in a few extras."

"What sort of extras?"

"Follow me and you'll find out." Danny winked as they went through the foyer towards the main staircase.

Both men went up the stairs into the large sitting room, the room that Karl had visited the previous night. Although the furniture in the room was of good quality, it was covered by piles of clothes and magazines.

Karl winced as they entered. "The maid's day off, is it?"

Danny merely shrugged. "There's another room through

here," he said opening the dual set of doors. The second room was equally as big as the first, and just as untidy. At one time it had been a dining room but the table was covered in books and magazines, and again there was an abundance of discarded clothing.

"Don't you ever put things away?" Karl frowned. He was used to having a clean and tidy home, and he found Danny's lifestyle disturbing.

"Sorry about the mess," Danny said unconvincingly. "Like I told you earlier, Billy's not fully housetrained yet. Anyway, it's the building that's for sale. I'm not applying for entry in 'Homes and Gardens' for Christ's sake."

"It's just as well. You live like a pig. This place is disgusting."

Danny suddenly became defensive. "If that's what you think, maybe we should call this off."

"Maybe we should, but I need to see the rest of this pigsty first. You said there were four bedrooms?"

"Yeah, they're through here." Sulkily, Danny led the way down the corridor. "I only use two as bedrooms," he said. "One is used as a storeroom and the other an office. That's down at the end."

Karl followed Danny down the corridor to the office. This room was sparsely furnished with a small desk and swivel chair, and to Karl's surprise, was very tidy. A couple of shelves containing box files were arranged neatly, and two chairs were on the back wall.

On one wall was a door which was slightly open, revealing a cupboard with files stacked neatly on the overhead shelf. Danny walked over to the cupboard.

"You remember I told you last night I had something special to show you?"

"What is it?"

"In here," he said, walking into the cupboard. He pulled on a concealed lever and the back wall opened, revealing a steep staircase. Karl followed Danny down the dimly lit stairs. At the bottom was a narrow corridor lined with shelves. Karl could see that the shelves contained boxes of alcohol, cigarettes, cigars and other contraband.

"Bloody hell," he exclaimed. "It's like Aladdin's cave down here."

"Not bad, is it? My old man had it built when he bought this place. Only a handful of people know about the passage so don't go spreading the word."

"As if," Karl smirked.

"What I really want to show you is this." Danny made his way further up the narrow corridor. "Look through there."

Karl pressed up to the wall and peered through the fleur-de-lis fretwork. He smiled broadly, realising that from here he was just feet away from the punters.

"Nothing gets said in here that I don't know about. It can be very useful."

"I bet it can. You say only a few people know about this?"

"Me and Victor, that's all. The bloke that helped my old man to build it died years ago."

"Well it certainly has possibilities, mate, that's for sure. I'll need to think about this."

As they walked back along the passage, Danny picked up a box of cigars.

"Here, these are for you." He handed the box to Karl. "There'll be plenty more if we can strike a deal."

"You're not trying to bribe me, are you?"

"Course I am. I'll tell you what, I'll even throw in Victor for free."

"What the hell do I want with Victor? I've got my own doorman, thanks."

"Victor's more than a doorman, trust me. Very handy to have around is Victor."

"No, I don't think so, but thanks for the smokes."

The two men made their way back into the living room just as Victor and Joe arrived. Joe nodded a greeting towards Danny.

"Is it alright to open up?" Victor asked. "It's twelve o'clock."

"Yes, you do that. I'll be down soon."

Victor hurried from the room.

"Can I have a word, boss?" Joe asked. "It's important."

"I'll leave you to it," Danny said, walking towards the door. "I've got things to do downstairs. Just make sure you keep your mitts off my whisky."

Left alone, Karl turned to face Joe.

"You've been to the house?"

"Yes, boss," Joe replied, handing over the money he had collected from Aggie. "But there's a problem. Aggie needs a hip replacement. She's going into hospital next week to have it done."

"Hospital? For fuck's sake, how long will she be away?"

"Well, that's the problem, boss. She won't be coming back. She's decided it's time to retire."

"Shit!" Karl snarled. "I don't have time for this."

"I think I might be able to help," Joe said hesitantly. "I know someone who's got experience in running a house and she's looking for a job."

"Who is she? Do I know her?"

"Her name's Marion Watson."

"Marion Watson? I know that name from somewhere."

"Marion worked for Graham Gibb a few years back before some punter threw acid in her face."

"Yes, I remember now. How badly scarred is she? I don't want her frightening away the punters."

"She's not too bad. We can give her a trial and see how it works out. We need to act quickly though, Aggie's having her operation next week."

"Okay Joe, I'll leave it for you to arrange," Karl sighed heavily. "By the way, I won't be at Cedar Road tonight. I've got some business on with Danny. Will you be alright watching the girls by yourself?"

"Sure," Joe grinned. "No probs. See you later."

NINE

Joe parked the car in his usual place on Cedar Road. He could see Shirley pacing up and down the street in an effort to keep warm. The other six girls working that night had already gone off with their punters, leaving Shirley alone on the street.

Joe watched intently as a white van slowly cruised along the road and stopped close to Shirley. Through the gloom he saw a large man emerge from the front of the van and approach her. Joe could see him talking to Shirley, and after a few minutes he began shaking her by the shoulders and slapping her across the face. Shirley yelled out in pain as she fell back against the wall but the man continued pushing and slapping her. Without hesitation, Joe leapt out of the car and raced to Shirley's aid.

"What the hell do you think you're doing?" he yelled as he grabbed the man from behind. Without warning the side door of the van slid open and three men jumped out. Before he had time to react, a baseball bat came crashing down on Joe's head, knocking him into the wall. He spun round to face his attackers as a second blow caught him on the shoulder. Soon kicks and punches were raining down on him and he slumped to the ground.

"That's enough," a voice said in a strong Scottish accent. "I think the bastard's got the message."

One of the assailants, a man with wild bushy hair, pulled Joe's head back roughly and leant menacingly over him.

"Tell that bastard Karl Maddox he's finished," he hissed. "From now on the Kennedys will be running the streets. Can you hear what I'm saying, pretty boy?"

Joe nodded faintly.

"This is just a friendly warning. If Karl wants to argue the point, we'll be waiting."

As Joe's head was released from the man's grip, he felt one more kick to his ribs before sinking into oblivion.

"Joe, wake up. For Christ's sake, babe, wake up."

Slowly Joe began to regain consciousness. He became aware of a familiar high-pitched voice and the smell of sickly sweet perfume.

"Shirley?"

"Yeah, it's me, Joe. You've got to get up, babe. Those bastards have gone now."

Slowly Joe struggled to his feet, assisted by Shirley. He felt dizzy and disorientated. He could feel blood pouring from his nose, and a sharp pain ripped through his ribs. Joe managed to get to his feet but his legs felt weak beneath him and he grabbed onto Shirley for support.

"Help me to the car," he said faintly. "I have to warn Karl."

"But Joe, you…"

"For fuck's sake, don't argue, Shirley, just get me to the car, now."

Step by slow painful step, Shirley managed to get Joe over to his car.

"I'll drive. We can be at the hospital in ten minutes."

"No," Joe protested. "No hospital. Take me to Danny's place."

"Where?"

"Just drive. I'll tell you the way."

TEN

Karl was in Danny's lounge enjoying his second glass of whisky when he heard a commotion outside the room. Before he could get to his feet, the door burst open and Victor entered. He was cradling Joe in his arms. Victor was closely followed by a hysterical Shirley.

"What the hell?" Karl gasped, rushing over to the two men. "What the fuck happened?"

"It was them Scottish Kennedy bastards," Shirley sobbed. "Three of them jumped out of the van and started beating up Joe. He didn't stand a chance."

"Kennedys? Who the fuck are the Kennedys?" Karl snapped, helping Victor to place Joe on the couch.

"They said they're taking over the street," Shirley sobbed. "They said the girls are working for them now, not you."

"Oh did they?" Karl growled. "We'll see about that."

"Let's see to Joe first," Danny said with concern as he began to examine him. "A couple of ribs broken, that's for sure, and I think his nose could be busted."

"Do you know anything about these Kennedys? I've never heard of them."

"They came to Leeds a couple of weeks ago from Glasgow. Bad lot by all accounts." Danny wiped the blood carefully from Joe's swollen face. "I think it would be best if we took him to the hospital. He's had a real kicking."

"No hospital," Joe pleaded, pushing himself up into a sitting position. "No hospital, Karl. I'll be okay."

"Drink this," Danny ordered, handing him a small glass of brandy. "I'll bandage your ribs, mate. It might make them feel easier." Skilfully Danny began winding the bandage around Joe's ribs, ignoring his cries of discomfort.

"Nearly done," he said reassuringly. "Here, take a couple of these." Danny handed Joe two small white tablets. "They'll help with the pain."

"What are they?" Karl asked suspiciously.

"Well, just let's say you won't get them at Boots, more's the pity. But they'll do the job, trust me. I think Joe had better stay here tonight."

Billy had been hovering nervously near the door. "I'll get the spare room ready," he offered, scuttling down the corridor. "It won't take a minute."

Carefully Danny and Karl helped Joe into the bedroom.

"You rest up," Danny said as he helped Joe into the bed. "You'll be back on your feet in no time."

Joe could already feel the effect of the tablets he had taken as he began drifting slowly into a deep slumber.

"Don't worry, mate," Karl said. "I'll get the bastards who did this, and when I do…"

But Joe was already unconscious, unaware of everything around him.

"You stay here and watch him," Danny ordered Billy. "Get him a drink if he wakes up but no more pills. Okay?"

Billy nodded obediently and sat on the chair at the side of the bed.

"Where are you going?" he asked meekly.

Danny ignored Billy's question as he walked back into the lounge with Karl close behind him. Shirley had helped herself to a brandy and was visibly shaking. Her face was streaked as her tears had caused her mascara to run.

"He hit me," she wailed. "That big bastard with the bushy hair, he punched me in the face and…"

"Yes, alright, Shirley, you're safe now," Karl said dismissively, handing her a twenty pound note. "Get a taxi and go straight home, do you hear me? I don't want you working tonight."

"But Karl, they…"

"Shirley, I said go home," Karl snapped impatiently. "I won't tell you again. Now get moving. I've got things to do."

Shirley drained the brandy from the glass before heading towards the stairs.

"I'll see her out," Victor said, opening the door.

When Shirley had left the room, Karl turned to Danny. "So? Where do I find these bastards?"

"They have a flat in Cheapside. I err… overheard them talking when they were in here the other night. You wouldn't believe what I overhear in this place." He gave Karl a sly wink. "They're in the protection racket. They operated out of Glasgow but things got a bit too hot for them up there so they came down to Leeds to try their luck."

"How many of them are there?"

"Two brothers and a cousin, and there's a big bloke with red bushy hair. I don't think he's related. He's a tough looking bastard. He's the main muscle."

Danny looked enquiringly at Victor.

"I've spoken to them, boss," Victor grinned. "They'll meet us there in twenty minutes."

"Good. Time to get tooled up, Karl, don't you think?"

"I need to make a couple of calls first," Karl said. "If there are four of them, we're going to need more men."

"Don't worry, it's taken care of," Danny said. "Victor has two brothers, both built like brick shithouses. He's already made the call. They'll meet us in Cheapside."

"Do they know what they're up against? I can't afford to lose this fight."

Victor walked over to Karl and placed his hand on his shoulder. "Mr Karl, where I come from, you learn to fight before you learn to walk. Don't you worry, my brothers will take care of business."

Danny went into the kitchen and returned a couple of minutes later carrying several baseball bats, two small axes, and a selection of knives.

"Name your poison," he grinned. "Do you want to bash their

brains in or cut off their bollocks?" All three men laughed. "I assume your brothers have their own?"

"Yes, boss, don't you worry about them."

Karl made his selection: a heavy baseball bat and a small axe.

"Let the games begin," Danny said, as all three men went out into the street and got into his car watched by a worried Billy.

Twenty minutes later they pulled into a side street behind the block of flats where the Kennedys were known to be staying.

"My brothers, they're here," Victor cried excitedly, getting out of the car and heading towards the large blue van parked a little further up the road.

Karl watched as two men, both carrying claw hammers, got out of the van and embraced Victor.

"Christ, they're big bastards," Karl murmured.

"Hard as nails, the pair of them," Danny said. "The Kennedys won't know what's hit them."

Karl and Danny got out of the car and walked towards Victor and the two men.

"These are my brothers, Mr Karl," Victor beamed. "Jan and Erik."

Karl nodded to the men by way of acknowledgement and all five went into the small foyer. Karl pressed for the lift.

"Which floor?"

"Fourth," Danny answered. "Flat forty-two."

Silently the lift made its way upwards.

ELEVEN

Stephen Kennedy tossed the empty lager can towards the plastic bucket in the corner of the room. The can hit the side of the bucket and fell onto the floor to accompany the heap already there.

"Did a good job tonight, boys," he said, for what must have been the tenth time that evening. "We've shown that bastard Maddox we're not to be messed with."

"You don't think he's going to take this lying down?" asked Freddie, his younger brother. "I've heard Karl Maddox is a bit of a nutter."

"So you think he can take us on?" Stephen asked menacingly. "He's a pussy. Good at pushing women around but when it comes to hard men, he'll be shitting himself. Trust me. Karl Maddox is an arsehole."

All four laughed coarsely.

"Talking of arseholes, where's that delivery?" asked George. "I'm starving."

"You're always starving, you fat bastard," said Harry. Harry was Stephen's cousin. "We only placed the order fifteen minutes ago. It'll be here."

George grunted loudly and flung himself into an armchair. He was tired of being disrespected by the Kennedys. After all, it was him that was the real muscle, the one who made things happen. They'd be nothing without him. It would serve them right if he took off and left them. See how tough they were then when he wasn't around to fight their battles. Before he could say anything, there was a sharp knock on the door.

"Finally," said Stephen. "I'll pay this time, but from now on…"
Stephen opened the door, two ten pound notes in his hand. He

had barely got the door open when a giant of a man pushed the door wider and head butted him full in the face.

"Hello," said the newcomer, smiling. "I'm Victor. It's very nice to meet you."

Stephen fell to his knees, blood spurting from his nose as the newcomers trampled over him as they rushed into the room. George was first to his feet, his adrenaline on full alert as the men rushed towards him. It was Karl who tackled him first. The baseball bat he wielded went crashing down on George's shoulder. Before he had time to recover, Danny cracked George's head hard with his own bat. George crumpled to the floor, semiconscious and writhing in agony.

Karl turned to see Jan and Erik holding Freddie and Harry by the hair and using their heads as battering rams.

"Again," Jan shrieked excitedly.

"Okay," Erik replied. "One, two, three…"

It was Stephen Kennedy who fired the gun. He was aiming at Karl but his hand was shaking so much that the bullet ended up hitting the ceiling and shattering one of the light bulbs. Instinctively, Victor sprang forward and punched Stephen hard in the face. The gun fell to the ground. It was quickly retrieved by Danny.

"That's not nice," Victor smirked maliciously, twisting Stephen's arm up his back. "You could seriously hurt someone firing a gun like that."

Victor forced Stephen to his knees placing his powerful arm around his throat. Karl walked over to him.

"So, you're the Kennedy gang, are you? Big, bad and tough, isn't that right? I hear you're going to take over my streets." Karl smirked as he kicked Stephen a couple of times hard in the ribs. "My girls are now your girls. Isn't that what you said?"

Trembling uncontrollably, Stephen raised his head to face Karl.

"Sorry," he said pitifully. "It was a stupid thing to do. Please, let us go and you'll never hear from us again."

Karl turned to face Danny. "What do you think I should do with these maggots?"

Danny pointed the gun at the terrified men. "We could blow their fucking brains out, if they have any brains that is."

Karl could barely remember a time when he had felt such excitement and exhilaration as he did right then. Tonight he felt invincible. He smiled as he surveyed the carnage. All four of the Kennedys had been thrown into a heap in the centre of the room, totally at his mercy.

It was then that Karl noticed Jan and Erik were dousing the men in petrol. They screamed for mercy as Victor leant over them menacingly.

"You leave now, tonight, or tomorrow we bring matches. Understand?"

They all nodded in terror.

Karl walked over to the men and pulled George from the tangled heap.

"This is for slapping one of my girls," he hissed, punching George several times in the face. "And this, you bastard, is for hurting my boy." Karl raised the baseball bat and brought it down repeatedly on George's shoulders and back.

"That's enough, Mr Karl," Victor said, pulling him away from George's crumpled body. "I don't think he'll be giving us any more trouble."

There was a sharp rap on the door.

"Who the fuck's that?" Danny spat. "If it's the cops we'll…"

"I'll go," Karl offered, walking towards the door. "Cops don't usually knock." He opened the door slightly. "Yes?"

"Pizzas for Mr Kennedy," answered the spotty faced youth. "Seventeen pounds fifty, please."

Karl turned to face his men. "Hungry, boys?" he grinned.

They all nodded enthusiastically. Karl picked up the two ten pound notes Stephen Kennedy had dropped on the floor and handed them to the young man. "Keep the change," he said smiling as he took the pizza boxes.

"Thanks, mate, have a nice day."

"Oh I will," Karl smirked. "I certainly will."

TWELVE

"Time I was going," Karl yawned. "It's nearly two o'clock."

"Lightweight," Danny said, laughing. "There's nothing to rush back for, is there? I thought Erica's not back until tomorrow?"

"That's right, but we've a busy day, don't forget. Oh and thanks for the gun. You never know, it might come in useful one day."

"Let's hope not, eh? But it's better with you than with them bastard Kennedys. Anyway, you just make sure you're at the solicitors by eleven. The sooner we get this deal done, the better."

Karl got up off the couch and stretched. "Don't worry, I'll be there. But I still think you're a robbing bastard. I'm paying you far too much for this run-down dump."

"Bollocks. You're way below the asking price. I wouldn't consider such a low offer from anyone else."

"Just make sure you don't forget the freebies. Cuban cigars and whisky, like we agreed. Oh and I've decided to take you up on your offer of Victor."

"Good move," said Danny. "You won't regret it. Like I said, Victor can be very useful. So, tell me, mate, what are your plans for this place once it's yours?"

"You'll have to wait and see."

"I bet you'll turn it into one of those joints where girls dance up sticks."

"Eh?"

"Pole dancing, they call it. Bloody perverts sit about drooling all night at half-naked women prancing around, and then they stick money in their knickers. I know where I'd like to stick it."

"I take it you won't be coming to opening night, then?" Karl said.

"You take it right. I'll be in some club in the heart of Benidorm having a fantastic evening with Billy and a few mates."

"And whilst you're doing that, I'll be coining it in, night after night."

Both men laughed.

"Joe's sleeping peacefully," Danny said. "He should be okay to go home tomorrow."

"Good. He'll be sorry he missed out on the fun tonight. By the way, I need to make a call. Can I use the office phone?"

"Sure. You know where it is."

Shortly afterwards Karl left the club and got into the waiting taxi. "Belvedere Mansions," he instructed the driver. The taxi drove the ten minute journey to the modern block of flats on the outskirts of the city.

"Wait here," Karl instructed the driver, handing him two twenty pound notes. "I'll be about an hour. Okay?"

"Right, mate," answered the cabbie. "You take your time."

Karl walked through the thick carpeted foyer, his heart beating wildly. He was still buzzing from earlier, and now, being here so close to her, his body tingled with excitement. An excitement that Erica should satisfy, he told himself, not leaving him alone so she could visit her bloody sister. Well, whatever happened tonight would be all her fault. After all, he had needs, needs that had to be fulfilled.

He got into the glass lift and pressed the button to the tenth floor. He had already telephoned for an appointment. Madam would be waiting for him to walk through her door and throw himself at her mercy, just like he'd done half a dozen times over the last year.

Karl's throat felt dry with anticipation of what lay ahead. Maybe tonight she would be wearing the black leather cat suit with thigh length boots and five inch heels. He liked her in that outfit. Or maybe she would be wearing the long white chiffon nightie revealing just a hint of what lay beneath. Karl wiped his brow with his handkerchief. Each time he visited her he swore it would be the last, but the truth was he enjoyed the experience too much. He needed this. Perhaps he needed it more than he needed Erica.

Karl got out of the lift, his heart pounding. The door, her door, was directly opposite. What lay beyond that door was drawing him like a magnet. The pleasure he would soon be feeling, and the pain too, of course.

He trembled slightly remembering the first time he had experienced her leather whip biting into his naked flesh. The degradation had been wonderful. What would Madam demand from him tonight, he wondered?

Taking a deep breath, he pressed the buzzer…

THIRTEEN

Erica arrived at the port in plenty of time for her connection, only to learn that the ferry had been delayed due to thick fog over the Irish Sea.

"It could clear in an hour," said the cheerful clerk behind the counter, "or it could last for the entire day. It's in God's hands."

"Do you have a telephone, please?" she asked.

"Yes dear, it's round the corner."

Erica rang her flat but there was no reply. She dialled Joe.

"Hello," said a faint, yet familiar voice.

"Joe? It's Erica."

"How's it going? Are you on your way back?"

Erica quickly explained the situation.

"I'll ring you when I know the new sailing time," she sighed. "Everything went to plan here. Mary…"

"Karl's here," Joe interrupted. "I'll put him on."

"What's the delay?" Karl barked down the receiver. "You should be on your way back by now."

Again Erica explained the reason for the delay.

"So when will you be back?"

"Later today hopefully. It depends when the fog lifts."

Karl slammed down the telephone abruptly.

"Bloody bitch," he hissed.

"It can't be helped," Joe soothed. "If bad weather's delayed the crossing, there's nothing she can do about it, mate."

Karl glared at Joe.

"She shouldn't be there in the first place," he said bitterly. "She should be here, with me."

"But if her sister's sick…"

"She's married to me not her bloody sister."

There was an uneasy silence as Joe sipped the coffee Karl had made him.

"I'll get Victor to pick her up," Karl said at last, "but you'll have to go with him. Erica doesn't know Victor. Will you be okay with that?"

"Sure, I'm feeling much better. I don't know what was in those pills Danny gave me but they certainly did the trick."

"Good, but, for Christ's sake, don't take any more." There was no mistaking the concern in Karl's voice. "Once you've heard from Erica, give Victor a call and he'll bring the car round."

"Sure. By the way, what's happening with the Kennedys?"

"There was no sign of them this morning when Victor's brothers went round to the flat. They're a pair of mad bastards. I wouldn't like to get on the wrong side of either of them two."

"Luckily you won't have to. I hear Victor's on the payroll now."

"That's right. We're gonna need all the muscle we can get with the plans I've got for the future."

"What plans? You mean the club?"

"Yeah, and a few other things besides. I'll talk to you about it when you're up and about."

"Karl, I've told you I'm fine, just a bit sore that's all. So tell me, what's in the pipeline that I should know about?"

"I'm thinking of opening up another house," Karl grinned. "I've found the perfect spot up on Percival Terrace. It's bigger than Broughton Street so we can get more girls in. What do you think?"

"Percival Terrace is a bit out of our league, isn't it?" Joe said thoughtfully. "I mean, it's quite a prosperous area around there. I don't think neighbours would take too kindly to a brothel on their doorstep."

"That's just it. They won't know anything about it. There's a public car park directly behind the street so punters would come in the back way. It's secluded with a high-walled yard and a solid wooden gate. Trust me, mate, it's perfect."

"The rent must be high, a lot more than Broughton Street."

"I know the bloke who owns it. Let's just say we came to an arrangement about the rent."

"What about staffing it? We can't have the street girls working in that house."

"No, of course we can't. You're going to have to recruit some high quality girls."

"Me? What do I know about recruiting high quality girls?"

"What about this Marion woman you were talking about? Does she have contacts?"

"I've no idea. I've arranged to meet her tomorrow with Aggie, I can ask her then. We're going to need someone to run the house too, don't forget. Have you got anyone in mind?"

"No, but that's your job. That's what I pay you for, to sort out personnel."

"You make it sound like a proper job. We'll be having board meetings next."

Karl laughed, despite his irritation.

"So that's settled," Karl said a little more sternly. "You're in charge of all recruiting and staffing. I'm concentrating on getting Danny's shitty Pool Hall into shape."

"It's going to be stretching the finances a bit, isn't it, boss? Danny's place is going to need a complete overhaul, and Percival Terrace will probably need a refurb."

"Don't worry about that. It'll be tight at first but nothing I can't handle."

"When does Danny move out?"

"He'll be leaving next week. Things should be settled by then."

"What about Erica? Will you be giving her a role in the club? She'd make a brilliant hostess and she could keep an eye on the girls. After all, they'll all be new to us, don't forget."

"Not a bad idea. I'll talk to her about it. I'm having an office there too, so it could work out quite well. Anyway, I'd better be off," Karl said, putting on his overcoat. "I need to visit Aggie this morning to collect."

"Why don't you take her some flowers? She'll be leaving us next week."

"Flowers? For Aggie? Trouble with you, Joe, is you're too soft."

"She'd appreciate them," Joe grinned. "She has worked for you for a long time."

"Alright, I'll take the old crow some flowers. Do you want me to get you anything before I go?"

"No, I'm fine, thanks. I'll just wait for Victor."

"Okay, I'll see you later."

As soon as Karl had left the flat, Joe walked over to the cabinet and poured himself a very large whisky. "Mission accomplished," he smiled to himself.

FOURTEEN

Erica went into the port lounge and ordered a coffee. Twenty minutes later the coffee was still on the table, cold and untouched. Other travellers sitting on the hard, orange plastic chairs seemed resigned to the long wait ahead. After half an hour Erica went to the desk and enquired if there had been any progress.

"Nobody will be leaving for at least two hours," said the same cheerful clerk she had spoken to earlier.

"Could I leave my case here whilst I go for a walk?" The thought of staying in the terminal for the next couple of hours seemed unbearable to her.

"Over there," the clerk beamed, indicating a door marked 'Left Luggage'. "Don't be too long, dear," she warned. "Remember, the fog can lift just as quickly as it came."

Once outside the terminal, Erica delighted in breathing in the cold salty air and feeling the cool breeze on her face. She crossed the road and walked down a pretty terraced street directly across from the ferry terminal. Each house was painted a different pastel shade and most of them had hanging baskets beside their door. At the end of the street the skyline was dominated by the impressive stone-built Sacred Heart Church. A large notice board boasted its existence since 1801. To her relief, Erica found the church unlocked.

It had been a long time since she had seen the inside of a church. When she was a child she had attended with her parents and sister every Sunday. Church was somewhere she had always felt safe and at peace. Inside she inhaled the familiar aroma of incense and candle wax. The icons and stained glass windows gave her a feeling of comfort and tranquillity.

Erica sat on a wooden pew near the back of the building and bowed her head. She had intended to have a few minutes of quiet prayer but her thoughts were of her sister. Erica had tried not to dwell on what had happened to Mary, but being in the church did strange things to the mind and she found herself transported back seven years. Their mother had died from cancer the previous year, and she and Mary lived at the house with their father Tom. He was the deputy headmaster at the local primary school.

Mary had been almost sixteen, three years older than Erica. She could still remember Mary's excitement when she first told her about meeting Liam. Liam had been working on the dodgem cars at the local fair. He was eighteen, and according to Mary, was gorgeous with the cutest Irish accent. Mary had made her promise not to tell their father about him and, of course, Erica had agreed. When the fair moved on a few weeks later, Liam had stayed behind to be with Mary and had got a job labouring for a local builder.

It was a couple of weeks after this when Erica's world came crashing down. She remembered the weather had been very hot and humid, and she had found it difficult to sleep. The hall clock had chimed three when she heard noises coming from Mary's room next door. Rubbing the sleep from her eyes, Erica had quietly got out of bed and gone onto the landing.

Mary's bedroom door was slightly ajar. The room was illuminated by the street light and Erica could see her naked father lying on top of her sister. Mary was crying softly as her father's body moved up and down, slowly at first, and then more quickly. After a few minutes there was a strange grunting sound and he suddenly stopped, climbed off the bed and picked up his dressing gown from the floor.

"Shut up with that wailing," he hissed as he made his way onto the landing. Quickly Erica went into her own room and closed the door shut. She remembered standing behind her bedroom door, trembling with fear at what she had witnessed. She could hear her sister's muffled sobs, but had been too frightened to go to her. The next morning Mary had been her usual cheery self and Erica had wondered if she had imagined the horrors of the night before.

"I saw what he did last night," she blurted as they walked home from school that afternoon. "You should tell somebody, Mary. Let's go to the police and…"

"No!" Mary had shrieked. "Please, Erica, don't tell anyone. You must promise."

"But Mary, what he did was wrong. He…"

"What will happen to us if he goes to jail? Have you thought of that?"

"I don't care. You can't let him get away with it. What if he tries to do it again?"

"Again? Erica, you don't think that was the first time, do you?" Tears began to run down Mary's cheeks. "I don't want to talk about it anymore. You must promise you won't tell anyone. Promise me, Erica."

Reluctantly, Erica had agreed not to report her father but she vowed not to let him anywhere near her sister again. She had moved her own bed into Mary's room, claiming that her bedroom was too draughty.

Shortly afterwards, Mary had had her sixteenth birthday. Their father agreed she could have a small party at the house whilst he was in the pub. It was that night Erica tasted wine for the first time. It was also the first time she had seen Liam. Mary hadn't exaggerated his good looks and Irish charm.

Perhaps it was the wine she had drunk, but it was mid-morning before she had woken. Rubbing her eyes, she had run out onto the landing shouting for Mary but the house had been empty. It was then she had seen the white envelope propped up on the dressing table. Mary had gone away with Liam.

It had been nearly a month before Sally, one of Mary's closest friends, had stopped her in the school corridor and handed her a letter.

"Mary wrote to me and asked me to give you this," she said, awkwardly handing over the letter. "I hope she's okay."

Erica had frantically torn at the envelope and read the contents half a dozen times. Mary was in Ireland with Liam. They were living with his sister but they were both working and should have somewhere of their own to live very soon. She had promised to write again in a few weeks.

"Are you alright, dear?" said a kindly voice. "Is there anything I can do?"

Erica looked up to see an elderly woman sitting beside her on the pew, a look of concern on her weathered face. Erica realised she was sobbing and her whole body was trembling.

"I'm fine," she said, smiling weakly, trying to regain her composure. "Just a little upset, that's all."

The woman gave an understanding nod and patted her arm comfortingly. "Well if you need to talk, dear," she said, "God is always there to listen."

After a few minutes Erica walked towards the doors of the church, leading onto the street. To the right she saw the confessional box, the green light indicating the priest's presence. Hesitantly, Erica entered the cubicle. Facing her was the familiar grill separating her from the priest.

"Forgive me, Father, for I have sinned," she began. "It's been several years since my last confession..."

FIFTEEN

It was almost four o'clock in the afternoon when Erica finally got back to England. Joe was waiting for her in the terminal and she was shocked to see his face swollen and bruised. Standing beside Joe was a big, heavy set man with a shaved head and a broad smile.

"Erica!" Joe greeted, walking towards her. "How was your journey?"

"Never mind my journey. What the hell's happened to you? You look awful."

"Nothing serious," Joe smiled, taking Erica's small case. "It looks worse than it is. By the way, you haven't met Victor. Victor, this is Erica, Karl's wife."

Victor gave a mock bow and took Erica's hand, kissing it lightly.

"Very nice to meet you," he beamed, showing his extremely white teeth. "Mr Karl is missing you very much."

Perplexed, Erica looked at Joe.

"Victor is working for Karl. He's going to be helping out at the club."

"What club?"

"Karl will tell you all about it. A lot has been happening since you went away."

"I've only been gone three days. What's this about a club?"

Joe grinned as he opened the rear door of the car for Erica. "Victor's driving," he said, as he climbed into the front passenger seat. "I'm still a bit sore."

"Joe, please tell me what's been going on."

"Karl will explain everything when you get home, so please, no more questions."

51

Victor was a fast driver and they arrived at Karl's flat in just over an hour. Joe removed the suitcase from the boot and he and Erica walked into the flat.

"Right, boss," Joe said cheerily. "One wife safely delivered. I'm off to Cedar Road now with Victor."

"Thanks, Joe. See you tomorrow."

Karl was in the lounge in his bathrobe. Erica went to her husband and kissed him lightly on the cheek.

"At last," he greeted, grabbing her tightly around the waist. "I thought I was going to have to drag you back myself."

"It was the bad weather, Karl, I told you that," Erica said defensively. "The ferry was delayed because of the fog."

"Well, never mind, you're here now, that's all that matters."

"Karl, what's this Joe mentioned about a club?"

"Business," Karl said abruptly. "I'll tell you all about it tomorrow. Now hurry up, you need to put your glad rags on. We're going out to dinner with Danny and his boyfriend."

"Do we have to?" Erica sighed. "I'm exhausted. I thought we could have a quiet night in."

"I said we're going out," Karl said sharply, turning to face his wife. "It's all arranged. Hurry up and get showered. I've put the dress I want you to wear out on the bed."

Reluctantly Erica made her way into the bedroom. She stared in disbelief at the dress Karl had selected. It was a pretty pale blue shift dress in a soft silky fabric with a matching bolero jacket, perfect for a warm summer's evening but much too flimsy for a bitterly cold November night. She suspected he had chosen the dress purposefully to punish her for going to see Mary. She quickly showered and applied her make-up, and, fastening her hair into an attractive top-knot, slipped into the dress.

"There's a drink waiting for you so hurry up, we're leaving in half-an-hour," Karl shouted through to the bedroom.

Quickly Erica put on the small silky jacket and went into the lounge.

"You look lovely," he smiled, handing her a gin and tonic. "You'll be the prettiest girl there."

"Where exactly are we eating?" Erica asked as she sipped the drink Karl handed to her.

"There's a new curry house opened up on the precinct. Danny wants to give it a try."

"Sounds lovely," Erica smiled unconvincingly. She hated curry and Karl knew it. Whatever silly games he was playing, Erica was determined not to rise to the bait. After all, she had had the last laugh. Karl just didn't know it yet.

SIXTEEN

Joe arrived at Broughton Street just after nine the following morning in the company of Victor. Aggie was looking even frailer than when he had seen her a couple of days earlier.

"Morning, Aggie," he greeted pleasantly as he entered the lounge. "Is the kettle on?"

Aggie looked concerned when she saw Joe's bruised face but she said nothing. Instead she handed him the takings from the previous day.

"You'll never guess what," she said, positively beaming. "When Karl came here yesterday morning to collect he actually brought me some flowers. Can you believe it? Maybe I've misjudged him all these years."

"Maybe you have," Joe grinned. "By the way, Marion will be coming this morning to meet you. I thought you could show her the ropes." Joe plumped up the cushions on one of the armchairs before sitting down.

Aggie merely shrugged and stared at the newcomer. "And who's this?"

Before Joe could respond, Victor took a step towards Aggie.

"Hello," he smiled. "I'm Victor. It's very nice to meet you." Victor gave his customary mock bow but made no attempt to kiss Aggie's hand.

"Victor is going to be working for Karl," Joe explained. "He'll probably be coming here to collect in future."

"Nice to meet you," she said unconvincingly.

There was a sharp rap on the front door.

"I'll get it," Joe said, making his way into the hallway. "Ah, Marion, glad you could make it. Please come in."

Marion Watson was in her early forties, tall and slim with shoulder-length auburn hair. She was wearing a grey tailored skirt and jacket with a lemon blouse and black court shoes. Marion would have been attractive but for the left side of her face which was a mottled purple colour. At first sight it looked like a birthmark, but on closer examination you could see that the skin had been burnt with acid. The disfigurement extended along her chin and down the left side of her neck.

"Nice to see you again, Joe," she smiled, holding out her hand.

Joe shook it and escorted her into the lounge.

"Please take a seat, Marion. Aggie's just making tea."

Marion sat elegantly on the couch, crossing her long, shapely legs.

"This is Victor. He'll be collecting every couple of days from the house."

"Nice to meet you," Victor smiled. Again the mock bow but this time he did reach for her hand and kiss it lightly.

Before Marion could respond, Aggie came into the room carrying a tray with four cups.

"Aggie, this is Marion," Joe said.

Aggie looked at the woman and nodded by way of acknowledgement.

"Who wants sugar?" she asked.

Only Victor responded positively. For ten minutes the four of them chatted pleasantly. Joe was surprised to find that Victor had a very dry sense of humour and he began to warm towards him.

"Well, we'd better be off," Joe said, finishing his tea. "We'll leave you two ladies to sort things out."

"I will see you very soon, Marion," Victor said rather stiffly. "Goodbye, Miss Aggie and good luck if I don't see you again before you leave us."

Both women smiled as Joe and Victor left the house.

"He seems a nice bloke," Aggie said when they had left. "He must be a friend of Karl's."

"I haven't met Karl yet. What's he like?"

Aggie shrugged her bony shoulders. "Karl's Karl. He's always been alright with me, but I wouldn't want to get on the wrong side of him."

"You mean he's violent?"

"He can be. I've heard he's given a couple of the girls a good slapping in the past, but they probably deserved it."

"Is he married?"

"Yes. He's married to a very nice girl called Erica. She's much younger than him, of course."

"Was Erica a working girl?"

"Oh no, not Erica. She came from a good home, so I heard. But someone said her father had been murdered a few years back and the poor little mite had been put into care. That's when she met Karl."

"Do they have any kids?"

"Kids? Karl? Don't make me laugh. He won't have anything to do with kids. He insists that girls who work for him don't have any either. That's one of his rules."

"Why's that?"

"I don't really know, it's just the way it is. He thinks they are too tying. I think he gets kids mixed up with dogs sometimes."

Both women laughed.

"Does Karl ever come to the house personally, or just send one of his men?"

"What is this, twenty bloody questions?" Aggie said irritably. "Take a word of advice Marion and keep your nose well and truly out of Karl's business. Now, let's get on. You've a lot to learn and not very much time to learn it in."

SEVENTEEN

Erica rose early that morning. Karl was still sleeping. By the time he did get out of bed, Erica had washed and tumble-dried her clothes from the suitcase and was half way through the ironing.

"Good morning," she greeted cheerfully as Karl came into the kitchen. "Want a coffee?"

"I want more than a coffee. Where's the aspirin? My head's killing me."

Erica got the packet of aspirin out of the kitchen cupboard and handed him two tablets along with a glass of water. He swallowed them and greedily gulped down the water.

"Christ, that Danny can't half put the booze away," Karl moaned. "I won't be going out with him again any time soon."

"He was telling me he is going to live in Benidorm with his boyfriend," Erica said as she turned on the kettle. "Do you want your coffee black this morning?"

"Yeah, black and strong," he said, walking through into the lounge.

Erica busied herself at the ironing board as she waited for the kettle to boil. "I thought I'd go to the supermarket this morning. The fridge is looking a bit empty."

"Never mind the supermarket. I want to talk to you first about something important."

"You're not going to have another go at me over Mary, are you? I've told you…"

"No, it's not about Mary," Karl snapped irritably. "I told you, this is important."

The kettle came to the boil and Erica busied herself making the coffee.

"What is it?" she asked as she walked into the lounge and handed him the drink.

"Sit down," he said abruptly.

Erica sat on the couch and her husband sat next to her.

"Next week you're twenty-one."

"Yes, next Monday. But Karl, I don't want a fuss, I told you that. Please don't organise a party."

"Party? No, it's nothing like that. Erica, I want to talk to you about the money that you will get from your parent's estate."

"I don't want the money, Karl. I told you that. I don't want anything from that pig after what he did."

"So what do you want to do with it? Give it to the government because that's what will happen."

"I thought I could give the money to a charity. Barnardo's, perhaps?"

"Erica, charity begins at home, our home. We need that money for the business."

"No, I don't want it. Nothing good will come of it. Mary felt the same about her share. She never accepted it when she was twenty-one either."

"What did she do with her share?"

"She gave it to me."

"So you're entitled to the full amount?"

"Yes, but I…"

"Erica, we need that money. It's for our future, don't you understand?"

"No!" Erica said defiantly. "I won't touch a penny of it. Never!"

Without warning, Karl slapped Erica hard across her face, causing her to yell with pain. She desperately tried to get up off the couch but he grabbed her by the hair and held his fist menacingly to her face.

"Do I have to remind you about what you did, you stupid little bitch?" he snarled. "One word from me and you're finished. Is that what you want?" He began shaking her violently. "Well, is it?"

"No," she whimpered through her sobs. "Please Karl, you're hurting me."

"I'll stop hurting you when you stop acting like a stupid selfish cow." He dragged her to her feet and frogmarched her into the kitchen. Reaching out, he picked up the hot iron and held it close to her face.

"Now, are you going to do as I ask or do I have to really hurt you?"

"Please don't," Erica screamed hysterically. "I'll get the money, Karl, I promise I will. Please don't hurt me."

Karl held onto his terrified wife for a few seconds before releasing his grip. He watched as she fell to the floor sobbing.

"Get up," he hissed.

Slowly Erica got to her feet. She could see Karl was still holding the iron.

"I'll... I'll ring the solicitor," she said through her sobs. "I'll make an appointment for Monday morning."

"Don't bother," Karl grinned. "I've already done it. Now, where's my breakfast?"

EIGHTEEN

Karl hadn't visited his younger brother, Jason in over a year. In truth, he hadn't even thought about him in all of that time, so it had come as a shock that morning to receive a letter from Jason in the distinctive HM Prison envelope.

"What the fuck…?" he muttered, tearing it open. Inside were a Visiting Order and a brief note. '*Need to see you, bro,*' it said. '*It's urgent.*' Karl felt irritated at the request and a little uneasy. Jason was volatile and aggressive, forever getting into trouble with the police. He stared at the note for a few seconds before picking up the phone.

"Joe, I need you to go to the club this morning and keep an eye on Danny for me. He's moving his stuff out and I want to make sure he doesn't take anything he shouldn't. I have some urgent business on but tell Danny I should be back to see him off at about four."

"Sure, boss," Joe answered. "No problem."

"Thanks, mate. See you later." Karl then dialled Victor.

"Victor, I need you to drive me to Manchester this morning. Be here as soon as you can, okay?"

"Yes, Mr Karl. I'll be there in ten minutes."

Karl poured himself a coffee and waited for Victor to arrive.

"Erica, I'm going out," he shouted from the lounge as he heard the car horn sound outside a few minutes later. "I'll meet you at the club at four."

"Alright, darling," she answered. "See you then."

Erica got out of the shower and began to dress. She chose the slinky new black lace underwear she had bought in Ireland, the set that Karl hadn't seen yet. Looking through her wardrobe, she settled on the red dress with the black lace overlay. The skirt came just above her knees and showed off her shapely legs, as did her patent stiletto heels. Carefully she applied her makeup and brushed her hair, leaving it loose to fall onto her slim shoulders. A spray of her favourite perfume and she was ready.

Karl sat on the hard plastic chair in the visiting room waiting for Jason. He drummed his fingers impatiently on the small table in front of him and looked anxiously at the door for sight of his brother. After a few minutes, a guard opened the door and came into the room followed by half a dozen inmates. They all went to sit at the various tables where their visitors were waiting. Jason was the last to enter the room. Karl was shocked to see how much his brother had changed since he had last seen him. His once thick black hair looked lank and greasy. His skin had a strange yellow pallor and his face looked gaunt. Jason strode into the room and sat across from Karl.

"Thanks for coming, bro. You're looking well."

Karl wasn't in the mood for pleasantries. "What's up?" he asked abruptly. "You said it was urgent."

"Yeah, well, it is urgent, at least to me." Jason smiled and Karl could see that his teeth were in a poor state.

"I'm up for parole next week, Karl. It looks like they're letting me out of this shithole at last."

"That's great news. So what are your plans?"

"Well, I thought you could put me up for a bit, just until I get on my feet."

"Sorry, Jason, I don't have the room. We've only got the one bedroom."

"I could kip on the couch. You wouldn't know I was there."

"Maybe not, but Erica would."

"Erica? Oh, you mean your wife Erica. I haven't met her yet. Does she know about me?"

"No. Why should she?"

"Come on, Karl, we're brothers. We're supposed to stand by

each other. After all the shit we've been through together, it's only right."

"Things have changed," Karl snapped. "I have a wife and a business to run now."

"You make it sound like you're legit," Jason smirked. "We both know you're nothing more than a lousy pimp."

"If you've asked me here to be insulting…"

Karl began to rise from his chair.

"No, no, sorry, bro. I didn't mean nothing, honest. I just need some help when I get out of here. I could be very useful to you."

"Useful? How can you be useful to me?"

"Word is you've bought Danny's place and you're making it into a club. You'll need plenty of bouncers on the doors when you open up. Pole dancing clubs attract all sorts of weirdos."

"That's taken care of," Karl said dismissively. "Anyway, working on the doors is the last sort of job you should be doing. With your temper, you'll end up back in here in no time."

"No, Karl, it's the perfect job. All that free pussy on tap. I can't wait." Jason became visibly excited.

"Don't be an idiot, that's not how it works," Karl said angrily. "The girls are there to work."

"I thought they were there for sex?"

"They are, but only if you pay them."

"But I'm the boss's brother. I wouldn't have to pay. Perk of the job, hey bro?" Jason laughed.

Karl sighed. "I'll see if I can find you a flat, but that's the best I can do. I don't want you anywhere near me or the business. Understand?"

"A flat?" Jason hissed, leaning menacingly across the table towards Karl. "You fucking bastard! You're my brother. You're supposed to stand by me and all you can offer is a poxy flat?"

"Take it or leave it," Karl shrugged as he walked towards the exit. "You fucked your life up the minute you started taking drugs. You've nobody to blame but yourself."

Suddenly Jason stood up and reached over attempting to grab Karl, knocking over the table in the process.

"I bet your precious Erica doesn't know about Lisa, does she?" he spat. "It would make things very awkward for you if she did."

Before Karl could respond, two prison officers ran over and pinned Jason's arms behind his back. Jason began spitting and kicking out at them.

"Get off me, you wankers!" he shrieked as they wrestled him to the floor. "Get your fucking hands off me."

Another guard pressed an alarm button and soon all the visitors were being escorted out of the room and the prisoners led back to their cells.

Once outside the prison, Karl got into the waiting car.

"I don't want you to mention this visit to anyone, Victor. Do you understand?"

"What visit, Mr Karl?" Victor grinned. "Do you want to go home now?"

"No, not yet, I have someone I need to see. Drive up the road. I'll direct you."

The car sped off up the street, making one stop before pulling up outside a block of flats.

"Wait here," Karl ordered as he made his way into the building.

Flat thirty-two had a red painted door and two terracotta flowerpots at either side. An outsider would never guess that behind the red door lived one of the most dangerous men on the planet. Karl rang the bell and it was opened almost immediately by a short, muscular man in his mid-forties.

"Karl!" he greeted. "Karl Maddox. Good to see you, mate. Come in."

Karl entered the well-furnished living room.

"You're looking well, Barney," Karl smiled. "Here, I've brought you a present." He handed him a bottle of single malt whisky.

"Thanks, mate," Barney beamed. "I'll have a glass now. Want one?"

"When have you ever known me to refuse?"

"So, big man, what brings you to this neck of the woods?" Barney asked as he sat on the brocade couch, indicating Karl to do the same. "Don't tell me you're starting up a business in Manchester."

"No, it's nothing like that," Karl grinned, taking a sip of the whisky. "I've just been to visit Jason in the nick."

"I heard he was banged up again, the stupid young bugger. Bit of a bad boy is your Jason."

"Bit of a bloody idiot."

"Well yes, he always was a feisty little bastard."

"I put it down to the drugs. I've warned him about it but… well you know what it's like once they get a taste for it."

Barney nodded in agreement. "It's a mug's game, that's for sure."

"Barney, the reason I'm here… I want you to do me a favour."

"Name it," Barney said as he swallowed his whisky in one gulp.

"I want you to arrange for Jason to be kept in jail for a while longer. He's due for release next week if he keeps his nose clean, but I would prefer it if he doesn't get out just yet. I'm in the middle of a big deal and I don't want that little twat messing it up."

Barney gave an understanding nod.

"No problem, mate. I'll get word out today. Consider it done."

"Thanks," Karl said, finishing his drink, "but Jason must never find out about this conversation."

"Don't worry. This is between you and me, and that big bastard inside that I'll get to provoke your little brother."

Both men laughed.

"One for the road?"

"Don't mind if I do."

Erica let herself into the flat and, hanging her coat on the stand, made her way into the neat kitchen. Smiling, she walked over to the fridge. There, on the inside of the door were two bottles of chilled Chardonnay. She removed one of the bottles and, taking two glasses from the cupboard, made her way into the bedroom. She didn't have long to wait before she heard the key in the lock.

"So, you decided to come over," Joe said, standing at the bedroom door smiling.

"Yes, darling. I've got a couple of hours free. I'm not meeting Karl until four."

"Did I ever tell you how beautiful you are?" he said, taking off his jacket and beginning to unbutton his shirt.

"You did, many times, but you can tell me again and again," she laughed. "Now come to bed. I'm feeling lonely."

NINETEEN

Joe was already at the club when Karl and Victor arrived at three-thirty.

"How's it going?" said Karl.

"Everything's on schedule," answered Joe. "Danny and Billy are upstairs finishing their packing. The removal van has already taken their furniture."

"When are the tables and lighting being taken out?"

"Tomorrow morning. Half are going to a club in Birmingham and the other half is staying local."

Karl nodded approvingly.

"I got a really good price for them. I didn't realise they would fetch as much as they did."

"The company who are remodelling the club will be here tomorrow afternoon. They've fitted out clubs before so they know what they're doing."

"Good. What about upstairs?"

"I've put three quotes on your desk. They're all available to start work immediately."

"It's all coming together," Karl grinned, rubbing his hands together. "This place will be ready for business in a few short weeks."

"Mr Karl," said Victor, "do you want me to collect money from Marion now? I didn't have time this morning."

"No, not now, I've told you about this before. You collect from the house before the girls start work. It puts the punters off if they see you there. I want you to call round tomorrow morning before twelve."

Victor shrugged and looked sulkily down at the floor. "Okay, I'll call tomorrow."

It was just before four o'clock when Erica walked into the club.

"Ah, there you are," Karl smiled, holding her head in both hands and kissing her on the mouth. "You look lovely, Erica. Is that a new dress?"

"Yes, I bought it when I was in Ireland."

"Ireland? I hope you didn't wear it over there."

"Of course I didn't. I was busy looking after Mary, not going out partying."

Karl frowned as he walked to the bottom of the stairs. "You'd better get a move on, Danny," he shouted. "The taxi will be here in a minute."

"Coming," Danny replied, somewhat breathlessly as he descended the stairs, a suitcase in each hand. He was followed closely by Billy. Erica walked over to Danny, her arms outstretched.

"Goodbye, Danny," she smiled, giving him a gentle hug. "I hope everything works out for you both."

"Thanks for coming, Erica. I appreciate it. Make sure you take good care of this man," he nodded towards Karl. "Try to keep him out of trouble."

"I'll do my best," Erica grinned.

The taxi pulled up outside and the driver pressed his horn.

"Well, time to go," Danny grinned. "This time tomorrow it will be sand, sea and…"

"Sex?" Karl joked.

"I was going to say sand, sea and Sangria, you dirty bugger."

Both men laughed.

"You take care of yourself, Karl," Danny warned. "Don't get into any more scrapes. Remember, I won't be here to patch you up next time you get slashed."

Karl walked over to Danny and held out his hand. "You're starting to sound like an old woman, do you know that?"

"Just be careful, that's all I'm saying. I did a pretty neat job, don't you think?"

Karl traced the three inch scar on his cheek.

"Not bad," he admitted.

Both men shook hands and Danny and Billy got into the taxi.

"I still think you got the club too cheap," Danny said, closing the taxi door. "I could have got a lot more for it than you paid."

"You're absolutely right," Karl winked. "It just shows what a shit businessman you are."

The taxi pulled away from the kerb and Karl and the others waved their goodbyes.

"Keep in touch," Karl shouted after the taxi.

"Keep in touch?" Danny mocked once the taxi picked up speed. "You must be fucking joking."

"Is everything alright?" Billy asked. "You're not upset to be leaving, are you, Danny?"

"Of course I'm not upset. I can't wait to get away. But there is one thing I forgot to mention to Karl, but it's too late now."

"What's that?"

"I forgot to warn him not to leave Victor alone with young girls. But I'm sure he'll find that out for himself soon enough."

TWENTY

The next day, Joe drove over to Percival Terrace. The house Karl had rented, number sixteen, was a stone-built end of terrace. It had a small garden to the front with a dwarf wall and a large bay window. Joe carefully surveyed the houses along the street and at the other side of the narrow road. All occupied by respectable, hard-working people, he surmised. Not the sort of people to tolerate a brothel on their doorstep.

Opening the front door, he walked inside to be greeted by a large, imposing hallway with a cloakroom to the side. His first impression was the house was well maintained and spotlessly clean. The hallway was carpeted in dark blue with immaculate white walls. Karl had told him the house was partly furnished so he was expecting to see the odd chair and table. On entering the lounge he was pleasantly surprised to see a large white leather corner suite and two matching armchairs. A thick, dark grey carpet covered the floor and bright yellow curtains were at the windows. The fire surround was white marble with a log-effect electric fire. A large mirror hung above the fireplace and a collection of eight landscape paintings covered the walls.

"Mm… not bad," he thought. "Not bad at all."

Joe made his way to the back of the house into a smaller sitting room, tastefully decorated in pale blue. This room had a two-seater couch and an armchair. On the other side of the hall was a modern kitchen with a door leading to the rear of the property. It was this that Joe was most interested in. He opened the outer door onto a flagged patio with a small lawn area. The whole of the outside space was surrounded by a high solid wooden fence with a sturdy gate at the far side. This ensured the property was completely private. Joe opened the gate and noted that a public car park was just feet away, enabling clients to park and enter the rear of the property without scrutiny from the neighbours. He smiled. Karl certainly knew what he was doing in choosing a location. He walked back into the house and up the broad, carpeted staircase. The landing opened out to four bedrooms, all large enough to house a double bed and side table. Two of the rooms were furnished and one of them had an en suite. There was a bathroom at the far side of the corridor.

"Perfect," he grinned.

He was halfway down the stairs when he heard a sharp rap on the front door. Opening it, he was surprised to see Shirley standing on the doorstep. He hadn't seen her since the night he had been attacked by the Kennedys.

"What the hell are you doing here?" he snapped, grabbing her by the arm and pushing her into the house. He looked anxiously up the street to see if anyone had seen her. Shirley was wearing her usual fake fur jacket and black leather mini skirt. Her make-up was heavy and poorly applied, and her long black hair looked unruly.

"Nice to see you too," she sneered. "That's not a very nice way to say hello."

"What are you doing here?" Joe repeated sternly.

"I heard Karl was opening up this house."

"And you thought you'd like to work here? Sorry, Shirley, but…"

"No, it's not that, Joe. I don't want to work here. I want Karl to let me run the house."

"What? You? You must be joking."

"Why not me?" Shirley cried indignantly. "I know the business inside out. You know you can trust me. Please, Joe, I'm begging you."

Joe sighed in frustration. "Shirley, running a house is a lot different from working in one. You can't sleep with the punters for one thing."

"I know that. What makes you think I want to?"

"Sorry, Shirley, but I don't think you'd be right for the job. If I were you, I'd stick to what you do best."

"Please, Joe, at least think about it. I know I can do it if you just give me a chance." Tears began to run down her cheeks causing her mascara to blotch

"Why do you want to run the house anyway? I thought you were happy working the streets."

"I was," Shirley sniffed into her handkerchief. "I was very happy. But when those Kennedys hit me and I saw what they did to you, I got really scared. I just can't face going back on the streets again. I'm terrified. I'll feel a lot safer if I was working inside the house."

"But, Shirley, you…"

"Damn it, Joe, you owe me!" she shrieked. "If it hadn't been for me…"

"I know, and I'm grateful, but I still think working here is not for you."

"At least give me a trial, say one month. What have you got to lose? I promise you won't regret it. Please, Joe."

"Alright, let me think about it," Joe said hesitantly. "No promises, Shirley, but I'll think about it. I'll have a word with Karl and see what he thinks. Okay?"

Shirley responded by throwing her arms around Joe and kissing him on the cheek.

"Thanks, Joe. I knew I could rely on you."

"I said I would think about it, Shirley, that's all. Are you still working in Broughton Street?"

"Yes. I work there three days a week."

"Okay, you carry on there and I'll be in touch."

Smiling, Shirley walked over to the front door, but Joe grabbed her arm.

"Don't use this door," he said sternly. "We're only using the back, it's more private." He guided her into the kitchen and into the rear garden.

"This place is a lot posher than Broughton Street," Shirley grinned. "Is Karl going up-market?"

Joe shrugged. "Business is improving, I suppose. Now you get yourself off, and keep your mouth shut. I don't want any more of the street girls pestering for work."

Smiling, Shirley made her way towards the gate. "See ya later, Joe, and thanks."

Back in the house, Joe made a list of what was needed, and feeling quietly confident that Percival Terrace could be a big money earner, he went into the street and carefully locked the door behind him.

TWENTY-ONE

Joe was busy supervising the workmen removing the last of the lighting fixtures when Karl arrived with Victor.

"How's it going?" Karl asked casually. "Did you visit Percival Terrace?"

"Yeah, it looks good."

"I thought you'd like it. Have you got it fully staffed yet?"

"Don't worry, we'll get the girls."

"Well, just make sure they're the right girls. I don't want any slappers in that house. Percival Terrace is going to have class."

"I know that," Joe answered indignantly. "Trust me, Karl, they'll be quality girls. Talking of slappers though, Shirley called to the house this morning."

"Shirley? What the fuck did she want?"

"You're not going to believe this. Shirley asked if she could have a job running the house."

"You are kidding me, right? Shirley?"

"She said she's too scared to work the streets since she was attacked the other night. She wants a job working inside the house."

"She works at Broughton Street, doesn't she? What's wrong with that?"

"She doesn't want punters any more. She wants to run Percival Terrace."

"I hope you told her to piss off."

"I did say no at first, of course I did, but the more I think about it, Karl, the more I think it might not be such a bad idea."

"No, absolutely not," Karl said emphatically. "I can't see Shirley as a Madam. She's a street girl, always has been."

"But just think about it. If we scrape some of her make-up off and dress her more appropriately, she might be alright. At least with Shirley you know she's straight."

Karl lapsed into silence for a couple of minutes.

"I suppose so," he said at last. "Shirley is the wrong side of thirty to be on the streets. Tell her we'll give her a trial, but no promises, mind. We can always bounce her out if she's not up to it."

"Okay. I'll get Marion to knock her into shape."

"I was thinking of advertising the house next week, if you're sure you can get the girls."

"No problem. I've already met half a dozen suitable girls and I've arranged to meet three more at the Black Swan later."

"Good. Let's hope they're up to it, but no slappers. You know the sort of girls I want in there." Karl walked towards the club's foyer, followed closely by Joe. "Come and look upstairs. I've made a few changes already." Both men began ascending the stairs. Suddenly, Karl stopped and turned to Victor. "Before I forget, I want you to watch the girls in Cedar Road tonight. Will you be alright on your own?"

"Yes, Mr Karl. I'll take care of your girls. No need for you to worry," Victor replied, giving Karl his broadest smile.

"Good, I'll speak to you later about collecting the money." Karl made his way up the staircase, Joe by his side.

Two stud walls had been erected in the corner and a door had already been hung.

"This is going to be my office. I've had it made twice the original size. When it's been decorated it will look the dog's bollocks." He walked over to a door in the far corner of the office. "Take a look at this, Joe," he said, opening the door and walking into the cupboard. He pressed the concealed lever and the back wall opened out revealing the stairs. "You can see everything that's going on in the club from down here."

Joe followed Karl down the steep stairs and along the corridor. From behind the fleur-de-lis he could see the builders in the club going about their work, all oblivious to their presence.

"Bloody hell, Karl, this is incredible."

"Danny's father had it built years ago. Don't say a word to anyone about it, mind. Only Victor knows about it and that's the way I want it to stay."

"Sure, boss. My lips are sealed."

Both men ascended the stairs and returned to the office. Karl walked over to the drinks cabinet.

"Drink?" he said, as he poured himself a whisky.

"No thanks, I've got some work to do later. I don't want to stink of booze."

"Very commendable," Karl grinned as he swallowed the whisky in one gulp. He walked over to his large new desk just as the telephone rang.

"Barney!" he said, leaning over the desk. "How's it going, mate?"

"Karl, I'm sorry but I have some bad news."

"What's happened? Is it Jason?"

"I'm afraid so." Barney lapsed into silence.

"Well?" Karl asked with concern. "What's up?"

"I did what you asked," Barney said solemnly. "I got my bloke on the inside to pick a fight with Jason in the canteen. He knocked his dinner plate out of his hands."

"Jason wouldn't like that."

"He mouthed off at my man, but that's all. He just went back to the counter and got another plate."

"He didn't retaliate? That's not like Jason."

"No, Karl, you don't understand. Jason did retaliate. It was later that day in the showers. He attacked my man with a blade."

"He did what?" Karl hissed, the colour draining from his face. "What happened?"

"My man got cut pretty bad. He thought Jason was going to kill him so he punched him hard and Jason fell backwards. He cracked his head on the tiled wall."

"Is he alright? Is Jason alright?"

"I'm afraid he's dead. It was all very quick, he wouldn't have known much about it."

Karl's body stiffened. He sat down heavily on the chair behind his desk.

"I'm so sorry, Karl. It was an accident. A fucking stupid accident."

Karl was silent for a minute. "Thanks for telling me," he said eventually, returning the telephone to its cradle.

He sat for a few minutes staring blankly ahead as the realisation of what he had been told slowly began to sink in. Jason, his baby brother, the brother that he had always felt responsible for, was dead. Jason was dead and it was his fault.

"Is everything alright, Karl?" Joe asked. "You look like shit."

Karl shook his head slowly, and then lowered it in his hands. Joe had never seen Karl cry before. He felt uncomfortable seeing his friend sobbing, his broad shoulders shaking uncontrollably. After a few minutes Karl stopped and handed Joe the empty glass, nodding towards the whisky. Joe refilled the glass and handed it to his friend.

"You met my brother Jason, didn't you?" Karl said eventually. "He was inside the same time that we were."

"Yeah," Joe replied, recalling the aggressive, vicious young thug. "I take it it's not good news?"

"He's dead. Jason got involved in a prison fight, the stupid bugger."

"I'm sorry, mate," Joe said with feeling.

Karl took a handkerchief out of his trouser pocket and wiped his eyes. "Jason started taking drugs when he was about fifteen. He was hooked by the time he was twenty. That's why I won't have drugs anywhere near my business. I've seen first-hand what it did to my brother." He walked over to the window and stared out onto the street for a couple of minutes. "He was always up for a fight was Jason. Do you remember that time he took on two of the guards in the exercise yard? It took five of them to get him back to his cell."

"I remember," Joe grinned. "He didn't take shit from anybody."

"That's right," Karl smiled weakly. "That was down to the

drugs. He was his own worst enemy, our kid. He didn't seem to understand when to fight and when to walk away."

"I will have that drink, if you don't mind," Joe sighed, walking over to the cabinet. "What was Jason inside for this time?"

"He half killed a copper when he tried to arrest him for pinching cars."

"I'm sorry for your loss, Karl," Joe said. "If there's anything I can do…"

"There's nothing anyone can do. He's dead. Gone. It's like he never existed."

Both men lapsed into silence as Joe poured himself a whisky.

"It's our mother's fault he turned out the way he did," Karl said angrily, breaking the silence.

"Your mother? What do you mean?"

"I told you she was a whore, didn't I?"

"You mentioned it," Joe replied, beginning to feel uncomfortable.

"But I didn't tell you what else she got up to." Karl got up from his chair and began anxiously pacing the room. "She would bring men back to the house at night. Jason and I were told to stay upstairs in our room and not come down when she was entertaining. That's what she called it, the dirty slag." He walked over to the desk and took out a cigar. "Want one?"

"No thanks, mate."

Karl lit the cigar and continued to pace. "Anyway one night, Jason would be about eight or nine, she was out on the streets as usual. Jason was thirsty so he went downstairs to the kitchen to get some water just as my mother and one of her men friends came into the house."

Joe could see Karl was physically trembling.

"Jason never told me what happened that night, but he came back to the bedroom about half-an-hour later and I could see he'd been crying."

"What did you do?"

"What could I do? I was thirteen. I was just a kid myself. He never spoke about what had gone on and I never asked him, but he changed. He became aggressive towards everyone, always fighting with the kids in school, when he bothered to go to school, that is."

"What about your mother? Didn't she try to sort him out?"

"My mother was too busy either getting high or getting laid to worry about Jason. I tried to help him but, well, you saw what he could be like. In the end I moved out when I was sixteen and left him to it."

"I'm sorry," Joe said sincerely. "Like I said if there's anything I can do."

"Thanks, I appreciate the offer, but I'll deal with it. Anyway, you'd better get yourself over to the Black Swan."

"If you're sure you'll be alright. I…"

"I'll be fine. Just make sure you staff the house."

"Yeah, it's a tough job but somebody's got to do it."

Both men laughed.

"See you tomorrow," Karl said as he drained the last of the whisky from his glass.

Left alone, Karl went over to the couch and began to sob uncontrollably.

TWENTY-TWO

Two weeks after Jason died, Percival Terrace was about to open for business. Joe had been pleasantly surprised to see the change in Shirley's appearance. Whatever Marion had said to her certainly had the desired effect. Her usual short skirt and fake fur jacket had been replaced by a smart dark blue suit with an attractive floral top. Her makeup was now skilfully applied and her long, unruly black hair had been shaped into an attractive bob. She even seemed to have lost weight, Joe noticed approvingly.

"The important thing to remember is to make sure both the girls and the clients use the rear entrance," Joe said sternly. "Don't let anyone use the front door."

"Of course not," Shirley sighed. "We've been over this a dozen times already."

"Well, make sure you remember. I don't want the neighbours seeing anyone other than you coming into the house through the front door."

"Don't worry, they won't. The door's locked so nobody can get in that way."

"Just make sure it stays locked. Another thing, don't forget what I said about the fees. If a girl doesn't have the hundred pounds rent upfront, she doesn't work. Never give credit, okay?"

"Yes, I do know that. I've been in this business a long time. I know every trick in the book, believe me."

"Another thing to remember, Shirley, is not to let anyone work who you suspect takes drugs. You know how Karl feels about that. Don't even let punters in if they look high."

"Yes, Joe, I know all that. Will you go now please? You're making me nervous. We're opening up in three hours."

"Alright I'm going, but be careful and remember everything I've told you." Joe took a last look around the room, and satisfied that everything was in order, made his way to the back door just as the telephone rang.

"Hello," Shirley answered in her huskiest voice. "You're through to The Love Nest. What can I do for you today? Oh, Karl it's you… yes, he's still here. I'll put him on." She handed the receiver to Joe.

"Good morning, Karl," Joe said. "Everything's fine here. We'll be opening on schedule this afternoon. Shirley's got everything organised." He winked at her as he spoke.

"Never mind that," Karl growled, "I need you over at the club now. It's urgent."

"What's up?"

"Not over the phone. Just hurry up and get here."

"I'll be ten minutes," Joe said frowning, as he put down the receiver and hurried towards the kitchen door. "Got to go, Shirley. I'll speak to you later in the day. Good luck."

TWENTY-THREE

As soon as Joe walked into the office he could see the tension on Karl's face.

"What's happened?" he asked anxiously.

"It's Victor. He's been arrested."

"Arrested? What the hell for?"

"The police said he raped a girl."

"Victor? I don't believe it. What girl?"

"That young skinny thing that started working in Cedar Road last week. Linda, I think she's called."

"Lindsay," Joe corrected.

"Linda? Lindsay? What the hell does it matter? The lying little bitch said Victor raped her in his car last night."

"Did he?"

"How the fuck do I know?"

"Has he been charged?"

"Not yet. The police are still making enquiries. The last thing I need is lily law poking their long noses into my business. You've got to make that girl withdraw her statement, Joe, for all our sakes."

"Me? Why me?"

"Because it's your fault, that's why," Karl snapped. "I told you she was too young to work the streets, but, oh no, you know best. Now look what's happened."

"Lindsay is eighteen, I checked her ID myself. And if you remember, it was you who said she'd be popular with the punters because she did look so young."

Karl glared at Joe and for a moment, Joe thought he was going to become violent.

"Here's her address," Karl said, handing Joe a small index card. "You'd better take Shirley with you."

Joe took the card and walked to the office door.

"I don't care what you have to promise her," Karl hissed, "just make sure the little bitch withdraws her complaint."

Joe shrugged. "I'll try but I can't promise. From what I remember, Lindsay is a feisty little thing. She wanted to work at the club but I thought she looked too young for that. You wouldn't believe the abuse I got when I said no." Joe frowned as he recalled the way Lindsay had cursed him, flinging herself at him in temper. It had taken ten minutes for him to calm her down. "I suppose I could tell her I've changed my mind about her working in the club. That might keep her sweet."

"I don't care what you have to promise the stupid little cow as long as she withdraws her statement."

"And what if she won't?"

"Do whatever's necessary to make sure she does. Threaten to cut her tits off if you have to. Just get it done."

"Okay, I'll see what I can do," Joe sighed. "What are you going to do about Victor?"

"Don't worry about that little bastard. I'll deal with him," Karl growled. "Now hurry up, we haven't got much time."

"I'm on my way," Joe said, raising his arms submissively. "Give Shirley a ring and tell her I'll pick her up in ten minutes, will you?"

"Alright, and thanks, mate. I owe you."

TWENTY-FOUR

Joe pulled up outside the address Karl had given him for Lindsay. It was a small flat above a kebab shop in a back street.

"You know what to say, Shirley?" Joe said sternly. "Be sympathetic but firm."

Shirley nodded. "Don't worry. I'm sure I can persuade her."

They walked over to the door and pressed the bell for flat three. After a few seconds a female voice answered through the intercom.

"Yeah, who's that?"

"Lindsay, open the door, love. It's Joe."

"What do you want?"

"I want to talk to you about what happened with Victor. Please let me in."

It was a couple of minutes before the door clicked open. The stairway was gloomy and uncarpeted with paint peeling from the walls. A single bulb provided the only light there was. Joe and Shirley climbed the stairs in silence. A young girl was waiting for them on the landing.

Lindsay Carter looked no more than fifteen. Her long black hair was tied back with a rubber band and her small, oval face was pale with dark shadows beneath her eyes. Lindsay was dressed in grey jogging bottoms and a pale blue tee-shirt with 'Princess' emblazed across the front. She was barefoot.

"Victor raped me," she cried, running towards Joe and flinging her slender arms around his neck. "I told him no but he wouldn't stop. He really hurt me." She began to cry. Joe guided her into the flat, a small dingy room with a single bed in one corner, two armchairs and a tiny kitchenette.

"This is Shirley, a friend of mine. She's come to make sure you're alright," Joe said as he gently led the girl to one of the chairs.

Lindsay glared at Shirley suspiciously for a moment before she spoke.

"It was horrible," the girl sobbed, clinging desperately to Joe's arm. "Victor's an animal."

"Tell me what happened' Lindsay," Joe coaxed. "From the beginning, that's a good girl."

Lindsay began twisting her fingers nervously and stared straight ahead. "I'd been working in Cedar Road." She faltered. "It was getting late and I was cold. Most of the girls had already gone when Victor drove down the hill towards me. He offered to give me a lift home." Her slim body began to shake.

Shirley handed Lindsay a handkerchief and the girl wiped her eyes and blew her nose before continuing.

"I was glad to get a lift home. I was cold and tired and the car was warm and comfortable. It made me feel safe."

"Go on," Joe encouraged.

"We were driving along chatting, and then I realised Victor had driven into the park. I told him I wanted to go home, but he just laughed. I screamed at him to let me out of the car but he had locked the doors and I couldn't get out." Lindsay began to cry once more. "I tried to get out, Joe, honest I did, but the doors were locked."

"What happened next?" Joe asked soothingly.

"Victor parked the car near the lake. He never spoke a word. Suddenly he jumped out and came round to my side of the car. He opened the door and grabbed me, pulling me outside. I tried to run away but he pushed me down on the grass and got on top of me. He put his hand up my skirt and pulled my pants down. I couldn't stop him, Joe, honest, I couldn't, he was too strong." Lindsay blew her nose once more and wiped her eyes before continuing. "He was on top of me, inside of me. I couldn't do anything to stop him."

"You're sure Victor couldn't have thought you wanted sex with him?"

"No, of course not," Lindsay cried indignantly. "He's an old man. He must be at least forty. I kept pleading with him to leave me alone. Eventually he stopped and lay on the grass beside me for a few minutes."

"Didn't you try to run away?"

"No, I was too scared. After a few minutes he told me to get dressed and then he pushed me back into the car. He lit a cigarette and after he had finished smoking, he drove me home as if nothing had happened."

"Did you ring the police straightaway?"

"I'd no credit on my phone so I couldn't ring. I walked round to the police station. It isn't far."

"Did the police take a statement from you?"

"The policeman on duty took me into an interview room and I told him what had happened. He said he would arrest Victor and speak to me again later."

"Did the police arrange for a doctor to examine you?" Shirley asked.

"No. The policeman gave me some leaflets to read and then he brought me home."

"Did you mention you worked for Karl?"

"No, of course not, but I think he knew anyway."

"What makes you think that?"

"When I told him I'd been working on Cedar Road, he said I must be one of Karl Maddox's girls."

"What did you say to that?"

"I didn't say anything. I just wanted to report Victor and go home."

Shirley walked over to Lindsay and crouched down in front of her, gently holding both of her hands.

"What Victor did was a very bad thing," she said softly, "and Karl and Joe will make sure that he gets punished for it."

"Good. He deserves to be."

"Of course he does," Shirley smiled sympathetically. "But the thing is, Lindsay, if the police prosecute Victor, Karl and Joe will get into trouble too. You don't want that to happen, do you? Joe's your friend, isn't he?"

Lindsay looked at Joe affectionately and nodded.

"Then you must go to the police and withdraw your complaint."

"No, I won't," Lindsay said defiantly. "That bastard raped me."

"Lindsay, Victor won't get away with it, love. Joe and Karl will see to that. They can hurt him a lot more than the police can."

"Tell you what I'll do, Lindsay," Joe said gently. "If you withdraw your statement, I'll make sure you get an audition to work in the new club. You said you liked dancing, didn't you?"

"Yes, but…"

"You'll make a lot more money in the club than working the streets, and you'll be safe. What do you say, Lindsay? Do we have a deal?"

"You promise Victor will get punished?"

"You leave that to us. Victor will get what's coming to him, I promise you that. Now, do we have a deal?"

Lindsay was silent for a minute. "Alright, Joe. I'll go to the police station and withdraw my statement," she said hesitantly, "but I don't want that pig anywhere near me again."

"I promise you'll never see him again. Now, we must hurry. I'll drive you to the station and tell you exactly what to say."

Lindsay put on her shoes and grabbing her coat from the hook behind the door, she followed Joe and Shirley down the stairs.

"I've got to drop Shirley off at work first," Joe said as he started up the car, "then we'll go straight to the police station."

TWENTY-FIVE

It was just after eleven when Shirley arrived back at Percival Terrace. The telephone was ringing and she hurried to answer it.

"Hello," she purred. "You're through to the Love Nest. What can we do for you today?"

"Is Nicola working?" a male voice asked.

"Nicola starts at twelve. Do you want to make an appointment?"

"Yeah. It's Mr Smith. Nicola knows me. She told me she was moving to the new place today."

"What time will you be calling, Mr Smith?"

"I'll be there just after twelve. I have a busy afternoon so I can't stop long."

"Very well, I'll tell Nicola to expect you. Do you know our new location?"

"I park at the back of Percival Terrace and come through the end yard, right?"

"Yes, that's right. I look forward to seeing you at twelve." Shirley wrote the appointment in the house diary when the telephone rang again.

"Hello, you're through to the Love Nest," she cooed seductively.

For the next half hour the telephone rang constantly with clients making appointments to meet the girls. Shirley grinned in satisfaction as she placed her hand down the side of the chair's cushion and felt the reassuring touch of the baseball bat she had put there earlier.

It was half-past eleven when Nicola arrived at the house, followed closely by Karen and Julie.

"Oh, this is lovely," Nicola cried excitedly as she inspected the ground floor. "It's much posher than Broughton Street. How many bedrooms, Shirley?"

"Four. There's still room for another girl to work on this shift. Joe's working on it."

"Joe can work on me any time," Karen giggled. "He's gorgeous."

"Joe never gets involved with any of the working girls, you know that."

"He wouldn't dare. Karl makes sure of that," Julie grinned. "Can I choose which room I want? I've been working for Karl the longest so it's only fair I get first choice."

"Alright, but I want your rent first. You know the rules. One hundred each, please, ladies."

Each girl handed Shirley their money.

"Thank you, now hurry up and get changed." The three girls went out into the hallway. "Oh, Nicola, before I forget, Mr Smith rang. He'll be here at twelve o'clock. He said he's one of your regulars from Broughton Street."

"I thought he wouldn't be too long in arranging a visit."

"I wish he was my client," Karen sighed. "Easiest money you'll make today. Done and dusted in ten minutes."

"Oh, he's one of those?" Shirley smirked. "A wham bam, thank you, ma'am."

"No, it's not like that," Nicola protested, glaring at Karen. "It's just that he has very… specific requirements."

"I'm intrigued. What sort of specific requirements?"

"Mr Smith likes to take photographs. Lots and lots of photographs."

"Allowing punters to take photographs is not allowed," Shirley said with concern. "You should know that, Nicola."

"Oh, there's no film in his camera, he just pretends there is."

"Eh?"

"Mr Smith always carries a smart briefcase and inside he has a camera. He instructs me which poses to adopt. He really can be quite inventive." She began to giggle. "Then he starts clicking away with his camera. After a few minutes he wanks himself off into a small paper bag he has in the briefcase, says, 'Thank you,

Nicola, that was very nice,' and then I get dressed. It's the same routine every time. I call him Mr Kodak."

"Sounds a bit of a weirdo to me," Shirley grinned.

"Oh, he's harmless. Just a silly bit of role play, but he does visit every week without fail and he pays very well."

"Has George phoned for me?" Julie asked as she began ascending the stairs. "He said he would be visiting me today."

Shirley checked the diary.

"Yes, George said he would be here at two o'clock."

"Good, I like George."

"Is he a weirdo too?" Karen giggled mischievously.

"No, he is not. George is nice, he's a gentleman, and he brings me presents. He brought perfume on his last visit."

"Perfume? He'll be taking you to meet his mother next."

"Jealousy is an ugly thing, Karen. You…"

"That's enough, you two," Shirley snapped irritably. "Hurry up and get ready. It looks like it's going to be a busy afternoon."

TWENTY-SIX

Karl was behind his desk when Joe came into the office, followed by a sorrowful looking Victor.

"How did it go?" he asked anxiously, addressing Joe.

"No problem. Lindsay withdrew her statement so the police won't be taking the matter any further."

"That's something, I suppose. Give us a minute, Joe. I need to speak to Victor."

Joe left the room, closing the door silently behind him.

As soon as Joe left the room, Karl sprang forward and grabbed Victor by the throat, his face close to his.

"What the fuck do you think you're playing at, you stupid bastard, attacking one of my girls?" he hissed.

"Mr Karl, I can explain," Victor spluttered. "The girl…"

"I ought to nail your dick to a cross," Karl spat, as he pushed Victor roughly back against the wall.

"I didn't attack her, Mr Karl. I just wanted to love her. Danny said I could love any of the girls that worked for you. He said it was a perk of the job."

"Danny told you that?"

Victor nodded as tears began to roll down his plump cheeks.

"Please, Mr Karl, I promise I won't do anything like that again. I'll tell the girl I'm sorry and…"

"You'll fucking keep away from her, from all of them, do you hear me? I don't want you anywhere near the girls. You can't be trusted."

"Please give me another chance, Mr Karl. I …"

Before Karl could respond, there was a sharp rap on the door and Joe came into the room.

"Karl, there's a policeman downstairs. He says he wants to speak with you."

"Did he say what about?"

"No, but he said it was important."

Karl quickly gathered up the papers on his desk and put them into the desk drawer. "You'd better show him up."

Joe left the room and Karl turned to Victor.

"Get in there," he ordered, indicating the cupboard door. "Not a sound."

"Yes, Mr Karl," Victor said as he quickly went through the inner door and descended the stairs.

Karl was at his desk when Joe returned with the visitor.

"Sergeant Glendenning," Joe said, standing to one side as the newcomer entered the room.

"Sergeant," Karl greeted, a faint smile on his lips. "What brings you here? I hope I haven't broken any laws."

The two men shook hands.

"No, it's nothing like that, Mr Maddox," he said politely, sitting on the chair across from the desk. "This is just a courtesy call to make sure you are aware of the rules. Running a club like yours can be a tricky business. There are lots of pitfalls, if you know what I mean?"

"Nothing that can't be sorted out, I'm sure," Karl replied, "and please, call me Karl."

"I'm David," he grinned, lighting a cigarette. "When are you planning to open?"

"We should be ready in about three weeks."

"I've had a quick look downstairs. It looks pretty impressive. I understand you're having a private members' lounge up here. That sounds interesting."

Karl reached for one of his cigars. "Perhaps you'd like to come to the opening night as my guest, David?"

"Perhaps I might."

"Can I get you a drink? Tea? Coffee? Or perhaps something a little stronger?"

"A coffee would be nice, black, no sugar."

Karl nodded to Joe and he left the room.

Karl put his cigar in the ashtray and leaned forward. "Now, David," he said, his tone suddenly menacing, "suppose we stop fucking about and you tell me the real reason you're here?"

"My! What a suspicious nature you have," David grinned.

Karl glared at the policeman and for a few seconds there was silence.

It was David who spoke first.

"Yes, you're quite right. I do have an ulterior motive for being here."

"Well, suppose we stop wasting each other's time and you tell me what it is?"

"All in good time. You and I could be a great help to each other, Karl, in all sorts of ways."

"I don't know what you mean. How can you help me?"

"Luckily for you it was me who was working last night when that young tart came in to report the rape. It wasn't easy covering it up, you know. Victor's done it before."

"Victor's raped a woman before? When?"

"Two years ago he half killed a young woman working in Canal Street. Danny begged for my help to cover it up and I did. Victor's a very dangerous man where young girls are concerned."

"Thanks for that," Karl muttered, somewhat begrudgingly. "But don't you worry about Victor. From now on I'll make sure he doesn't get near any more young girls. But tell me, David, what's in it for you?"

"I'm a police officer," David said, a broad grin across his face. "A very ambitious, well-connected police officer, but not a very honest one, I'm afraid." He took out another cigarette and lit it before continuing. "You run a vulnerable business, Karl. You could benefit from having someone like me looking out for you."

"Go on, I'm listening."

"I have access to information, information that could keep your business out of trouble in the future." David drew heavily on the cigarette causing a plume of smoke to rise into the air. "I don't mean just this club. I mean the whorehouses you run and the girls up on Cedar Road that work for you. I could be very useful to you, very useful indeed."

"And what is all this information going to cost me?"

"Well, there will be a cost of course, but don't worry, I'm not a greedy man. No, what I really want is a sort of payment in kind."

"What the fuck are you talking about, payment in kind?"

"Karl, I'll be honest with you. I have a weakness for working girls. All types of working girls."

"Well if it's sex you want, I suggest you visit one of the brothels, they're full of girls. Or you could go down Cedar Road, that's teaming with 'em too."

"No, you don't understand. I have to be discreet, after all I have a position to maintain. I can't be seen picking up some slapper off the street, although I have to admit that's the type that turns me on the most." He laughed. "No, what I want is for you to send me a girl every now and then to my flat, a little hideaway I have in town. I'll tell you which girl and when, and of course, it goes without saying that there'll be no charge."

"Are you crazy?" Karl snapped, rising from his chair. "You want free shags whenever the mood takes you?"

"Well, that's a crude way of putting it, but yes. That is what I want. And I want the utmost discretion of course."

"And what do I get out of the deal? I presume you do have something to offer?"

"Of course," David smiled. "Like I said before, you get information."

Karl walked over to the cabinet and poured himself a whisky. "What sort of information are you offering exactly?"

"Well, for starters, this weekend there's going to be a series of police raids on sex workers on the streets, including Cedar Road. You need to get your best girls off the street for a couple of days."

"If there's going to be a raid, I need to get all of them off the street."

"No, don't be bloody stupid. The police will have to pick up some girls, or they'll smell a rat. Just put the scrubbers out that don't earn as much. Put your best girls in the houses, or give them a couple of nights off."

Karl glared at David suspiciously. "If you're fucking with me…"

"Don't be a prat, just do as I say. I'll be back in touch in a couple of days. We'll talk more then." David got up to leave just as Joe entered the room with a mug of coffee.

"Thanks, but I have to go," David said, stubbing his cigarette out in the ashtray. "I'll see you soon, Karl."

"What did he want?" Joe asked once David had left the room.

"I'm not sure yet," Karl said thoughtfully, "but we have some sorting out to do for this weekend." He quickly outlined to Joe what David had said.

"Leave it with me. I'll make sure the quality girls lay low."

"Just make sure you don't stand all the girls down, the police mustn't be made suspicious."

"You trust this bloke then?"

"I'm not sure yet. If he's genuine, he could be very useful."

"And if he's not?"

The expression on Karl's face hardened. "If he's not, he's going to regret fucking with me."

Joe shrugged. "Well, I'd best get on. When you're ready, come and have a look downstairs. The poles are all up now, it's looking great."

"Yeah, I'll be down in a minute."

When Joe left the room Karl opened the cupboard door to release Victor. He was sitting on the top step, his head in his hands.

"Hurry up and get out," Karl ordered.

Victor quickly got out of the cupboard and attempted to get to the office door. Karl grabbed his arm, pushing him back against this wall.

"Not so fast," he said sternly. "This is your last warning, Victor. You keep your dick in your pants from now on, or next time I swear I'll cut it off myself. Do you understand?"

Victor nodded vigorously.

"Yes, yes, Mr Karl," he faltered. "I'm very sorry for what I did."

"Don't forget what I've said," Karl glared. "I don't make idle threats. Now, get downstairs and give Joe a hand, and remember, I'll be watching you."

"Thank you, Mr Karl," he gulped. "I won't let you down again."

"You'd better not."

TWENTY-SEVEN

It was nearly nine o'clock in the evening. Business had been slow at Broughton Street, partly due to the heavy rain that had been falling all day and partly due to the football match on the television that evening. Marion knew from experience that whenever England played Germany it always affected business. The three girls working the late shift had barely made their rent and were sitting on the couch looking miserable.

"Anyone want a cup of tea?" she asked cheerfully.

"No thanks," chorused all three girls.

"Cheer up, for goodness sake. There's still another three hours to go. The match will be finished soon and you know how blokes love to celebrate."

"What if England lose?" asked Rosie, a pretty mixed race girl of nineteen. "They'll probably go down to the pub and drown their sorrows."

"Happy little soul, aren't you? There's nothing..." There was a sharp rap on the door. "Ah, what did I tell you? You just have to be patient." Marion got up from her chair and went to the door.

"We have three girls working at present," she said smiling as she led the two middle-aged men into the room. Both men were smartly dressed in suit and ties. "This is Rosie, Hannah and Lucy."

"I'll take Hannah," said the first man. He was tall and thin with a crop of thick sandy coloured hair. "I love redheads. My mother was a redhead."

Hannah gave her sweetest smile and took the man's hand.

"Follow me," she smiled. "My room's up here."

Marion turned to the second man. He was short and chubby with a ruddy complexion and thinning grey hair.

"I'll take that one," he said, pointing to Lucy. "I love tall women."

Lucy jumped up from the couch and locked her arm in the man's. She was almost a foot taller than him.

"This way," she grinned. "What's your name, love?"

"It's Edward, Eddie to my friends."

Lucy began to climb the stairs, followed closely by Eddie.

"Are you sure you don't want a cup of tea?" Marion turned to Rosie when they were left alone. "I'm making one for myself."

"I don't want a bloody cup of tea," Rosie snapped. "I want to earn some money. I've only made fifty quid today. This is ridiculous."

"That's how it goes sometimes," Marion soothed. "There's still time. You're here until twelve." Rosie picked up a magazine, only to throw it down in frustration after a couple of minutes. Marion went through to the kitchen and filled the kettle.

"I might as well empty the kitchen bin whilst we're not busy," she called out to Rose, as she took out the white plastic bag from its container. "I won't be a minute."

The rain had stopped but the air was still cold and damp as Marion made her way to the far side of the yard. She quickly lifted the lid and put the white plastic bag inside. On returning to the kitchen, the kettle began to boil. After washing her hands, Marion quickly made herself a drink and went back into the lounge to find Rosie standing by the window.

"I think I'll call it a night," Rosie sighed heavily. "It doesn't look like there's going to be much business about tonight." Before Marion could reply, there was a loud commotion from upstairs.

"What the…" Marion ran into the hallway. Looking up to the landing she saw Eddie shaking a hysterical Lucy by the shoulders.

"Where's my wallet, you thieving little whore?" he yelled. "You've got five seconds to hand it back or I'll ring your scrawny little neck."

"I don't have it," Lucy whimpered. "Please stop. You're hurting me."

"Hurt you? I'll bloody kill you, you thieving little bitch." He raised his clenched fist above her head menacingly.

Marion rushed up the stairs, two at a time.

"That's enough," she yelled, pushing Eddie back against the wall. "Leave her alone, there's no need for violence."

"This bitch has stolen my wallet. I want it back now or I go to the police," he hissed.

"Please, Eddie, let's stay calm," Marion soothed. "I'm sure we can sort this out without involving the police."

"Do you know who I am?" he shrieked, the veins in his thick neck pulsating. "I can close this place down in an instant, and believe me, I will."

Marion turned to face the girl, who was slumped against the wall, quaking with fear.

"Lucy, did you…?"

"No, I bloody didn't," Lucy protested. "I was in the shower with him all the time. I never left him, Marion. Someone must have come into the bedroom and taken the bloody wallet."

The second bedroom door opened and Hannah, wearing only a silk dressing gown, came out onto the landing.

"What the hell's going on?" she asked.

Eddie ignored her. "I don't know who's taken it but I better get it back pronto or there'll be trouble."

Hannah shot an enquiring glance at Lucy who shrugged her shoulders.

"It wasn't me," she protested. "I never touched it."

"Well, it hasn't grown wings and flown away," Eddie shouted. "Arthur, Arthur come out here, mate." The second man, who had been with Hannah, came onto the landing.

"Is everything alright, Eddie?" he asked, covering his modesty with a blue fluffy towel.

"No, it bloody well isn't," Eddie growled. "My wallet's missing."

"Are you sure you had it with you when you came in?" Marion asked, trying to defuse the situation.

"Are you saying I'm stupid?" Eddie said angrily, turning to face Marion. "Do you think I go around leaving my wallet wherever?

I know I had it when I came into this dive and I'd better have it when I leave or there'll be trouble."

"Have you had a good look round the room? It could have fallen onto the floor and got kicked under the bed, or…"

"Of course I've looked. The wallet's gone, I tell you."

Marion turned to the girls.

"You two get dressed. Go and sit downstairs with Rosie. I'll be down in a minute."

Both Lucy and Hannah went into their rooms and closed the door.

"Eddie, I'm sorry about what's happened. I'm sure there's an explanation. Please, come downstairs and have a drink and I promise I'll find your wallet."

"Fuck this," Eddie growled. "I've had enough of this bullshit. I'm calling the police."

"Eddie, for fuck's sake, calm down and think," Arthur pleaded. "If this gets out it could ruin both of us."

"What are you suggesting that I let these whores get away with it?"

"How much cash did you have?"

"About three hundred, but it's not just the money, it's the other stuff. Bank cards, identity cards for work. I can't let some little whore have access to that."

Marion suddenly remembered Rosie. Quickly she descended the stairs and went into the lounge. It was empty.

"Rosie, Rosie love, where are you?" she called. She went into the kitchen but the girl had gone.

"Can you give me an hour, Eddie?" Marion pleaded. "I'm sure I can sort this out."

"One hour," Eddie growled. "If I haven't got my wallet back in one hour, I'm going to the police."

Marion went into the lounge and picked up the telephone. After a few seconds it was answered by a familiar voice.

"Joe, it's Marion. I'm sorry but we have a problem…"

TWENTY-EIGHT

Erica withdrew the money from her account and handed it back to the bank clerk.

"Put the money into this account, please," she instructed, handing the second account details to the woman behind the counter.

The clerk looked enquiringly at Erica.

"I can transfer directly from one account to another, dear," she said in a slightly patronising voice. "It would be much quicker."

"No," Erica insisted. "I want two separate transactions."

"Very well," the clerk said sulkily. "I was just trying to make it quicker for you."

"Thank you, but I want you to pay the cash into the second account."

When the transaction was completed, Erica left the bank and walked along the High Street, calling at the florist where she purchased a large bunch of white lilies. Hurrying out of the shop, she managed to get onto the bus before it pulled out of its bay.

"Church Lane, please," she said to the driver, handing over her fare.

"Nice flowers," he smiled. "Going to the cemetery?"

"Yes, that's right."

"A relative, is it? I have my dad and two brothers buried there."

"A friend," Erica replied.

"Well, you haven't picked a very nice day for it. The forecast says to expect more rain."

The journey took ten minutes and when Erica got off the bus it was raining heavily. She carefully made her way to the far side of the cemetery to a grave close to the boundary fence.

Carefully she laid the flowers down and stood with her head bowed respectfully for a few minutes. The gravestone bore the name Gladys Winterbottom. Gladys had died on the first day of November, aged eighty-seven.

"Hello dear," said a cheery voice. "They're lovely flowers. Mam always did like lilies."

Startled, Erica turned to see a chubby, middle-aged woman in a black coat and headscarf standing close behind her. The woman was holding a red and white golfing umbrella advertising Dunlop sports equipment.

"Come and stand under the brolly, love," she invited. "You look soaked."

Erica smiled weakly at the woman. "Thank you," she said, "but I was just leaving."

"How did you know my mum? She didn't get many visitors in the home."

"She was a friend of my parents."

"Were they neighbours?"

"Yes, a long time ago. Now I really must be going or I'll miss my bus."

"Alright, love," the woman smiled. "Perhaps next time we can go for a cup of tea?"

But Erica didn't hear the invitation. She was already hurrying along the muddy path back to the bus stop.

TWENTY-NINE

Karl walked slowly around the ground floor of the club doing his final inspection. He gave a smile of satisfaction. The club was a far cry from the gloomy pool hall it had been just a few weeks previously. Apart from the oak panelling at the far end of the club, all the walls had been painted charcoal with large, ornate mirrors strategically placed. There was a scattering of both green and black leather couches around the room. Six booths were at the far side where girls would give private dances. Five podiums, each with a gleaming silver pole were positioned along the centre of the room and a dozen tables and chairs were placed in front of the panelled wall. A glass and chrome bar ran almost the whole length of one wall and above it, in fluorescent green lighting, were the words 'Emerald Club'.

"Well, mate, we did it," Karl beamed. "We bloody well did it."

"It looks great," Joe nodded in agreement.

"Great? What do you mean, great? It looks bloody fantastic." Karl walked over to the bar and turned on loud music and strobe lighting. Joe stifled a laugh as Karl attempted to spin on one of the poles landing unceremoniously on his knees.

"Don't give up your day job," Joe chuckled as he helped Karl to his feet.

"Talking of day jobs," Karl said trying to regain his composure, "did you sort that incident out at Marion's the other night?"

"Yeah. One of the new girls we set on made off with a punter's wallet. I found her on Canal Street, wallet and contents intact."

"I take it you dealt with her?"

"Of course I did. Don't worry, Rosie won't be hanging around here anymore."

"Christ, Joe, you didn't…?"

"No, of course I didn't. What do you think I am? No, just let's say Rosie has learnt her lesson."

"What about the punter? Was he happy to get his wallet back?"

"I wouldn't say happy exactly," Joe smirked. "What made him happy was when I offered him and his mate six month's free membership of the VIP lounge."

"You did what? Do you know how much that's worth?"

"Karl, believe me it'll be worth it. When I looked in the bloke's wallet I saw he was Edward Williamson MBE. Councillor Williamson, to be exact, Chairman of the local Planning Department."

Karl was silent for a moment, absorbing the enormity of what Joe had told him.

"The shit would really hit the fan if the press found out he'd been to Broughton Street," Joe smirked. "I told him the club would guarantee absolute discretion."

"Who was the other punter with him?"

"Arthur Reed, he's another council big-wig. Karl, do you realise what getting these two on board would mean? Six months' free membership seems a small price to pay."

"And you're sure they won't take the matter any further?"

"Absolutely positive, so stop worrying. They'll both be here on Friday for opening night."

"Good job," Karl grinned, patting Joe affectionately on the back. "Now, let's take a look at the real gold mine upstairs."

Both men went into the foyer, an attractive area with the same charcoal walls and high-gloss tiled floor as the club. A toilet block was to one side with a public telephone on the wall. A large counter with a smoked glass screen faced the entrance. The screen had two hatches. The first one was for the club and the second hatch to the left was for the VIP lounge upstairs. Both men went through the door marked 'Members Only'.

The staircase had a thick, dark green carpet and soft wall lighting. A silver handrail, similar to the poles in the club, ran up one side. A small table bearing a vase with early spring flowers was at the bottom of the staircase.

"This looks great, Karl, really classy. You've done a good job, mate."

"I thought you'd like it," Karl said proudly.

Tucked in one corner of the broad landing at the top of the stairs was a small table and chair.

"I thought I'd put Victor up here. He can't get into any more mischief then."

"Okay, if that's what you want, but I was hoping he could still come with me to Cedar Road. It's always best to have two in the car. You can't be too careful."

"Yes, I suppose you're right," Karl said thoughtfully. "He could be with you until about ten and then come here for the last four hours. But for Christ's sake, don't let him near the girls on his own. After what happened last time, he just can't be trusted."

"Don't worry, Karl, Victor will be with me in the car the whole time."

Joe opened the oak door leading into the VIP lounge and both men walked through. The walls in the lounge were decorated in a pale silver grey flocked paper. Each of the six windows was draped from floor to ceiling in grey velvet. A dozen dark green couches were placed around low smoked glass tables, each bearing a small lamp. At the rear of the room were the private booths, each curtained to the front which could be closed for privacy. To one side of the room was a small bar stocked with wines and spirits.

"So, this is what a VIP lounge looks like," Joe smirked. "I've never been in one before."

"Neither have I, but this is what I think one should look like."

"I take it the drinks and nibbles are served to the punters by waitresses?"

"Joe, we don't have punters up here, we have guests," Karl chastised, wagging his finger playfully. "For the prices they'll be charged, we have to give them respect."

"If you say so, boss. Can I see the office now that it's finished?"

"This way," Karl said, walking to the far side of the room towards a substantial oak door. The door bore a brass plaque which read 'Private. Strictly No Admittance'.

The spacious office had a thick grey carpet with the same wall covering as that in the lounge bar. In the centre of the back wall was a large oak desk and leather swivel chair with two similar chairs in front. A large green velvet couch with two matching armchairs was placed to one side of the room and a small drinks cabinet was against the wall. In one corner was a door to the concealed staircase leading down to the club.

"So this is where you'll be hanging out from now on?" Joe laughed. "Office bound, that'll be you, Karl."

"Not bloody likely, I was thinking Erica could work up here, helping with the accounts. She's good with figures. Talking of Erica, where the hell is she? I told her to be here at twelve."

"It's only just," reasoned Joe, looking at his watch. "Anyway, I've got the dancers coming to audition so I'll leave you to it."

Joe left the room and went downstairs, just as Erica was entering the foyer.

"He's upstairs," Joe grinned mischievously, "and you're late. I hope you've got a note."

Erica rushed past Joe and made her way to the office.

THIRTY

"Everything okay, Si?" Joe asked, addressing Simon, the senior doorman at the Emerald Club.

"Sure, Joe," he grinned. "These two ladies are here for the audition."

Joe nodded to the women and opened the door leading into the club.

"This way, ladies," he invited. "If you want to get changed, I'll put on the music."

Both women took off their outer clothes. The first girl, Candy, was in her late twenties, tall and slim with short blonde hair and piercing blue eyes. She was wearing a dark blue leotard and high platform shoes. Joe watched intently as she seductively wound her body around the pole.

"Thanks, Candy, that was great," he said as she concluded her dance. "Can you sit over there for a moment?"

Candy smiled at Joe and then turned to the other woman auditioning.

"Beat that," she hissed through clenched teeth.

The second girl, Daisy, was younger than Candy. Her hair, the colour of golden syrup, almost reached her waist. As she whirled round the pole, she leant back and her hair brushed the floor. When she had finished her dance, Joe invited her to take a seat, along with Candy.

Simon entered the room accompanying two more young women.

"There are four more waiting in the foyer, Joe. Do you want me to bring them all in?"

"No, just two at a time, I don't want to start any cat fights."

Both men laughed.

For the next hour, Joe watched as girl after girl performed on the pole. Most were experienced dancers, some of them from other clubs in the area, whilst some were enthusiastic amateurs. Joe had been surprised to see how well Lindsay had danced, despite his earlier misgivings.

It was getting towards the end of the session when Simon came into the club followed by a young black woman in her mid-twenties.

"Just one more, Joe," he said. "This is Cocoa."

Joe turned to face the newcomer and stared at her in disbelief.

"What the hell are you doing here?" he spat.

"I need a job," Cocoa replied defiantly. "I can dance, Joe. You know I can dance, and I need a job."

Joe pushed past her and addressed the ten girls he had already selected.

"Here are the rules of the club," he said, handing each one a sheet of paper. "I want you all here tomorrow at two o'clock for rehearsals. The club will provide your outfits, okay?"

Each of the women nodded excitedly.

"Show them out, Simon, then you can go."

Once they had left, Joe turned angrily to face Cocoa.

"What's with the stupid bloody name? Your name's Angie, not Cocoa."

"Cocoa's my professional name."

"Your professional name? Please don't tell me you're on the game?"

Angie glared at Joe.

"How dare you? I'm a dancer, nothing else."

"I thought you were going to be a nurse? What the hell happened?"

Angie stared at Joe defiantly but said nothing.

"Come on, Angie, tell me what went wrong," Joe encouraged, reaching out to hold her hand.

Angie pulled away violently.

"For Christ's sake Joe, leave me alone. All I want to do is dance. Is that a crime?"

"Dancing in this sort of place is," Joe said sternly. "This isn't for you, Angie. You're better than this, you know you are."

"Better? Joe, you are so naive. You have no idea what my life has been like since…"

"That's all over," Joe said reassuringly. "It's in the past. Forgotten."

"Forgotten? How the hell can I forget? I killed a man. I was sixteen, I was drunk, I stole your car and I killed a man. How can I forget that?"

"Angie, I sorted out the mess."

"No, you lied to the police. You took the blame for something that I'd done. You went to prison when it should have been me. I ruined your life. I'm so sorry." Tears began to run down her cheeks and her slim body began to tremble. Joe put his arm around her shoulders and kissed her lightly on the cheek.

"Don't be silly, you didn't ruin my life. You're my baby sister and I'd do anything for you, you know that."

"If that's true, then give me a job here."

"I've told you no. This is not for you."

Angie pulled away from Joe's embrace, anger flashing in her large brown eyes.

"Why aren't you working in a hospital like you planned?" Joe said softly. "The only thing that kept me going when I was inside was the thought of you going to college and getting a good career. What happened?"

"I'll tell you what happened," Angie said angrily. "I couldn't get the grades to get into college. I couldn't hold down a job, not even in a burger bar. Can you believe that? Your baby sister, who everyone thought was so clever, couldn't hold down a job flipping burgers."

"Oh Angie, I don't know what to say."

"Don't," Angie snapped. "Don't you dare feel sorry for me, I'm really not worth your pity. Let's face it, Joe, I'm a screw-up. I always was."

"Please don't say that. You're not a screw up. You're my sister and I love you." He put his arms around her protectively and kissed her lightly on the cheek. "Where are you living?"

"I'm in a squat off Eldon Mews."

"You're in a squat? Angie, you can't live in a squat. You're coming home with me. No arguments," he said firmly, stifling the girl's protest. Joe released a Yale key from the ring in his jacket pocket.

"Here, take this," he said, handing her the key. "It's to my flat. I'll put you in a taxi and I'll be there about eight. There's food in the fridge and…"

"Joe, you don't have to."

"Yes, I do. You're the only family I have and…"

Before he could finish, Angie threw her arms around his neck and kissed him on the cheek.

"I love you, big brother," she whispered in his ear.

"And I love you, little sister," Joe replied affectionately. "There's a phone in the foyer, I'll ring for a taxi from there."

Neither Joe nor Angie noticed that Karl and Erica had entered the club and were standing near the bar.

"Looks like Joe's got himself a woman at last," Karl grinned. "Pretty little thing, isn't she?"

Erica stared at Joe and the girl, her eyes glistening with unshed tears.

"Good for him," she said quietly. "I hope they'll both be happy."

THIRTY-ONE

It was shortly after eight when Joe got back to his flat. On opening the door he immediately became aware of the strong smell of marijuana. He rushed into the lounge, his anger mounting with every stride. Angie was lying on the couch in her underwear. Next to her was a tall, thin black man in his late thirties. He wore jeans but his chest was bare.

"What the hell do you think you're doing?" Joe asked angrily, "and who's he?"

Angie struggled into her jeans and top.

"What's going on?" Joe demanded, grabbing her by the arm.

Angie pulled away from Joe and sat on the man's knee.

"This is Ray," she said defiantly. "Ray's my friend, my partner."

Joe walked over to the man and leant over him menacingly.

"How dare you use that shit in my home?"

"Cool it, man," Ray grinned as he pulled on a bright orange hoodie. "It's only weed. Want some? Or maybe you'd like something stronger? There's nothing I can't get hold of, mate."

"I'm not your mate," Joe spat, pulling Angie off Ray's lap. "Now get the fuck out of my house and take that shit with you." He grabbed Ray's arm and roughly frogmarched him to the door.

"Get off him," Angie screamed. "If Ray leaves, I'm leaving too."

"You're staying put," Joe said angrily, pushing her back into the room. He opened the outer door leading to the street, still holding onto Ray. When they were outside, Joe turned to face him.

"If I see you anywhere near my sister again, you're a dead man. Understand?"

"Don't tell me what to do," Ray sneered. "Angie's my girl and…" He never got to finish the sentence. Joe head-butted him in the face and Ray crumpled to the ground. Joe kicked him in the ribs a couple of times before a hysterical Angie ran out into the street, flinging herself between them.

"Leave him alone, don't hurt him," she pleaded.

Joe grabbed Angie by her arm and pushed her back inside the flat. "Stay in there," he hissed. "I won't tell you again."

Whilst Joe was distracted with Angie, Ray got to his feet and hurried along the road cursing. Joe was tempted to give chase but decided instead to go back into the flat and speak with his sister.

Angie was curled up on the couch, sobbing loudly when Joe entered the flat.

"You bastard," she hissed. "You hurt Ray."

"If he comes here again I'll fucking kill him," Joe spat. "Now, I want you to tell me everything that's been going on, and I mean everything."

Angie stared defiantly at her brother but said nothing. Joe sat next to her on the couch and slowly his anger began to subside.

"Come on, Angie, I want to help. That's what big brothers do, right?"

She turned to face him, but remained stubbornly silent.

Joe went to the cupboard and got out the whisky.

"Want one?" he asked. Angie nodded.

He handed her a glass, but still she didn't speak.

"So what happened, Angie? Why aren't you living with Aunt Renee like we agreed?"

"She wasn't the saint everyone thought she was. I hated living with her."

Joe could see Angie's lips trembling as she fidgeted nervously with her hair.

"I know Renee wasn't the easiest person to get along with, but…"

"She was horrible," Angie hissed. "She was constantly going on about what a bad person you were, and how she was glad you were in prison where you belonged. I wanted to tell her it was me that should be there, not you, but I was too scared."

Angie turned to her brother and began to cry softly. Joe put his arm around her shoulders and gave her a squeeze as he handed her a tissue. She dried her eyes.

"So tell me what happened, sis?"

Angie took a sip of whisky before she spoke. "After you went to prison, I bunked off school all the time, so when it came to exams, it was a joke." She blew her nose on a tissue before continuing. "When I was seventeen, Aunt Renee sold the house and retired to the Caribbean. She didn't care what happened to me. I went from one squat to another. That's how I met Ray."

"You're not stupid. Surely you can see that Ray's no good."

"That's not true," Angie protested. "He was there for me when nobody else was."

"He's a junkie and he'll make you a junkie too if you stay with him. You haven't taken any of that shit he's peddling, have you?"

Angie turned her face away from Joe.

"Tell me," he snapped. "What have you taken?"

"Nothing, I swear. Just a couple of pills now and then, nothing heavy. I'm not hooked if that's what you think."

"I want you to promise me you'll not see him again."

"But Joe, I love Ray. He takes care of me and…"

"Angie, I'm serious. If you want me to help you, you have to promise to keep away from him."

There was an uneasy silence.

"Can I stay here with you?" she asked eventually. "Just until I get myself sorted out. I won't be any trouble, I promise."

"You can stay as long as you need, you know that," Joe smiled, putting his arm comfortingly around her slender shoulders. "Tomorrow I'll see about getting you a job at the club."

"Dancing?"

"No, Angie, not dancing. I was thinking you could help Erica in the office. What do you think?"

Angie turned to face her brother. She was smiling.

"That sounds good. When do I start?"

THIRTY-TWO

David Glendenning was in a foul mood. It was the opening night of the Emerald Club. He had been looking forward to it for days. It had been a shock when Lydia announced her father was having a birthday dinner that same night and they were both invited. David reluctantly agreed to attend, after all he couldn't say no to the Chief Constable, but he was determined to go to the club that evening, however late.

Lydia's parents lived in an impressive detached Edwardian house set in three acres of grounds. The family's wealth came from Lydia's mother, Sonja. Sonja was not generous with her money however, a trait shared by her daughter. Although David enjoyed the benefits of a wealthy lifestyle, Lydia had always made it quite clear that it was her money, not his.

David knew the evening would be the same routine as it had been every year with Sonja taking credit for the meal, even though she had employed the best caterers in the county. David had recently taken the police exams and was hoping George would confirm his promotion during the evening. If he had been successful, this would make him one of the youngest inspectors in the Force.

"Darling, there you are," Sonja greeted her daughter, kissing her lightly on the cheek. "Let me get you a drink." She nodded to David by way of acknowledgement. "Vodka, isn't it? What about you, David?"

"I'll have the same, Sonja," David smiled, sitting on the elegant brocade couch next to his wife. David had always admired the house, the sheer size, the location, the décor, everything about it screamed money. Lots and lots of money.

"Who else has Daddy invited?" Lydia asked casually.

"The Fitzpatricks are coming, of course," Sonja said, handing out the drinks, "and Geoffrey and Amanda Lawrence, although why on earth your father wants to have that dreadful man at his table I cannot imagine."

"Geoffrey Lawrence is a Chief Superintendent," David said. "He's tipped to take over eventually when George retires."

"Well, he'll have a long wait. George won't be retiring for some time yet."

"Where is Daddy? We have a present for him."

"He'll be down in a minute, darling. He's in the study making a phone call."

As if on cue, George Butterfield strode into the room. He was a large man, both in height and girth, with an unmistakeable aura of authority. His once black hair was now speckled with grey giving him an imposing dignity. His hazel eyes were exactly the same colour as those of his daughter.

"Ah, there you both are. So glad you could make it," he greeted, holding out his arms to welcome his daughter.

Lydia ran to her father and kissed him on the cheek.

"Happy birthday, Daddy," she cried as she handed him a card, together with a white envelope.

"What's this?" George smiled as he tore it open.

Inside was confirmation for a three night stay at St Andrew's Golf Hotel, together with three rounds of golf for two people. "Darling, that's perfect," George beamed. "Thank you. Thank you both. I'll really enjoy this."

"Will you be taking Mummy with you?"

"I don't think your mother is quite ready for three days golfing, dear. No, I think I might ask Geoffrey Lawrence, he's a keen golfer. He's coming to dinner tonight."

"Yes, Mummy said."

"David, if you have a minute, I'd like a word in private, please," George smiled. "We can go up to my study."

"Daddy, your guests will be here any time. Can't police business wait until later?"

"Darling, the others won't be here for half an hour yet. This won't take long, I promise. David?"

David rose from the couch and followed his father-in-law up the impressive staircase and along the minstrel gallery to the study. Once inside, George closed the door and walked over to his desk.

"Sit down," he said, his tone suddenly becoming stern. "You and I need to talk."

"George, what's wrong?" David asked anxiously as he sat on the chair across from George's desk.

"Wrong? What's wrong? I'll tell you what's wrong, you lying, cheating little bastard."

"I don't know what you mean," David protested, rising from his chair.

"Sit down. You sit down and you listen to what I have to say." David sank back into his chair.

"I know you've been having an affair, David. I don't know her name but I do know she is some creature selling sex on the street."

"That's a lie," David protested. "I've never…"

"Don't you fucking lie to me. Don't you dare lie to me."

David could feel his heart racing, and struggled to keep his composure.

"You were seen, man. Twice you were seen by fellow officers driving around with some tart in your car." George's face contorted with anger.

"George, I can explain. I…"

"Enough! Geoffrey Lawrence has been approached twice by junior officers reporting seeing you. How dare you?"

"I haven't," David protested. "On my life, I wouldn't cheat on Lydia. She's the love of my life. She and Matthew mean everything to me."

"David, I don't believe you. I think you're a liar and a cheat, and I won't have it. Do you hear? I simply won't have it." He banged his fist down heavily on the desk. "You'll be informed officially on Monday morning that you've been successful in passing

115

your inspector's exams. Your promotion will depend upon my recommendation. I can make it happen, David, and believe me when I say, I can just as easily destroy you."

"George, please, you have this all wrong," David wailed. "It's true that I meet informants from time to time, and occasionally some of them are women, but that's all part of the job. You know that. Sometimes I speak to them inside my car. Maybe that's what was witnessed. Believe me, I'd never cheat on Lydia, I give you my word."

There was a sharp rap on the door and Sonja stepped into the room.

"Our guests have arrived, dear," she said quietly.

"Thank you, darling, we'll be down in a minute."

When Sonja had left the room, George turned to face David.

"If I receive any more reports about you and prostitutes, I swear to God, I'll finish you. I hope you understand that. Nobody cheats on my daughter." He walked over to the study door and opened it. "Now that we understand each other, shall we join my guests?"

Silently, David followed George downstairs, feeling somewhat shaken by their encounter.

"Dinner is served," Sonja announced, smiling. "If you would all follow me into the dining room."

David was seated facing Geoffrey Lawrence. Lawrence was in his early forties, tall and thin with an unruly crop of bright ginger hair and eyes the colour of boiled gooseberries.

"Good evening, David," Geoffrey greeted. "I understand congratulations are in order."

David smiled weakly.

THIRTY-THREE

It was eight o'clock and the Emerald Club was about to open its doors for the very first time. Karl wore a dark grey suit, white shirt and green tie embossed with the words 'Emerald Club'. Each of the male staff had been supplied with the same tie. All twelve dancers wore identical outfits, a silver and green sequined bikini and silver stilettos. Behind the bar were four experienced bartenders. Simon, as well as Victor's two brothers were standing by the doors.

"Everything looks ready," Karl said anxiously as he lit one of the Cuban cigars given to him by Danny. "I just hope nothing goes wrong tonight."

"Calm down, boss," Joe soothed. "It will go like clockwork, you'll see. By the way, what time do you want me to pick up Erica?"

"Shit, I'd forgotten about her. Can you go now? I told her to be ready for eight."

"Okay, I'll be back in half an hour."

Karl decided to do one last check upstairs. He had taken on eight girls to work the VIP lounge. All had been recruited by Joe.

"Good evening, ladies," he said jovially as he entered the lounge bar. "May I say how lovely you're all looking this evening." The women ceased their chatter and smiled at their new employer. "We'll be opening up downstairs in a few minutes. You all know what to do, right?"

Sharon, the self-appointed spokesperson, moved forward.

"Mr Maddox, we are all professionals, darling. We have done this before. Trust me, there's nothing for you to worry about. We all know how to keep the punters happy, isn't that right, girls?"

"Bring it on," cried a shapely brunette.

"They won't know what's hit them," said another.

"Don't forget, when you go downstairs I want you to persuade as many punters as you can to buy a membership for up here. There's a bonus for each new member you sign up."

"By the time we've finished, you'll have more members than you can cope with," Sharon laughed.

Satisfied, Karl turned and walked onto the landing where Victor was stationed behind a small table.

"Everything alright, Victor?" he asked.

Victor, looking smart in his new grey suit, smiled warmly at Karl. "Yes, Mr Karl, everything's good."

Karl walked downstairs and into the foyer. Angie and another girl, Kerry, were behind the glass screens.

"You two alright?" he asked.

"Yes, Karl," Kerry answered giving him her sweetest smile. "We're fine."

"If you get grief from anyone, and I mean anyone, remember the guys are just outside to sort it, okay?"

Both girls nodded.

Karl walked back into the club, content that everything was as it should be.

"Okay, people," he grinned, "it's time to open up."

On unlocking the doors, Simon was greeted by a crowd of punters, all eager to see what the Emerald Club had to offer.

Just after eight-thirty, Joe entered the club with Erica. Karl was standing near the bar being complemented by a local businessman on how he was bringing a little much needed spice into the town. It was usually Erica's beauty that caught Karl's attention. She was indeed a strikingly attractive woman. Tonight she was wearing a long black velvet gown which he had chosen. This was offset by an emerald pendent he had bought to mark the opening of the club. But it was something else that caught his attention that night. Was it his imagination he wondered, or was Joe being a little too familiar, placing his arm around Erica's slender shoulders? When she smiled at Joe, it was a sexy, welcoming smile, the type of smile that should have been reserved for him alone.

He walked over to his wife. "I was expecting you ages ago."

"Sorry, darling, the traffic was horrendous."

"I've reserved a table over there," Karl said, indicating the far side of the room. "Joe, get me a whisky, will you? I'll be back in a minute."

Joe escorted Erica to the reserved table in front of the panelled wall.

"Champagne?" he asked lightly.

"Yes, please, I love champagne."

"And I love you, Erica," Joe whispered. "I wish you would leave him and come away with me. I could make you so happy."

"Darling, you know that's impossible. Karl would kill you. He'd kill me too. No, that isn't true. He wouldn't kill me, he'd destroy me."

"I don't understand. You keep saying that but how can he destroy you?"

"Trust me, he can, and he will. There are things about me that…"

A waitress came to the table.

"What can I get you to drink?" she smiled. "All drinks are half price tonight. I… Oh, Joe, I didn't realise it was you."

Joe grinned at the girl, a pretty brunette with sparkling green eyes. "I don't think you've met Karl's wife, Erica. Erica, this is…?"

"Milly," the girl beamed. "Isn't this exciting, Joe? The lights, the music, the dancing. I wanted to be a dancer but…"

Joe smiled at the girl, remembering her audition a few days earlier. He had never seen anyone crash with such force as Milly had done as she slid screaming down the pole.

Joe ordered the round of drinks when he suddenly became aware of a faint yet familiar aroma, the aroma of Cuban cigars. He looked around but there was no sign of Karl. Out of the corner of his eye, Joe saw a faint plume of smoke through the fleur-de-lis. He discreetly signalled to Erica to be quiet as he silently mouthed 'Karl' and pointed to the panelling.

"I can't thank Karl enough for giving Angie a job in the club," he said casually. "It's really helped me out."

"Karl thinks very highly of you," Erica smiled. "He was only too happy to help."

She moved her leg seductively closer to Joe and entwined her foot with his leg beneath the table. A few minutes later Karl joined them, looking much more relaxed than he had earlier.

"Erica, you look beautiful tonight," he smiled, kissing her on the lips. "That dress is perfect. It's elegant and classy, just like you, darling."

Erica blushed and felt a little uncomfortable at the unexpected attention.

"Thank you for the pendant," she smiled. "It will always remind me of tonight."

Karl turned to Joe. "That sister of yours, she's a very bright girl. She picked things up straight away. I think she'll be a real asset to the club."

"Karl and I didn't know you had a sister," Erica smiled. "Do you have any more surprises, Joe?"

"No, there's just Angie. She's had a rough time recently so it will be great to get her settled. Thanks for that, Karl."

"No problem, mate. Now the good news is the membership for upstairs is doing great. We've already got over fifty. This place is going to be a proper goldmine, I just know it is."

"Well, it's certainly filling up downstairs," Joe grinned. "It looks like it's going to be a busy night."

"To the Emerald Club," Karl toasted.

All three raised their glasses.

THIRTY-FOUR

It was almost midnight when David Glendenning finally got to the Emerald Club. He walked into the foyer and was greeted by a pretty black girl.

"Good evening, sir," she smiled politely.

"Good evening, Angie," David responded, noting her name badge. "Is Karl about?"

"He's upstairs in the private lounge, but I'm afraid you can't go up there unless you're a member."

David grinned at the girl and produced his lounge pass. Angie smiled sweetly in response. Just then, the door to the club opened and Lindsay came into the foyer carrying a glass of coke.

"Angie, I've brought you a..." she stopped abruptly at the sight of David. "Oh, it's you," she said taken aback. "I never expected to see you in here."

David scowled at the girl for a second.

"Work," he snapped as he turned and walked quickly through the door leading to the VIP staircase.

"He's cute," Angie grinned when David was out of sight.

"Don't get ideas, Angie. He's a policeman."

"You're joking. He doesn't look like a cop."

"Well, believe me, he is. When I was attacked, he was the one who..."

"Stop gossiping, you two," Simon snapped. "Haven't you got work to do? Lindsay, take a coke upstairs to the lounge doorman and Angie, you make sure the cash tallies with the tills."

Sulkily, Lindsay got a coke from the bar and made her way up to the VIP lounge. The lighting was dim on the stairwell and she was almost at his side before she realised the doorman was

Victor. In panic she screamed, dropped the drink on the carpet and began descending the stairs as quickly as she could.

"Get away from me," she shrieked. "Leave me alone."

In her haste she tripped and fell down the bottom three steps. Hearing the commotion, Joe came out of the lounge to see Victor standing at the top of the stairs and Lindsay, a crumpled heap at the bottom, screaming profanities at him.

"What the hell's going on?" Joe demanded. "Are you alright, Lindsay?"

"Keep that pig away from me," she sobbed. "You promised I wouldn't have to see him again, Joe. You promised."

"Alright, calm down," Joe soothed. "Did Victor touch you?"

Tears streamed down her face as she shook her head. Joe looked up the stairs to see Victor looking forlorn.

"I never touched her, Joe, I swear I didn't. She just came upstairs and started screaming at me. Look what she did." He pointed to the drink spilt on the carpet. "She's a crazy woman."

Joe helped Lindsay to her feet. "Get a cloth from behind the bar," he instructed. When she had gone, he turned to Victor.

"We can't have this sort of thing happening again. It's not good for business. I'll speak to Karl later."

Victor hovered sulkily at the top of the stairs. A couple of minutes later Lindsay came into the foyer holding a cloth. Joe took it from her.

"Get back to work Lindsay. I'll speak to you tomorrow."

"But Joe, Victor…"

Joe raised his hand.

"Enough. I said I'll deal with this tomorrow, now do as I say and get back to work."

Muttering under her breath, Lindsay gave one last defiant look at Victor before returning to the club. Joe handed the cloth to Victor.

"Clean up the mess before someone sees it," he ordered.

Victor peevishly did as he was asked.

THIRTY-FIVE

The Emerald Club had been open two weeks and business was good, in fact business had been very good, exceeding all expectations. Joe and Karl were in the office having their usual morning meeting.

"How did Victor take it, being kicked out of the club?" Karl asked Joe.

"He was a bit sulky at first, but he seems alright now."

"Tough. I can't afford another incident like the other night."

"He doesn't have a good word to say about young Lindsay, but I suppose that's understandable."

"Lindsay's a good little dancer, and she's popular with the punters. She's adamant that she won't work at the club if Victor's there."

"You can't blame her, I suppose," Joe shrugged, "but don't worry about Victor, he'll be with me most of the night in Cedar Road. He won't be able to get into mischief."

"Let's hope not," Karl sighed. "Talking of Lindsay, she didn't turn up for her shift last night. You'd better get round there today and see what the silly bitch is playing at."

"Is she still at the same address?"

"How the fuck do I know? Just find her and don't take excuses. If she wants to keep her job she turns up on time for her shifts."

"Okay, I've got stuff to do this morning but I'll call round to Lindsay's this afternoon." He turned to leave.

"By the way, Joe, there'll be a fat bonus for you at the end of the month. You've earned it, mate."

Joe smiled his appreciation.

Joe was feeling happy as he drove to Lindsay's flat. Everything in his life was going well. Angie was still living with him and seemed to be enjoying her work at the club. Working with Victor in Cedar Road had meant he was able to spend time with Erica, leaving Victor on his own for a couple of hours.

Joe parked his car outside Lindsay's flat and pressed the buzzer on the street door. There was no response. He tried again, still nothing. He pressed for the other flats and eventually one of Lindsay's neighbours spoke into the intercom.

"Yeah?" said a gruff male voice. "What do you want?"

"I'm looking for Lindsay. Is she in?"

"How the hell do I know? She was in at eight last night making a bloody racket, shouting and screaming at some bloke, but I haven't seen her today."

"Thanks, mate, can you let me in?"

The door opened and Joe went into the foyer and up the dingy staircase to Lindsay's flat. He knocked on her door but there was no reply.

"Fuck this," he muttered pushing his shoulder hard against the door. It flung open immediately. The room was much the same as he had remembered it on his previous visit with Shirley. Looking over towards the bed, he could see Lindsay beneath the duvet.

"Get up, Lindsay," he snapped. "Do you know what time it is?"

There was no response. Pulling back the covers, he gasped at the sight before him. Lindsay's once beautiful face was swollen and bruised with congealed blood around her nose and mouth. Her eyes were lifeless and protruding and her neck was heavily bruised. Even before he touched her icy cold hand Joe knew that Lindsay was dead.

He reeled back. "I don't fucking believe this."

Joe stood motionless for a moment staring at Lindsay's battered and lifeless body. His first instinct was to ring the police but he quickly dispelled this. He didn't want to get mixed up in whatever had happened here. Instead he put the duvet back over her and quickly left the room.

Driving straight to the club, Joe went up to Karl's office. Karl listened calmly as Joe described what he had found. Eventually Karl walked over to the cabinet and poured two large whiskies, handing one to Joe.

"Victor," he said at last.

"Victor was with me last night, boss. He couldn't have killed her. We were both working on Cedar Road from six. We didn't finish until two this morning."

"He could have killed her earlier. You weren't with him in the afternoon."

Joe shook his head and relayed the brief conversation he had had with Lindsay's neighbour.

"This doesn't make any fucking sense. Who'd want to kill a kid like Lindsay?"

Joe shrugged. "Why don't you have a word with your policeman friend? Make him start earning his freebies?"

"I'll speak to him if it gets sticky. The best thing we can do is act dumb."

"You're probably right," Joe agreed, draining his glass. "Anyway, I've got stuff to do before I pick Victor up."

"Are you sure he was with you all night, Joe? He couldn't have sneaked off for an hour?"

"I'm absolutely certain. Victor did not leave Cedar Road last night. You have my word."

Left alone, Karl paced the office impatiently. The first week of the club opening and one of his dancers had been murdered. What was it Erica had said when he had demanded she hand over her inheritance? 'No good will come of it'. Perhaps she had been right. Perhaps the money was cursed and would bring nothing but bad luck.

"Don't be so fucking stupid, man," he muttered as he poured himself another drink and took out a cigar from the drawer. "There's no such thing as bad luck. Luck is what you make it."

Finishing his drink, he made his way downstairs into the club. The girls were just arriving for the early shift as he walked purposefully over to a booth.

"Hurry up and get changed," he commanded one of the girls, "and put some music on, something loud and sexy. I fancy a private dance."

THIRTY-SIX

It had been almost two weeks since Joe had found Lindsay's body. The only reference to her death had been a short paragraph in the Evening Post the previous week stating that the body of a known prostitute had been found by neighbours and that the police were treating the girl's death as suspicious.

It was just before midnight. Saturday was the busiest night of the week and both the club and the lounge bar were at full capacity. Simon was in the foyer talking to Jan when Erik suddenly burst through the door.

"It's all kicking off in the car park, Si," he cried breathlessly. "There's at least a dozen punters fighting."

Without hesitation, Simon bounded up the stairs to the lounge.

"Victor, get downstairs quick, there's trouble in the car park. I'll fetch Joe."

Grinning, Victor ran down the stairs, two at a time, only too glad to prove his worth since his reinstatement in the club. A few seconds later he was joined in the foyer by Simon and Joe. All three ran out to the car park to see Jan and Erik confronted by a large group of men. Most of the men seemed to be very drunk and were shouting profanities at one another.

Joe grabbed hold of one man who was kicking furiously at another who was huddled on the ground.

"That's enough," he yelled angrily, as he grabbed his arm and roughly pushed him away. The man spun round and tried to head-butt Joe. Victor was standing close by and grabbed the man by the neck encircling it with his muscular arm. Whimpering, the man quickly gave up the struggle before Victor released his grip. Gradually the fighting was brought under control, and one by one the men began dispersing, watched by a vigilant Joe and Victor.

"Si, you get back to the foyer. We don't want any of this lot trying to get into the club," Joe said, taking charge of the situation. "Jan and Erik, patrol around the building. Make sure they don't come back. I'll stay out here for a while with Victor."

"Okay, Joe, but be careful," Simon warned, as he made his way back to the club.

Simon had entered the foyer before he realised something was wrong. Kerry, the young girl working behind the counter, was crying and holding a tissue to her bloody nose. Angie pushed her roughly to one side.

"Get out of the way," she hissed as she ran round to the front of the counter. She was carrying a dark blue holdall. It was then that Simon became aware of a tall black man standing by the door.

"Come on, Ray," Angie cried. "Let's go before they all get back."

"What the hell are you doing, Angie?" Simon cried. "What's going on?"

"She's taken the money," Kerry sobbed. "They're robbing the club, Si. You've got to stop them."

Before Simon could respond, he felt a sharp pain in his back and realised he had been stabbed as he fell to the ground. Ray leant over him, still holding the knife.

"Don't," Angie cried hysterically. "For fuck's sake, leave him alone and let's get out of here." She opened the door and Ray followed her out into the night.

Within minutes, Joe and Victor were back inside the building.

"It was Angie," sobbed Kerry. "Angie and her boyfriend, Ray. They've robbed the club and stabbed Simon. Joe, I think they've killed him."

THIRTY-SEVEN

Joe drove Simon to the hospital in his car, reasoning it would be quicker than waiting for an ambulance. He'd been in A&E about half an hour when the doctor who had been treating Simon came over to him.

"Your friend's been very lucky," he said. "Another inch to the right and…"

"Can I take him home?"

"I think it would be best if he stays here tonight for observation. He's had six stitches under local anaesthetic, besides the police will need to speak to him."

"Police? What for?"

"Any assault, especially a stabbing, has to be reported to the police. It's the law."

"Can I see him?"

"Of course, but just for a few minutes. He's very weak."

Joe rang Karl once he was outside the hospital.

"I managed to speak to Simon before the police got there," he said. "Simon knows what to say."

"Well, that's something, I suppose." Karl sighed heavily. "I want you to find them, Joe, and when you do, you bring them to me. Okay?"

"Sure, boss, but it's like looking for a needle in a haystack. They could be anywhere by now."

"Don't make excuses," Karl growled. "You introduced that girl into the club. That makes her your responsibility. Over eight thousand that bitch took me for. When I get my hands on her, I'll…"

"But Karl, I…"

"And then there was Lindsay," Karl continued. "It was you who brought her into the club and look what happened there. It's like you're trying to get me closed down with all the stupid tarts you're fetching to work at the Emerald."

"That's not fair," Joe protested. "Lindsay was…" but Karl had already slammed down the telephone.

Karl rang David Glendenning. "I want you to make sure the cops don't come snooping around asking questions," he said after he had explained what had happened to Simon. "Make sure it's recorded as an incident occurring in the street and is nothing to do with the Emerald."

"Leave it with me," David said. "I'll take care of it."

"Make sure you do," Karl snapped, putting down the receiver.

There was a sharp rap on the door and not waiting for an invite, Victor came into the office.

"Mr Karl," he said slightly breathlessly, "one of the men fighting outside, he… he…"

"For fuck's sake, calm down, man, you'll give yourself a heart attack."

"His name is Lucas, he is a friend of mine. He said he didn't know I worked here or he wouldn't have…"

"Wouldn't have what?"

"Lucas said he was paid money to cause fight, Mr Karl. Him and two others. The black man paid them to make big fight in car park."

"The clever bastard," Karl hissed. "Causing a diversion so he could rob me, but nobody makes a fool out of Karl Maddox. Nobody." He slammed his fist down hard on the desk.

"Thanks, Victor, you'd better go home. I'll see you tomorrow."

"Goodnight, Mr Karl."

Left alone, Karl sat quietly behind his desk deep in thought. Tomorrow, he decided, he would get David to find out everything there was to know about Angie and Ray. In the meantime, he would invest in security cameras.

Joe spent the rest of the evening trawling the streets looking for Angie and Ray. Kerry said they had driven away in a dark saloon but her description of the car had been vague.

It was almost seven o'clock the following morning before he arrived back at his flat. As he approached, he knew something was wrong. The door to his flat was slightly ajar and all the lights were on. Inside he was horrified to see that his home had been ransacked. Drawers were wide open with the contents strewn about the floor, glassware had been broken, furniture overturned and pictures vandalised. Rushing through into his bedroom, he saw his mattress had been ripped open and the contents of his wardrobe flung around the room. He rushed over to the concealed floor safe beneath his bed and was relieved to find it had not been touched.

"Oh Angie," he whispered. "What have you done? You stupid, stupid girl."

THIRTY-EIGHT

David arrived at Karl's office just after lunch. Karl hadn't slept well and felt tired and irritable.

"Drink?" he asked, walking towards the cabinet.

"No thanks, I've got a meeting this afternoon. I can't go stinking of booze."

Karl shrugged in response and poured himself a whisky.

"So," Karl began, ignoring any pleasantries, "what's happening about last night?"

"Don't worry, I've sorted it. The night crew have been told Simon was attacked in the street by a gang of drunken thugs. The Emerald wasn't mentioned."

"What about Angie and that bloke she was with, Ray?"

"I've made enquiries about them. There's nothing of any significance against Angie. A couple of shoplifting charges last year and drunk and disorderly, but Ray Walters is quite a different matter."

"What's that bastard been up to?"

"He's been inside a couple of times for dealing drugs, and more recently for GBH. He stabbed a bloke in a fight a few years back, nearly killed him by all accounts. A very unpleasant character is Mr Walters."

"Where can I find him?"

"I can check his old haunts in Manchester, I suppose," David said hesitantly, "but you do realise that if he gets arrested it could come out that your man was stabbed inside the club. That will lead to questions as to why it wasn't reported."

"I don't want the bastard arrested, I just want to know where he is. You find him. I'll take it from there. Understand?"

"Karl, you can't…"

"Just do it," Karl cried angrily. "One phone call, that's all I want from you. Okay?"

David nodded. "I'll see what I can do."

"Good enough," Karl said. He walked over to his safe and took out a bulky envelope. "There's a grand in there, David. Make sure you earn it."

David took the envelope and placed it in his inside pocket.

"Thanks, Karl," he said. "Actually, I was wondering about that girl working last Saturday, the one wearing the red dress."

"Oh you mean Honey? She dances downstairs and then comes up to the lounge to entertain."

"I don't suppose she could visit me tomorrow night at the flat?"

"I'm sure that can be arranged," Karl grinned. "I have to say, David, you're a sneaky bastard having your own little hideaway. You sure the missus doesn't know about it?"

"Positive," David smirked. "It's just a very small flat in a very big block, but it serves its purpose, if you know what I mean." He winked mischievously at Karl.

"What time should I send the delightful Honey?"

"About eight, if that's possible."

"Alright, eight it is, but make sure she's back here for ten. Honey's a popular girl."

"Don't worry, she'll be back," David said, walking towards the door.

"And David, don't forget about the phone call," Karl said. "I'll be waiting."

THIRTY-NINE

Karl was busy supervising the installation of security cameras at the club the following afternoon. He had settled on two cameras in the foyer and four overlooking the car park.

"No Joe today, Mr Karl?" asked Victor.

"Joe's having a few days off," Karl said sulkily. "It's just going to be me and you tonight in Cedar Road."

"What time do you want to go down?"

"About six," Karl answered.

Karl had tried ringing Joe earlier but had got no reply. It wasn't like him not to answer his phone and Karl was getting worried. Perhaps he had gone a little too far the previous evening in blaming Joe for what happened with Angie. After all, you can't be responsible for what your sibling gets up to. He knew that only too well with what had happened to Jason.

"Victor, I want you to drive me over to Joe's flat before we go to Cedar Road."

"Alright, Mr Karl, I'll bring the car round to the front."

It was just after six when they arrived at Joe's flat.

"You wait in the car," Karl said. "I won't be long."

Karl gave one sharp rap on the door and not waiting for a reply, walked into the flat.

He was startled at the sight before him. "Bloody hell, Joe, what's been going on? Who's done this?"

Joe shrugged and shook his head. "I think it must have been Ray. I found it like this when I got back from looking for Angie."

"You can't stay here, mate," Karl said sympathetically, surveying the broken furniture and crockery strewn around the room. "I'll get you into a hotel for a few nights while we get this fixed."

"Thanks, but I have to find her. Anything could be happening to her whilst she's with that vicious bastard."

Karl leaned against the wall, his hands thrust deep into his coat pockets. "Joe, this isn't easy for me to say, but I'm sorry for the way I spoke to you yesterday. I was out of order."

Joe stared at Karl. He'd never heard him apologise for anything in all the time he'd known him.

"Thank you." He held out his hand.

Karl moved towards him and instead of shaking Joe's hand, he put both arms around him in a hug.

"You're like a brother to me, Joe, you know that. Your pain is my pain, mate. Don't worry, we'll find Angie."

Joe smiled weakly. "I'd offer you a drink but everything's been smashed."

"Don't worry about that, we'll get it sorted. It'll just take a couple of phone calls. I guarantee it will be as good as new in no time."

Karl walked towards the door, and then turned to face Joe. "Will you be coming back to work tomorrow night?"

"Sure," he smiled weakly. "The show must go on, right?"

"Good. I'm going to Cedar Road for a couple of hours tonight with Victor. I want to see if there's any talent suitable for the club."

"Good luck with that," Joe smirked. "See you tomorrow."

It was just before eleven when Karl got back to the Emerald. There was a note on his desk requesting he ring David Glendenning urgently.

"Karl, thanks for getting back to me," David said. "I've got some news about what we were talking of earlier."

"Where is he?" Karl snapped, ignoring pleasantries. "Where is the thieving little bastard?"

"Before I tell you that you have to promise not to get me involved. No one must know you got the information from me, okay?"

"Where is he?" Karl repeated, the aggression in his voice unmistakable.

David took a deep breath. "Manchester. He's staying in Manchester with the girl. But Karl, you must promise…"

"Stop fucking about David," Karl growled. "Where in Manchester?"

David read out the address and Karl scribbled it down.

"Thanks," he said coldly. "I'll take it from here."

"Karl, listen to me, you can't…" But Karl had already hung up the receiver and was dialling another number.

"Barney? Barney, it's Karl Maddox. How are you, mate?"

"Karl, it's good to hear from you," Barney greeted warmly. "How are things over there in the wilds of Yorkshire?"

"I need your help," Karl said abruptly.

"Anything, mate, you know that. After what happened to Jason, I owe you big time."

FORTY

Erica was wearing the green satin dress Karl had chosen for her when working at the club. He had insisted that three nights a week she should network with guests in the lounge bar for a couple of hours before working on the accounts in the office. A small desk had been put in the corner for her use. Above the desk were screens for the newly installed cameras.

It was Friday night. Erica had already worked at the Emerald for three consecutive weekends. She hated being there, but she knew better than to complain. Working in the office was no better, being constantly under Karl's scrutiny.

"Keep an eye on those screens," he instructed her, "especially the ones in the foyer. We don't want a repeat of last month, do we?"

"It's Joe I feel sorry for," Erica sighed. "Just imagine, your own sister doing that to you, the wicked girl. Poor Joe must be devastated."

"He'll get over it," Karl said dismissively. "I've had his flat fully refurbished. I can't do more than that."

"I don't think it's about the flat, it's more the misplaced trust. He thought a lot about Angie. I don't think he'll ever come to terms with what she did to him."

"Well, I've done all I can. I just wish everyone would keep their personal problems away from work."

There was a sharp rap on the door and Victor entered the room.

"Mr Karl," he said, giving his usual broad smile, "there's someone to see you. He says it's urgent."

"Does this someone have a name?" Karl asked sarcastically.

"Yes, Mr Karl," Victor answered, oblivious to the sarcasm. "His name is Colin Clutterbuck."

Karl frowned. The name was vaguely familiar. "Did Colin Clutterbuck say what he wanted?"

"No, Mr Karl, only that he needed to speak to you urgently."

"Well, you'd better show him in." Karl grinned, suddenly remembering where he knew the name from. "Erica, you can go into the lounge and mingle for a while. I'll let you know when I need you."

Erica shrugged. "Okay," she said. "I need to stretch my legs."

As she went through the door, she almost collided with Karl's visitor.

Colin Clutterbuck was a short, stocky man in his early forties. His bald head and round chubby face gave him the appearance of a large egg. Steel rimmed spectacles sat halfway down his long, thin nose and behind the thick lenses were a pair of shrewd grey eyes.

"Karl, good to see you," he greeted, holding out his hand. "Long time no see, eh?"

Karl smiled at his visitor and shook his hand warmly. "It must be ten years, no, nearer twelve."

"You haven't changed a bit," Colin said smiling. "I heard you were doing well for yourself. I always knew you would."

"What about you? What are you up to these days?"

"Not much I'm afraid," Colin sighed, sitting down heavily on the leather couch. "It's not easy getting a job once you've been inside, especially in my line of work."

"I suppose not," Karl said sympathetically. "Would you like a drink?" He walked over to the cabinet and began pouring himself a whisky.

"No, thank you. I never touch the stuff."

"That's right, I'd forgotten. You don't drink and if I remember rightly, you don't smoke either. So tell me, what do you get up to?"

"I embezzle," Colin said proudly. "I steal from rich bastards, right from under their bloody noses."

"Two million, wasn't it?" Karl asked, sitting next to him on the couch.

"Nearer three," Colin corrected. "I'd have got away with it too if I hadn't got bloody shingles the week before the auditors came in. Nasty thing, shingles."

"Bad luck. So how long did you get?"

"Eight years. Can you believe it? Eight bloody years for doing what those rich bastards do all the time. I was just unlucky to get caught, that's all."

Karl nodded. "Well, Colin, it's very nice to see you after all these years, but why are you here? Don't tell me you're looking for a job?"

"Well actually, that's exactly what I'm looking for. I desperately need a job and, if I'm not mistaken, you need someone who knows what they're doing where finances are concerned." Colin gulped excitedly, his breathing becoming more irregular. "You need someone working your books who won't ask too many questions, right? I could save you a king's ransom in taxes, I know every dodge there is, and as far as investments go…"

"Whoa!" Karl interrupted. "Just hold on a second, Colin, not so fast. Are you seriously asking me for a job?"

"I'm not asking, Karl, I'm begging." Colin took out his handkerchief and dabbed at his perspiring brow. "I don't know where else to go."

"Colin, mate, I'm sorry you're on hard times but you can't work here. This is a business that's cash only, dodgy cash at that. The temptation would be too much for you. Think of the pressure you'd be putting yourself under."

"Bloody hell, you don't think I'd be daft enough to try and steal from you, do you? You're my friend. You proved that more than once in prison. Please, just give me a chance to show you what I can do."

Karl frowned. "Colin, I don't think…"

"Please, Karl, a month's trial, that's all I ask. For old time's sake?"

Karl studied the little man sitting next to him. He knew that

Colin had a brilliant mind where finances were concerned. Even the judge at his trial had commented on the cleverness of his crime. Newspapers had written about his brilliance, declaring him to be a genius, a totally dishonest, unscrupulous genius, but a genius nonetheless.

"I'll tell you what I'll do," Karl said, somewhat reluctantly, "come to the office at nine o'clock on Monday morning and we'll see if you can still work your magic, but no promises, mind. It's only a trial, remember that."

"Thank you, Karl," Colin beamed, taking off his glasses and polishing them furiously with his handkerchief. "You won't regret it."

"I'd better not because I'll promise you this…" Karl's tone suddenly became menacing, "if I ever have reason to think you've had your sticky little fingers in the till, it won't be prison you'll be going to, it'll be the morgue. Do you understand what I'm saying?"

Colin took a deep breath, replaced his glasses and dabbed his brow yet again with the handkerchief.

"Well?"

"I give you my word. You have nothing to worry about on that score. I've learned my lesson. From now on I'm going straight."

Karl began to laugh, lightening the mood.

"There's no need for that. I never said you had to go straight. What I said was where my money is concerned, you resist all temptation or else."

"Karl, all I want is to earn a decent living again and get back my self-respect. Surely you can understand that?"

Smiling, Karl walked over to the office door and opened it. "In that case, Colin, I'll see you on Monday morning. Ask Erica to come through on your way out, will you?"

"Erica?"

"The woman you collided with earlier. Erica's my wife."

"Right," Colin grinned as he walked through into the club. "And thank you for giving me this chance, Karl. You won't regret it."

"I'd better not, for your sake."

Karl couldn't help feeling that perhaps he had invited a wily fox into his chicken coup.

"Who was that funny little man?" Erica asked as she came into the office.

"That funny little man, as you call him, is Colin Clutterbuck. He's probably got the best financial brain in the country. I've just set him on to do the accounts."

"Does this mean I don't have to work here anymore? Please say I don't."

"Are you saying you don't like spending time with me?" Karl glared at his wife suspiciously.

"Of course not, darling, but I want our time together to be something special. The cinema or out for dinner perhaps, not stuck in this room working until the early hours. Do you know when we went out together last? It was when we went to dinner with Danny and Billy. That was ages ago."

"Alright, I'll see what I can do," Karl said peevishly, "but the Emerald Club doesn't run itself, no matter how many staff there are. I still have to be here to make sure it runs smoothly."

"I suppose so, but what's going to happen if you expand like you were talking of doing earlier. You can't be in two places at once."

"Opening a second club won't be happening for a couple of years yet. I thought maybe Joe could manage it. What do you think?"

Erica shrugged in response.

"You know Erica, the more I think about it the more certain I am that Joe would be the right person to run the Topaz Club."

"The Topaz Club? You've got a name planned already?"

"Of course I have. The next club I open will be the Topaz and following that will be the Sapphire. What do you think?"

"I think you need to make sure the Emerald is on its feet first," Erica said thoughtfully. "Running three clubs isn't going to be easy."

"The trouble with you is that you have no ambition." Karl took out a cigar from the desk drawer. "Trust me, if I say I will have three successful clubs in the next few years then that is exactly what I will have."

"I suppose we'll just have to wait and see what the future holds," Erica shrugged. "Now, can we go home? It's getting late."

PART TWO
2OO8

FORTY-ONE

It was the clock striking nine that caused Charlotte to wake from a troubled sleep. Her neck felt stiff and her body ached through the uncomfortable position she had been laid in. Turning on the light, she walked over to the dresser and retrieved the letter she had received that morning.

The envelope was a heavy cream wove with the name of the solicitors, Maguire & Flynn, heavily embossed in gold lettering on the left-hand side. The notepaper was equally impressive with the firm's Dublin address and contact details along the top of the page. *'Dear Ms O'Connor,'* it read, *'We act on behalf of your late parents, Mary and Liam O'Conner. Firstly, please accept our deepest condolences for your loss. I met your mother on several occasions over the years and found her to be a most remarkable woman.'* Charlotte re-read the opening paragraph again. Why would her mother be visiting a firm of solicitors in Dublin she wondered? What business could she have with them? The letter continued, *'We would be obliged if you could please visit our offices this coming Monday at, say, ten o'clock. There are some important matters which we need to discuss with you as a matter of some urgency.'* The letter was signed *'Shamus J Flynn – Senior Partner'.*

Charlotte frowned. What matters could there be? The cottage was rented from her Aunt Maureen and the souvenir shop that her parents ran had only been leased. After a few minutes, she picked up the phone and rang her Aunt Maureen.

"What do you think it's about?" she asked after reading her the letter. "What can solicitors want with me?"

Maureen was silent for a moment.

"Charlotte, I don't know all the facts but I think you need to speak to your Aunt Erica."

"Erica? What on earth for? I hardly know her. Dad said she was married to a gangster so we didn't have much to do with either of them."

"Oh Erica's a decent woman. Did you manage to speak to her at the funeral?"

"Yes, briefly, but I was too upset to get into conversation. Besides, Erica only stayed the one day. She did invite me to visit her in England, though."

"Well, if you take my advice dear, that's what you should do. Have you told Rory about the letter?"

"Yes, I told him this afternoon."

"What did he think?"

"He's as much in the dark as I am. He wanted to go to Dublin with me on Monday but I'd rather go on my own."

"Yes, perhaps that's for the best. I suppose you two will be thinking about getting married now, eh?"

"Oh, don't you start, I've enough with Rory. He'd get married tomorrow if I agreed."

"Well, you are eighteen, Charlotte. I was married with a baby when I was eighteen."

"I'm sorry but that's not for me. I don't want to get married until I'm at least twenty-one. Besides, if I married Rory and went to live on his farm, who would teach 3B their letters? Tell me that."

"So is it a career you're wanting?"

"I'm not sure what I want, to be honest. I just know that settling down isn't right for me, not yet anyway."

"Take my advice and be careful, Charlotte. Men like Rory won't hang around for ever."

Charlotte giggled, despite herself.

"I'm going to bed now, Aunt Maureen. I'll let you know what happens on Monday."

"Alright, darling. Goodnight."

FORTY-TWO

Dressed in a smart dark grey suit and white blouse, Charlotte arrived at the offices of Maguire & Flynn at a quarter-to-ten. She had tied her long blonde hair in a ponytail and her porcelain complexion bore only the minimum of makeup.

"Good morning," said the middle-aged receptionist in a somewhat nasal voice. "Can I help you?"

Charlotte introduced herself and said she had an appointment with Mr Shamus Flynn.

"Oh dear," sighed the receptionist, who Charlotte could see from the nameplate on her desk was called Deidre. "Poor Mr Flynn had a bump in his car this morning. He's at the hospital with a suspected broken leg."

"I'm sorry to hear that," Charlotte said sympathetically. "I suppose I'll have to make another appointment when he's recovered."

"No need for that dear," Deidre sniffed. "His son Patrick has taken over his father's clients for the time being." Deidre pressed the intercom on her desk. "He doesn't normally work from these offices but … Mr Flynn, there's Ms O'Conner in reception. She has an appointment with your father but…"

"That's alright, Deidre. I'll be through in a minute."

"Will it be tea or coffee you'll be wanting?" Deidre asked cheerfully, getting up from her desk. "Personally I prefer tea but we do have some instant coffee somewhere."

"Nothing thanks," Charlotte smiled. "I don't drink tea or coffee."

"Is that a fact? Why ever not?"

Before Charlotte could reply, one of the doors leading off

Reception opened and a tall, dark-haired man walked into the room

"Ms O'Connor?" he smiled, holding out his hand in greeting. "I'm Patrick Flynn. I'm so very glad to meet you."

Charlotte held out her hand and was impressed with his strong grip.

"Mr Flynn, I'm sorry to hear about your father's accident. Is he alright?"

"Oh, he'll be fine. Silly old sod crashed his car into a lamppost again, that's the third time in less than two years. I keep telling him he needs to change his glasses but well, you know how stubborn fathers can be?" He smiled and Charlotte became aware of how handsome Patrick Flynn was with his broad forehead and square chin, straight nose and penetrating deep blue eyes.

"Mr Flynn, I'm not sure what I'm doing here exactly," Charlotte said hesitantly. "Your father's letter wasn't very specific."

"If you'll come through to my office, Ms O'Connor, I'll explain everything." He smiled and Charlotte became aware of his perfect white teeth. The faint aroma of his cologne made her feel slightly aroused as she followed him through to his office.

"Please, take a seat," he smiled pulling back a black leather chair at the front of his large, imposing desk. "Have you been offered tea?"

"Yes, but thank you, no."

"Alright then, Ms O'Connor, let's get down to business." Patrick sat behind the desk and opened a buff coloured file. "There is in our client account, a substantial amount of money in your name. Our instructions were that on the untimely death of your parents before your twenty-first birthday, you were to receive that money in full."

"I don't understand," Charlotte said perplexed, "my parents didn't have any money."

"The money wasn't from your parents, Ms O'Connor. Oh no indeed. For the past eighteen years, money has been sent regularly from England by Mrs Erica Maddox, who I believe is your aunt?" He lifted an eyebrow quizzically.

"Yes, that's right, Erica is my aunt, but why on earth should she be sending me money? I hardly know her."

"We have been further instructed, Ms O'Connor," he continued formally, "to give you this letter." He handed Charlotte a small white envelope which she tore open immediately. Inside was one sheet of paper bearing her mother's familiar handwriting. *'My darling Charlotte,'* it read, *'if you are reading this letter it will mean that both your father and I are no longer alive. I want you to go to your Aunt Erica as soon as you can. Erica will explain everything to you personally. That's much better than reading it in a letter. I want you to know Charlotte, that everything we did was what we thought would be best for you. All our love my darling girl'.* It was signed *'Mammy and Daddy.'*

Charlotte read and re-read the letter several times.

"Do you know what this is about? I really don't understand. I hardly know Erica."

Patrick took the letter from her and read it. "I'm sorry, Ms O'Connor, I can't help you, I'm afraid. Of course I never actually met your parents, they were my father's clients, and there's nothing relevant in the file."

Charlotte folded the letter and put it in her bag. "You said there was a substantial amount of money put aside for me?"

"Yes, there's just over one hundred thousand euro," Patrick said smiling. "Your Aunt Erica must think a great deal about you, Ms O'Connor. I will arrange for our finance department to transfer the money into your account immediately. Can you confirm the details are still correct? Your mother provided them some time ago." He handed Charlotte a slip of paper.

"Yes," she nodded, "but I can't accept this money until I know why I was given it."

"I suggest you do as your mother asks and visit your aunt."

Charlotte sighed heavily. "I've only been out of Ireland once, that was a family holiday in Benidorm a couple of years ago. Apart from that I've rarely been outside County Wicklow."

"Well, I'm sure the foreigners don't bite," Patrick grinned. "I see your aunt lives in Yorkshire. I've heard there's some beautiful countryside over there."

"She doesn't live in the countryside. She lives in Leeds."

"Well, look upon it as an adventure," he smiled. "Do you have anyone to go to England with you? A family member or boyfriend perhaps?"

"Not really. My mum only had her sister Erica. All of my dad's family are travellers. They'll be busy with the fairs at this time of year. Dad has a sister, Maureen, but she's got four young children so she couldn't leave them."

"What about a boyfriend? Surely a pretty girl like you has a boyfriend?"

She felt herself blushing under Patrick's gaze. "There is Rory, but he won't be able to go to England. He has a farm to run. No, if I have to go, I'll go alone." Charlotte rose from her chair, "Well, thank you, Mr Flynn," she smiled. "You've been very helpful."

"You're very welcome, Ms O'Connor, and please, call me Patrick. Mr Flynn is what they call my father." He smiled and she smiled back.

"Alright, Patrick, then you must call me Charlotte."

They walked out into the foyer and he handed her his business card. "If there's anything I can do, Charlotte, anything at all, please don't hesitate to call me. My private number's on the back."

"I might just do that," she smiled, walking out through reception and into the busy Dublin street.

FORTY-THREE

The years had taken their toll on Karl. Still powerfully built, if not a little overweight, his once handsome face now bore lines that had not been caused through laughter. His once thick black hair was peppered with grey and closely cropped, giving him a hard, menacing appearance. An old scar ran down his left cheek.

Karl was at home in his study that afternoon, a newly acquired computer in front of him.

"Erica, come here a sec," he bellowed in frustration. There was no response. "Erica, where the hell are you? I need you here now."

The study door opened and Erica rushed into the room. She had hardly changed with the passing years. Fine lines around her eyes and mouth were the only indication that she was approaching forty. Still with a trim figure, her blonde hair was now shaped in a short bob.

"What on earth's the matter?" she asked with concern. "You can hear you across the park."

"It's this bloody computer," Karl growled. "How do I get the stupid thing to print?"

Erica leant over her husband and expertly operated the keyboard.

"There," she said with satisfaction as a copy of the document on the screen came out of the printer. "It's easy."

Karl glared at her.

"Get me a whisky, will you?" he snapped, taking out a cigar out of his desk drawer.

"Darling, you know what the doctor said about drinking. You must stop or at least cut down. It's not good for your heart."

"What are you talking about, woman? I have cut down. These days I only drink whisky if it's diluted with soda."

Erica sighed and walked over to the drinks' cabinet.

"Alright, but just a small one. You don't want to make yourself ill again."

"Stop nagging, for goodness sake," he hissed, taking the glass from her. "It's probably you nagging that made me ill in the first place."

Erica gave a disapproving look but remained silent, choosing instead to rearrange the flowers on the windowsill.

"What are you doing anyway?" she asked casually. "I didn't think you liked working on the computer."

"I don't, but Colin has designed a new website for the clubs. He's done a pretty decent job."

Erica walked over to her husband and, looking over his shoulder, she studied the screen.

"You can have a virtual tour of any of the three clubs," Karl said proudly. "This is bound to get more punters in."

"I suppose so," Erica gave a disinterested sigh, "but according to the papers the police are cracking down hard on sex workers. They raided three brothels only last week."

"Why do you think I closed Broughton Street and Percival Terrace when I did? I knew this would happen eventually. It's getting so a punter has nowhere decent to go for a shag."

"Well, let's hope they don't come after the clubs."

"Don't be daft, woman, half my punters are the police. Besides, all the clubs are legit. I have the certificates to prove it."

"I hope you're right, Karl. Shirley said Cupid's Angels are…"

"Shirley? When the fuck did you talk to Shirley?"

"We meet for coffee sometimes, me, Shirley and Marion."

"Why would you do that? They're paid to answer the fucking phone at the agency and arrange bookings. What's Shirley been saying?"

"Nothing, darling," Erica said soothingly. "She just said that the agency was getting busier by the day and…"

"It's just about the biggest in Leeds," Karl interrupted. "By the time I've finished, it will be the biggest in the north."

"Shirley was just saying how she enjoyed working there, a lot less stressful than running the brothel, that's all."

Karl snorted and finished the whisky in his glass.

"By the way, Karl," she said. "I saw Victor in town yesterday. He's looking well."

"Still doing security work in Sheffield with his brothers?"

"Yes. He says it's going great, they're very busy."

"Good for him," Karl sniffed somewhat begrudgingly. "At least I don't have to worry about what he gets up to with the girls anymore."

"He was saying how pleased he was that his boys are working for you."

Karl grinned.

"What I'll never understand is why Victor chose to name his kids Peter and Paul?"

"I think his wife wanted them to have English names."

"Peter and Paul Borowicz? Yeh, very English," Karl chuckled. "They're like chalk and cheese, those two. Peter's like his dad, all brawn and not a lot of brain."

"And Paul?"

"Paul couldn't be any different if he tried. He's a clever bloke though is Paul. Nothing much gets past him."

He handed his empty glass to Erica.

"Get me another whisky, will you? Not so much soda this time."

Erica frowned disapprovingly at her husband but poured him the drink.

"What do you fancy for lunch?" she asked, handing him the glass. "I was thinking a chicken salad or..."

"I hate salad," Karl growled. "I fancy something with chips. Have you got any steaks in the fridge?"

"You shouldn't be eating red meat," Erica scolded. "It's not good for you, neither are chips. You know what the doctor said."

"Doctors, doctors," Karl growled. "I'm fucking sick of hearing what the doctor said. He wants to mind his own bloody business and keep his nose out of mine, if he knows what's good for him."

"Karl, they're trying to keep you well. You should…"

A ringing sound came from the kitchen.

"Isn't that your phone?" Karl said dismissively, turning to face the computer screen. "It's probably your best mate, Shirley, wanting to gossip about my business again."

Erica gave a disapproving look as she hurried through into the kitchen, picking up her phone from the table.

"Hello," she answered, not recognising the number displayed on the screen. "Oh Charlotte, how lovely to hear from you. I was expecting you to ring…"

FORTY-FOUR

The private car that Erica had arranged to bring Charlotte from the ferry port, stopped outside the Westbrook Hotel in the centre of Leeds. Charlotte had declined Erica's offer to stay with her and Karl at their home. Instead, it had been agreed that she would stay at the hotel and Erica would visit her the following day.

Charlotte had never stayed in a hotel before and was finding the experience a little daunting. She began to unpack her suitcase when the telephone rang.

"Hello," she said slightly hesitantly. "Oh, Aunt Erica, it's you… Yes, I arrived about half an hour ago. It's a beautiful hotel you picked." She giggled excitedly. "The room is bigger than the whole of my cottage back home."

"I'm glad you like it, dear. I'll let you get settled tonight and meet you in the lobby at ten o'clock tomorrow morning, if that's okay? We have a lot to talk about."

"That's perfect, Aunt Erica. I'll see you then."

It was almost six o'clock when the telephone rang again. Charlotte answered it at once.

"Hello?"

"It's me, darling. Is everything alright?"

"Oh Rory," she said excitedly. "I was just going to ring you."

"Maureen told me you were staying at the hotel," Rory snapped irritably. "You told me you were staying with Erica at her house."

"I decided not to. I don't know Erica and her husband that well so I thought it better to stay at a hotel. Oh Rory, you should see my room, it's amazing, there's…"

"You shouldn't be there on your own," Rory interrupted angrily. "Anything can happen to a young girl alone in the city."

"For goodness sake, stop fussing. It's perfectly safe. Actually, it's quite exciting. My window looks down onto the street. I've never seen so many people."

"City streets are dangerous. You don't know who you're standing next to. I don't want you to leave your room until Erica gets there tomorrow."

"For goodness sake, Rory, don't be such a worrywart," Charlotte teased.

"I mean it. Promise me you won't leave the hotel."

"Alright, I promise if it makes you happy. I'll have dinner brought up to my room and have an early night, okay?"

"Make sure you do. You can't be too careful. I have to go now, so remember what I've said. Goodnight, Charlotte. I'll call again tomorrow."

"Goodnight, Rory," Charlotte replied softly.

Grinning mischievously, Charlotte replaced the receiver and, putting on her coat, made her way down to the foyer and out into the busy street.

FORTY-FIVE

The following morning was warm and sunny. Charlotte rose early and on entering the dining room, was shown to a small table to the rear.

"Orange juice, please," she requested of the young waitress standing by her table.

"Anything else, Madam?" the waitress asked in a strong east European accent. "The buffet table is over there," she said indicating a trestle table on the back wall, "or you can order breakfast from the menu." She held out a red leather-bound book.

"No, thank you," Charlotte smiled, "just orange juice, please."

The waitress disappeared and returned a few minutes later with the drink.

Charlotte sipped the juice and turned her attention to her surroundings and fellow guests. The elegant dining room was only half full. Four women were breakfasting at the table in front of the large window. They're probably attending some sort of convention, Charlotte reasoned, noting their smart suits and briefcases. Next to them, a young couple, both casually dressed, were chatting and laughing. She noticed that the man was holding the woman's hand. They look so much in love, she thought as she watched him lean over and kiss her hand lightly.

At the table next to her, a middle-aged man dressed in a smart suit and dark blue tie was finishing his meal. His companion, an attractive woman in her mid-twenties, was still eating her breakfast. The woman had long red hair, almost to her waist. She was wearing a tight black leather skirt and pink sweater. On her feet were red shoes with very high heels. Holy Mary, Charlotte thought, if she were to go to my town dressed like that they'd throw her into the sea. After a few minutes the man whispered something to the woman and got up from the table. Charlotte watched as he walked out into Reception and spoke to the desk clerk.

The young woman finally pushed her plate away and joined her companion.

"Call me next time you're in town," she cooed. The man turned to her and nodded, before hurrying to the exit and into the street. As the woman made her way to the exit, Charlotte noticed that she had left her handbag on the floor beneath the table.

"Your bag," she called, picking it up and hurrying into the foyer towards the woman. "Don't forget your bag."

"Oh, my God! I don't know where my head is this morning. Too much champagne last night, I expect," the woman smiled, taking the bag from Charlotte. "Thank you for returning it."

Charlotte smiled and turned to go back into the dining room.

"Can I buy you a coffee to say thank you?" the woman asked, following her back into the room. "I really am grateful."

"I don't drink coffee, but you can buy me an orange juice, if you insist."

The two women returned to Charlotte's table.

"You're not eating?"

"No, I'm not hungry. I'm too excited to eat. I've never been to England before."

"Are you on holiday?"

"No, not a holiday exactly. I'm meeting my aunt and… oh, is that your phone ringing?"

"Bloody nuisance," muttered the woman as she rooted around the inside of her bag, eventually retrieving her pink mobile. "Yes, Shirley? What have you got for me? The Marriott? What time? Okay, text me the details and I'll give him a ring." She turned to face Charlotte. "Well, it's been very nice meeting you but I'm afraid I have to get back to work. Thanks again for returning my bag. I'll have to buy you that drink another time. What's your name by the way?"

"Charlotte. Charlotte O'Connor."

"Well, you take care of yourself, Charlotte O'Connor. I'm Bunny, by the way."

"Bunny? That's an unusual name."

"Actually it's Bonita," she laughed as she headed towards the foyer, "but everyone calls me Bunny."

Charlotte finished her juice and decided to visit the shops. It would be another hour before she was due to meet Erica. She was still buzzing from the previous night when she had ventured up to Millennium Square. She had never seen so many bars and restaurants, some with tables on the street with people eating and drinking. The night air had been filled with music and laughter, a far cry from the small village where she lived. If this was what it was like to live in the city, Charlotte grinned, she liked it. She liked it very much.

FORTY-SIX

Carrying two shopping bags in each hand, Charlotte arrived back at the hotel just after ten o'clock. Erica was already in the foyer.

"Aunt Erica," she greeted, rushing towards her, "it's lovely to see you again." Charlotte kissed Erica lightly on the cheek. "Isn't Leeds wonderful? I've never seen so many shops."

"It looks like you've visited most of them this morning," Erica smiled. "Here, let me take some of those." She reached out and took two of the bags.

"Aunt Erica, I…"

"Charlotte, can you call me Erica? Aunt Erica makes me feel very old."

"Alright, if you're sure. Let's go up to my room, the lift is over there."

"I've invited Marion, a close friend of mine to join us later. You don't mind, do you, dear?"

"Of course I don't mind, I want to meet as many people as I can whilst I'm here."

Both women got into the lift and remained silent until they reached the second floor.

"What room number is it?" Erica asked.

"231, it's just round the corner."

Once inside the room, Charlotte flung the bags onto the king-sized bed and turned to face her aunt.

"It really is a beautiful room you got for me. Thank you."

"You're very welcome, dear," Erica smiled. "I'll text Marion and tell her where to come."

Whilst Erica busied herself with the phone, Charlotte placed the dresses she had bought in the wardrobe.

"I adore this dress, don't you?" Charlotte grinned, holding up a pale pink floral dress. "I bet Rory will love it too when I show him."

"I'm sure he will. It's very pretty."

Charlotte put the dress on a hanger before turning to her aunt. "Erica, I have so many questions I need to ask you, I really don't know where to begin." A deep frown crept over her face. "There's my mother's note for a start. What was it she wanted me to know that was so important? Then there's the money. The solicitor said you've been sending money every month since I was a baby. I don't understand why would you do that? And…"

"Please, darling, let's sit down," Erica soothed, placing her arm affectionately around the girl's shoulders and guiding her to a large wing-backed chair in front of one of the windows. Erica sat on the couch opposite. "Charlotte, what I'm about to tell you will come as a shock but it's very important that you know the truth." Erica could see the confusion on the girl's face.

"You're scaring me. What is it?"

"Darling, Mary and Liam loved you very much, you do know that, don't you?" Charlotte nodded. "The thing is Charlotte, Mary and Liam were not your biological parents. They adopted you when you were a baby."

There was a gasp from Charlotte and she put both hands up to her face. "No, no that can't be right. I don't believe it."

Erica reached out and gently took Charlotte's hand. "Your mother was my best friend. Her name was Paula."

"No, that's not true. Mary was my mother and Liam was my father." She pushed Erica away and strode over to the window. She was silent for a minute before turning angrily to confront Erica.

"So where is this Paula? Why isn't she here?"

"Paula died," Erica said softly.

"Died? When did she die? How?"

"I don't want to go into that right now. I think it would be best if…"

"Erica, if Paula was my mother like you say, I have a right to know what happened to her."

Erica took a deep breath. "Yes, you're right," she said solemnly. "I'm sorry, darling, but Paula was murdered."

"Murdered? Who murdered her? Why was she murdered?"

"It all happened a long time ago. Nobody has ever been charged, so they probably never will be now."

"What about my father? Is he dead too?"

"No, your father's not dead. He was a married man with a family," Erica said quietly. "He wasn't prepared to give that up and…"

"I want to meet him. If he's my father I have a right to meet him."

"Liam was your father. He provided for you and cared for you. He loved you very much."

There was a sharp rap on the door.

"That'll be Marion."

"I don't want to see her, not now. Please tell her to go away."

"I think you should hear what Marion has to say. It's very important, darling."

Charlotte remained stubbornly silent for a moment. "Alright," she sighed reluctantly. "You'd better let her in."

FORTY-SEVEN

Erica opened the door and Marion came into the room. She was dressed in an elegant navy blue dress and matching shoes. Her hair was styled in a neat bun.

"Charlotte, this is my friend, Marion," Erica smiled. "And this young lady is Charlotte, all the way from Ireland."

"It's very nice to meet you at last," Marion greeted. "I've heard a lot about you from Erica."

"Did you know my mother?" Charlotte asked abruptly. "Did you know Paula?"

Marion was silent for a moment and gave a worried glance at Erica.

"Charlotte needs to know the truth, Marion," she said quietly. "We owe her that much."

Marion walked over to Charlotte. "Yes, dear, I did know Paula, she was my daughter. My beautiful, beautiful child."

"What?" Charlotte gasped. "Paula was your daughter? I don't believe you. You're lying. You're both lying."

"Please calm down," Erica soothed. "Marion is telling you the truth. We both are."

Charlotte flung herself into the armchair and glared at Marion. "Well, go on then," she cried defiantly, "tell me about Paula."

Marion walked over to the bed and sat on the edge facing Charlotte. "When Paula was a baby, her father abandoned us. I had no money, there was no family to help me. I was desperate, you can have no idea how desperate."

Erica put a comforting arm around Marion's shoulders.

"Tell her the rest," Erica encouraged.

"I soon realised that the only person who could do anything

about the situation was me, that's why I took the decision to become a sex worker."

"A sex worker? Is that a fancy English name for a common prostitute?"

"Yes, I suppose it is. I became a common prostitute. I got paid for having sex with strangers. I didn't like what I did but at the time I had no choice. The work put food on the table and a roof over our heads."

"I don't believe I'm hearing this," Charlotte spoke in a whisper, shaking her head slowly.

"My pimp, that's the bloke who's supposed to keep you safe, was called Graham Gibb. A few days before Christmas I was out on the street working when a car pulled up and a man threw acid in my face. He'd been in a dispute with Graham and decided to attack his girls out of revenge."

Charlotte sat rigid in her chair, staring hard at Marion. The shock of what she was hearing was taking its toll as tears began to run down her cheeks. "What happened?" she asked quietly.

"Up to this point I'd managed to keep Paula under the radar, but after I'd been attacked I was in hospital for months. The authorities took her into their care, she'd be about seven or eight by this time. When I eventually got out of hospital I looked like this." Marion lightly traced the scars on her face with her index finger. "I knew I could never work the streets again and Social Services made it clear that I'd never get my daughter back, so eventually I moved out of the area."

"You abandoned her?"

"I had no choice. I kept in touch with Paula as best I could, but it wasn't easy. When she left care we lost touch for a while and then I got a phone call from her to say she was expecting you. I came back to Leeds after you were born and helped take care of you so your mother could work."

"Paula wasn't a prostitute too, was she?"

"Yes, Charlotte, she was," Marion said defensively. "That's what she did for a living."

"You were just a few months old when she died," Erica said

softly. "I knew Marion wouldn't be allowed to take care of you so we decided to take you over to Ireland to my sister, Mary. She and Liam were desperate for a child of their own."

Tears began to stream down Charlotte's face. "You mean I've been lied to all of my life? Erica, how could you?"

"Darling, we all did what we thought was for the best. Mary and Liam couldn't have loved you more if you had been their own child. They were going to tell you the truth when you were twenty-one but well, things didn't turn out that way."

"What about the money? Why did you send me all that money Erica?"

"The money was to ensure you had a secure future. Paula was my closest friend. It seemed the least I could do."

Slowly Charlotte began to regain her composure, wiping her eyes with a tissue.

"Did Aunt Maureen and dad's family know about this?"

"They knew Mary and Liam weren't your birth parents, nothing else, and there's no reason why anyone else should know."

"I'll have to tell Rory," Charlotte said quietly. "If we're to be married one day he'll have to know the truth about my past."

"That's up to you, darling, but you don't have to."

"I have something for you," Marion smiled picking up the small blue case she had been carrying. "In here are some of your mother's things I thought you might like. There are a few pieces of costume jewellery, some old photographs, a few silk scarves and some of her papers. I thought you might find comfort from them." She handed the suitcase to Charlotte who reluctantly took it and placed it on the bed.

"I'll look at it later," she sighed. "Right now I need to rest. I feel very tired."

"Alright, dear," Erica said kindly. "I know it's been a shock. There's been a lot for you to take in but you know where I am when you're ready to talk."

Charlotte nodded as she opened the hotel room door.

"We'll see you again soon," Marion smiled, kissing Charlotte lightly on the cheek, "and don't forget about the case."

When the two women had left, Charlotte sat quietly on the bottom of the bed feeling both confused and betrayed. Her head ached and her heart was racing. She suspected Erica knew a lot more about Paula's death and her father's whereabouts than she had told her. She was determined that when she met Erica again she would make her tell her everything. Just then the telephone rang.

"Oh Rory, thank goodness it's you," she said wearily. "Darling, before you say anything, I've got something to tell you…"

FORTY-EIGHT

To the outside world, David Glendenning had it all. Living in the impressive Georgian mansion he had inherited from his in-laws five years earlier, he was married to one of the wealthiest women in the county. His police career, which had so far reached Chief Superintendent, was expected to rise even further, some thought he'd be the next Chief Constable one day. In reality however, David's life was far from idyllic.

Lydia Glendenning sat at the breakfast table, pushing the scrambled eggs aimlessly around her plate. "What time will you be home this evening?" she said.

"I'm not sure," he replied, turning the page of the newspaper he was reading. "I will probably be late so don't wait up."

"Of course you'll be late," Lydia snapped. "It's Friday. You're always late on Friday. You'll be visiting that bloody club you're so fond of."

David lowered his newspaper and glared at his wife. "Perhaps if I had something a little more interesting to come home to I wouldn't want to spend time away," he sneered.

"You bastard. After all that my father did for you, you bloody bastard."

"What exactly has he done for me?" he said, the anger rising in his voice. "What I have achieved has been through my own merit. Your father had nothing to do with it."

"We both know that's not true. You'd be nowhere without my father's help."

"If that's what you want to believe," he said dismissively, folding his newspaper. "I have to go to work. What committee is it you'll be chairing today? Helping the homeless or is it substance abuse?"

David rose from the table just as their son, Matthew entered the room.

"What time do you call this?" David demanded. "It's after eight."

"It's my day off," Matthew answered as he poured himself a coffee. "What are you two arguing about at this time, as if I couldn't guess?"

Lydia poured herself another coffee. "Your father will be off visiting his whores again tonight. Isn't that right, dear?"

David glared at her. "Stupid cow," he hissed, leaving the dining room and slamming the door loudly behind him.

"I don't know why you put up with it, mum," Matthew sighed, taking his mother's hand. "Grandad did warn you about his philandering years ago. I don't understand why you stay with him."

Lydia pushed her plate away and picked up her coffee cup. "It's complicated," she said at last. "Your father has always had a weakness for a pretty face. I don't think anything I do or say will change that."

"But you're his wife. You can't just sit back and do nothing whilst he gets up to god knows what."

"None of the women are important to him, Matthew. It's always me and you that he chooses in the end."

"That's not the point. He can't just…"

"Please stop," Lydia said sharply raising her hand. "Your father needs other women in his life, I've come to accept that. But it's me he really wants. He would never leave me."

"I don't understand you," Matthew sighed, slowly shaking his head. "Why do you let him get away with treating you like this?

"Because I love him, that's why," Lydia said softly, tears running down her cheeks. "I've always loved him since the first time I set eyes on him."

"But he doesn't feel the same way or he wouldn't treat you like this."

"Your father can't help himself, Matthew. A few years ago I had him followed by a detective agency. I found out he rented a flat in the block across from the canal. He had done for years. That's where he would take his women, a different one each time apparently."

"And you did nothing?"

Lydia sighed and rose from the table. "I challenged him about the flat, of course I did, but I realised he was conducting his sordid affairs discreetly. That's very important to this family."

"I don't understand."

"Divorce is not something we do, ever. There has never been a divorce in my family and there never will be. Appearance is everything. Do you understand that son?"

Matthew stared at his mother. "Will he be with one of his women tonight?" he asked coldly.

"Yes, he probably will. He'll be at that damned club, The Emerald."

"Karl Maddox's club? I've heard about that place. I've a good mind to pay them a visit."

"No, Matthew, you mustn't," Lydia cried. "Please promise me you'll stay away from the club and away from your father."

Matthew made no reply but stared defiantly and poured himself another coffee.

"I must go," Lydia sighed. "I have committee meetings all day. I'll see you tonight, darling, and please Matthew, do as I ask."

David frowned as he started up his car. Arguments with Lydia were becoming more frequent and more hostile. He turned on the radio and the soothing music of Simon and Garfunkel filled the car. Bridge Over Troubled Water was playing. That had been Paula's favourite song. Tears began to sting his eyes as he remembered Paula, his true love from all those years ago. Where was she now, he wondered? What had she made of her life? If he could turn the clock back, would he still have made the same decision not to go away with her?

Still pondering, David pulled the vehicle into the police station car park. Checking his appearance in the car mirror, he picked up his hat and briefcase and headed for the entrance lobby.

He had been asked to attend a meeting with Geoffrey Lawrence, Deputy Chief Constable Lawrence as he now was. David was hoping it was news of him heading up a new task force dealing with violent street crime in the city. Afterwards he was meeting Karl Maddox for lunch at the Italian restaurant in Wetherby. He had some important information that Karl had to be aware of as soon as possible. That would be worth a few quid. Grinning, he made his way up to his office.

FORTY-NINE

David arrived at Deputy Chief Constable Laurence's office a few minutes early for his appointment. His secretary, Pamela, was behind her desk looking very solemn as she rattled away on her computer keyboard, barely acknowledging his presence.

"DCC Laurence said to go straight through, Superintendent," she said stiffly, avoiding eye contact. "Everyone else is here."

Everyone else? Who else would be attending an internal meeting? David wondered. He gave a sharp rap on the door and entered the room.

Geoffrey Laurence was seated behind his large mahogany desk. David thought he was looking even more smug than usual. To his right was Lucas Bonnington, Assistant Chief Constable of a neighbouring force, and whom David had met on several social occasions. To Laurence's left was a tall, thin man with thick black hair and glasses. He was dressed in civilian clothing.

"Good morning, Superintendent," Geoffrey Laurence began. "I think you already know Assistant Chief Constable Bonnington."

David smiled and nodded, "Yes sir," he said.

Bonnington made no acknowledgement.

Laurence indicated to the man on his right. "This is Detective Chief Inspector Williams. DCI Williams heads up Internal Affairs, or Discipline and Complaints as it used to be called."

"I don't understand sir, why am I here? What's going on?"

"You are here, Superintendent, because certain allegations of a very serious nature have been made against you."

"What allegations?"

"I believe you are familiar with Karl Maddox?"

"Karl? Yes, I know him slightly."

"I think you know him a little more than slightly. My information is that you are a frequent visitor to his club, the Emerald Club, and to the VIP lounge in particular."

David remained silent.

"Superintendent, you are aware of the Police Rules of Conduct are you not, and that frequenting such establishments is in breach of those rules? Furthermore, your association with a known criminal is…"

"The Emerald Club is a good place to pick up information," David interrupted. "I have several sources there and…"

"You have been seen indulging in inappropriate behaviour with women in the club, Superintendent. You were observed on several occasions and…"

"That's simply not true," David protested. "I've only…"

"Do not interrupt me again, Superintendent Glendenning," Laurence said. "Your actions are to be fully investigated by ACC Bonnington and DCI Williams. In the meantime you are suspended from all duties starting immediately. Please hand over your warrant card."

"This is ridiculous," David hissed, removing his warrant card from his wallet and placing it on the desk.

"Furthermore, Superintendent, you are to have no further contact with Maddox or the Emerald Club until this matter is resolved. Do you understand?"

David remained silent.

"I said do you understand, Chief Superintendent Glendenning?"

"Yes sir," David replied, staring defiantly ahead.

"You will be informed when we need to interview you formally under caution. Make sure you bring a Force Representative with you to that interview. Is that clear?"

"Yes sir."

"Good. You may go."

David made to leave the room, turned as if to say something to his accuser, then changing his mind, he went silently through the door.

Was this down to Lydia, David pondered as he drove his car

through the town. Had she finally plucked up the courage to report him? No, if she wanted to do that she would have done it years ago. Knowing it would be too dangerous to ring Karl on his mobile phone, David stopped the car outside a telephone box and rang Karl's number.

"Damn it," he hissed. It was engaged. He waited a few minutes before dialling the number again. When Karl's number was still busy after his third attempt, he ripped the telephone from the wall, screaming profanities. Getting back into his car, he drove at speed in the direction of the Emerald Club.

FIFTY

It had been a quiet morning at the club. Colin Clutterbuck was busy at his computer, and Karl was reading through the printouts.

"It looks like Joe's doing a good job over at the Topaz," Karl said, smiling. "We're up almost thirty per cent on last month."

"It's the hot weather," Colin chuckled. "Men always feel more randy when the sun shines. It's a known fact." Before Karl could reply the telephone on his desk rang.

"Where's Peter this morning?" Karl grunted irritably. "He should be answering the bloody phone."

"He had to go to the brewery and sort the delivery out. They've messed up the order again."

"They're bloody incompetent," Karl growled, picking up the receiver. "Emerald Club, sorry but we don't open until six so…"

"Karl," said a familiar voice, "Karl, it's me, Lisa."

"Lisa?" Karl gasped in astonishment. "Lisa, is that really you?"

"Karl, I have to see you urgently. Can I come round to the club now?"

"I… I…" he spluttered.

"I'll be there in twenty minutes. We have to talk, it's important."

Before Karl could respond, Lisa hung up the receiver. Karl leant back into his chair, his heart racing.

"Is everything alright?" Colin asked with concern. "You look like you've seen a ghost."

Karl sat motionless for a few moments, staring in front of him. He reached into his desk drawer and took out the bottle of tablets. "Colin, I need some privacy for the next hour or so. Find something else to do."

"Okay, boss. I could go and see Shirley."

"See who you want but I need you out now." He took out two tablets from the bottle and swallowed them.

When Colin had left, Karl began to pace nervously up and down the office. What the hell did Lisa want after all these years, he wondered? The shock of hearing her voice gave way to anger as, with one swoop of his arm, he swept the telephone and papers from his desk onto the floor. "Bloody bitch," he hissed through clenched teeth. "When I get my hands on her, I'll…" Although it was only ten thirty in the morning, Karl went over to the cabinet and poured himself a large whisky, purposefully omitting the soda. He checked his appearance in the mirror, straightening his tie in the process. "At least Erica isn't about this morning," he consoled himself as he picked up the debris from the floor and placed it neatly back on his desk.

Exactly twenty minutes later there was a sharp rap on the office door and Peter came into the room, followed closely by Lisa.

"There's a lady to see you, Karl," he grinned.

"Thanks, Peter. Please make sure I'm not disturbed."

Now in her early fifties, Lisa was still a beautiful woman. Her once golden hair was streaked with grey but her eyes were still as blue as Karl remembered them. She wore a floral sun dress with a white cotton jacket, and low heeled court shoes. Lisa wore very little makeup.

"Karl," she said smiling as she walked gracefully towards him. "How are you? You look well." She attempted to kiss him on the cheek but Karl pulled away.

"What the hell do you want?" he snapped, staring at her suspiciously.

"All in good time, darling. Do you mind if I sit down? I've had a long journey." She walked over to the couch.

"You haven't answered my question. What are you doing here?"

"You don't look happy to see me."

"I'm not," he hissed, walking towards her menacingly. "You left me. I thought I'd seen the back of you for ever."

"I still am your wife, Karl. We never got divorced, remember?"

She took out a cigarette from her bag and lit it. "I hear you have a new wife now. Erica, isn't it?"

"You keep Erica out of this."

"Oh I've no quarrel with her, in fact I feel sorry for the poor girl if you treat her like you treat me. But at the end of the day, Karl, I'm your legal wife, not Erica."

"So what is it you want after all this time? A divorce?"

"No, I don't want a divorce. What would be the point? We've both put the past behind us and moved on." She drew on the cigarette and exhaled, causing a plume of smoke to rise. "I've read all about you over the years. You seem to be quite the successful businessman these days. 'Mr Sleaze of the North' that's what it said about you online."

"If it's not for a divorce, why are you here?"

"I need money, darling. Legally half of everything you own belongs to me. You do realise that?"

"Over my dead body," Karl snarled, bringing his fist down hard on the desk. "You left me twenty-five years ago, remember? You won't get one penny of my money."

"I think you'll find that I will. But don't worry, I didn't come here for half of your grubby little empire. I only want fifty thousand pounds, and I want it in the next seven days."

"Fifty thousand? You must be crazy if you think I'll…" Karl suddenly began to gasp and clutched at his chest. "Heart," he whispered as he slumped heavily to the floor. "Get help."

Lisa dropped to her knees and cradled his head in her arms. "Hang on, Karl," she soothed, taking out her mobile phone from her bag. Karl was already unconscious.

Peter was in the bar when he heard the ambulance sirens. Suddenly the club's front door opened and two paramedics ran into the building.

"Where is he?" demanded the first one, a short, powerfully built man of about forty."

"Where's who?" Peter answered, perplexed. "What the hell are you doing here?"

"Up here," Lisa cried. "He's up here. Please hurry."

Both men made their way up the staircase and, directed by Lisa, made their way into the office, an anxious Peter followed.

Karl was lying on his back on the floor when they entered the room. Quickly the two men approached and began their checks.

"What's his name?" one asked.

"Karl," Lisa answered. "Karl Maddox."

"What the hell happened?" Peter asked Lisa. "What the fuck have you done to him?"

"He's had a heart attack, I think," Lisa said. "He'll be alright, I'm sure."

Karl moaned softly and his eyes slowly opened.

"Take it easy, Karl," said the first paramedic. "We're going to take you to hospital, mate. You're gonna be fine."

Karl looked anxiously over at Peter.

"You stay here," he said in almost a whisper. "Tell Joe what's happened but not Erica, okay?"

"Sure, boss," Peter nodded. "Don't you worry, Karl, Joe and I will take care of business."

Karl's breathing was shallow as he attempted to speak. He slipped back into unconsciousness as he was placed on a stretcher and carried downstairs to the waiting ambulance.

"I'll go with him," Lisa said quickly as she followed the paramedics. "I'll ring you when I have news."

Peter stared after her but said nothing. As soon as the ambulance was out of sight, he went up to the office and telephoned Joe.

FIFTY-ONE

"You've been very lucky," the nurse said quietly. "If it hadn't been for your wife's quick thinking…"

Karl slowly began to focus, taking in his surroundings. The sight of medical paraphernalia around his bed made him anxious. He sank back into the pillows and closed his eyes. He'd never been in a hospital before and it terrified him. A heart attack the nurse had said. How the hell had that happened, he wondered?

"I need to get home," he said weakly, attempting to sit up.

"Not so fast, Mr Maddox," the nurse said as she gently plumped the pillows. "I want you to lie back and relax. The doctor will be here shortly to speak to you."

Karl grunted in dismay by way of response.

"Your wife's outside. She can stay for a few minutes." The nurse, bristling with efficiency, walked over to the door. "Just five minutes, Mrs Maddox," she said, addressing Lisa.

Lisa came into the room and sat on the chair by the side of Karl's bed. "How are you feeling?" she asked with concern as she reached gently for his hand.

"I hear you saved my life, is that right?"

"I did what I could," she said softly. "The paramedics seem to think it was just a mild heart attack so you've been lucky. It could have been a lot worse."

"Mild? They should have been lying where I was lying. They wouldn't think it was fucking mild then."

Lisa smiled and for a second, Karl saw in her the sweet girl he had married all those years ago.

"So Lisa, here you are at last," he said, his tone softening. "Where have you been living all this time?"

"That doesn't matter now," she said dismissively. "That's all water under the bridge. You must concentrate on getting well."

Karl lay silent for a moment, staring suspiciously at her. "Tell me, what is it that brings you back after all these years?"

Lisa released her hold on Karl's hand and her posture stiffened slightly.

"You know why I came," she said abruptly. "I need fifty thousand pounds. You owe me that much."

"I owe you nothing," Karl responded abruptly, pushing himself up onto his elbows. "You haven't been a wife to me in over twenty-five years."

Lisa began to pace nervously around the room, pausing by the window.

"There's something I need to tell you," she said at last, "something that perhaps I should have told you a long time ago."

"Go on, I'm listening."

Lisa breathed deeply and Karl detected a faint tremor in her voice. "When I left you I… I was pregnant."

"Pregnant? You were pregnant? I don't believe you. Why the hell didn't you tell me?"

"Have you forgotten how bad things were between us? You were violent and cruel. I couldn't bring a child into that toxic relationship."

"But it was my child, damn it. I had a right to know."

"The way things were back then, you'd have made me have an abortion. You always said you never wanted kids."

"So you waited until I was banged up inside so you could sneak off. Tell me, where did you go when you left?"

"I have a cousin in Cornwall. I stayed with her for a couple of years."

"Cornwall? What did you do for money?"

"I worked in a pub at first and after the baby was born I went to evening class and learnt secretarial skills."

"Are you still living in Cornwall?"

"Karl, where I live now is nothing to do with you. Once I get the money you'll never see me again."

"So where is this kid?"

Lisa opened her bag and removed two photographs. "This is your son. His name is Alex." She handed Karl the first photograph. It showed Lisa as a teenager holding a small baby. Karl stared at the photograph in disbelief.

"Nice try," he said coldly. "This could be anybody's kid. It's probably not even yours."

"Of course he's mine… ours. Alex has grown into a fine young man." Lisa handed him the second photograph. This showed a smartly dressed man in his twenties. His physique and features were unmistakably the same as Karl's. "Alex is a doctor," Lisa said proudly.

Karl stared hard at the second photograph. "Alex, you say? A doctor. Where is Alex now?"

"He's working at the City Hospital in Manchester, but he has a fantastic opportunity to buy into a private practice in Canada. That's why I need the money, to give our son a good start in life."

"Canada? Why the fuck does he want to go to Canada?"

"It's a great chance for him Karl, for him and his wife."

"Alex is married?"

"She's a lovely girl. Alex and Sarah have been married almost a year now."

Karl sank back into his pillows. He could feel the sweat trickle down the back of his neck like it always did when he was angry. He closed his eyes for a few seconds before speaking. "Tell me, Lisa, are you still using the name Maddox?"

"No, not any more. After I left I reverted back to my maiden name, Sutton."

"So, my son is known as Dr Alex Sutton?"

"Yes, that's right."

Karl studied the photograph of his son. It was a couple of minutes before he finally spoke. "I'll tell you what I'll do. I'll give Alex the fifty thousand if, and only if, I get to meet him personally."

"That's never going to happen," Lisa snapped, glaring at her husband. "I don't want you anywhere near my son, do you understand?"

"Why? What are you afraid of? You don't think I'll corrupt him, do you?"

"Please Karl, leave him alone. Alex is a good boy and…"

"Take it or leave it, Lisa, it's up to you. If you want my money, bring Alex to the club to meet me."

"You always were a stubborn bastard," she hissed.

"I'm not swapping insults, Lisa. Just let me know when you've arranged the meeting. You'd better go now," he said dismissively, closing his eyes. "You heard what the nurse said. I need to rest."

Casting a defiant stare, Lisa hurried from the room. Once she had gone, Karl rang for the nurse.

"Yes, Mr Maddox," said the pretty first year student as she hurried into the room. "Is everything alright?"

Karl was about to snarl at the girl but instead he gave her his warmest smile.

"A telephone, please, dear," he said, "and a cup of tea, milk but no sugar."

"Yes, of course," she answered. Returning in less than five minutes, the nurse had the telephone trolley and a cup of hot tea.

"Is there anything else I can get you?" she asked nervously. Nurse Jones knew exactly who Karl Maddox was. All the staff on the ward were talking about him.

"No, thank you," Karl grinned as she turned to leave the room. "Thank you for the tea, Nurse Jones."

Carol felt the colour rising in her cheeks under Karl's gaze as she hurried out of the room. Smiling to himself, Karl dialled a familiar number.

"Joe? Joe I need you to come and collect me from the hospital."

"Hospital? Are you alright?"

"Yes, I'm fine. I just had a funny turn. I'm feeling a lot better now. Come and pick me up as soon as you can, and Joe, not a word to Erica. I don't want her fussing."

"Alright boss, if that's what you want. I'll set off now."

Karl made a second call.

"Peter? Peter, it's me. Is Paul with you?"

"Yes boss, I'll put him on."

"Hello, Karl," Paul Borowicz answered. "Is everything alright? I hear you went off in an ambulance earlier."

"Oh, nothing to worry about," Karl sighed. "I'll be back at the club later. Paul, I want you to do something for me. Do you have a pen?"

FIFTY-TWO

When Joe arrived at the hospital he went straight up to the ward. "Karl, are you alright? What the hell happened?"

Karl was sitting up in bed finishing off a shepherd's pie and chips. "The food's not bad in here," he grinned. "I don't suppose you've brought me a drink? Whisky would be nice."

"Never mind whisky, I rang Peter and he said you'd been carted off in an ambulance."

"A minor heart attack, that's all." Karl smiled faintly. "I'll be good as new in a couple of days."

"Do you want me to ring Erica?"

"No, I don't. What I want you to do is get my clothes out of that cupboard over there."

"No chance," Joe protested. "Not until the doctors say you can go."

"Joe, stop fucking about and do as I ask. I'm absolutely fine. It was just a minor attack, a warning that's all."

Joe looked at Karl suspiciously.

"They did an angiogram earlier and everything was okay," Karl grinned. "Now stop pissing about and get me my clothes."

Half an hour later, both men were in Joe's car and heading for the Emerald Club.

"Not a word about this to anyone," Karl warned as they entered the club.

"Alright, but I think you should tell Erica. She has a right to know."

"I said no one must know, especially Erica. Is Colin still at the Emerald? I have to speak to him urgently."

"I'm not sure if he'll still be there at this time. I've heard he's sweet on Shirley. He might be with her."

"Shirley?" Karl frowned. "Shirley and Colin Clutterbuck? I don't believe it."

"Well, it's what the girls are saying. Colin didn't deny it when I asked him."

"Bloody hell, Colin Clutterbuck and Shirley? Who'd have thought it?"

"Just goes to show there's somebody for everybody. Do you want me to give Colin a ring and get him back to the office?"

"No, it can wait until tomorrow. You'd better get back to the Topaz."

"Okay," Joe sighed. "If you're sure you're okay, Karl. I'll ring you tomorrow."

"See you then, Joe, and thanks for the lift."

When Joe had left the office, Karl poured himself a whisky, this time making sure to add the soda. He telephoned Erica.

"What time are you coming over?" he asked abruptly when she answered. "It's nearly seven o'clock. We'll be opening up soon."

"I've been trying to ring you all afternoon. Where have you been?"

"Since when do I answer to you?" Karl snapped. "Are you coming in tonight or not?"

"Well, that's why I was trying to ring you. Marion has invited me out for a drink. We haven't had a catch-up in ages and…"

"Marion? What the hell are you doing going out for a drink with her?"

"She's alright, in fact I like her. I think she's at a bit of a loose end since the house on Broughton Street closed."

"What do you mean 'loose end'? I would have thought running the agency would have kept her occupied."

"It's not the same though, just working on the computer and telephone all the time. I think she misses the banter with the girls."

"Where are you thinking of going with your new best mate?"

"Marion suggested the Westbrook. I thought we might have a bite to eat in the restaurant."

Karl hesitated a moment before speaking.

"Alright, I suppose you're due a night off, but I don't want you out late. Make sure you're in before midnight, okay?"

"You make me feel like Cinderella," Erica grinned. "I'll see you when you get home. Goodnight, Karl."

But Karl had already hung up the receiver.

FIFTY-THREE

David Glendenning parked his car at the far side of the car park and made his way to the back of the Emerald Club. He walked furtively over to the three steps leading to the rear entrance. He knocked just once before the door was opened by a large man whose frame almost filled the doorway.

"I need to see Karl urgently," David said, pushing past Peter.

"Karl's in his office," he replied. "Wait here."

Peter walked over to the internal phone and rang Karl's extension. After a brief conversation he turned to David. "The boss says to go straight up."

David ascended the familiar back staircase leading directly to Karl's office. Karl was waiting for him at the top of the stairs.

"Bloody hell, David, I thought I looked rough. What's the matter?"

David entered the office, flung himself on the couch and lit a cigarette. "I don't suppose there's a whisky going, is there? I've been trying to get in touch with you for hours."

Karl poured two drinks and handed one to David. "What's with the dark glasses and baseball cap?" he smirked. "Getting down with the kids, are we?"

"Ha ha, very funny. Where've you been all day anyway? I've been trying to get hold of you."

"Not another one who thinks I have to report my every move. I've enough with Erica. Now, are you going to tell me what's rattling your cage?"

David relayed the conversation he had had earlier that day with the DCC. "I'm finished. Those bastards are going to hang me out to dry."

"Bollocks. Just deny it. They can't prove anything."

"They'll have a bloody good try. I thought you vetted everyone who came to the lounge? It sounds like there's been an undercover cop snooping."

"We do vet applications as much as we can, but this is a sex club not MI5." The internal phone on Karl's desk rang. "Yeah," Karl snapped. "I'm busy, Peter. What is it?"

"There's a policeman here, Karl. He says he wants to talk to you. His name is Glendenning." Karl turned to face David.

"Fuck!" David snarled. "That's my son. What's he up to?"

"You'd better hide in here," Karl said opening the cupboard and releasing the back wall. "Don't make a sound." David looked quizzical at Karl but walked into the cupboard as directed and Karl closed the door.

"Show him up, Peter," Karl said sitting back behind his desk.

When Matthew entered the room, followed closely by Peter, Karl was struck by how much Matthew resembled his father.

"What can I do for you, officer?" he said cordially.

"You can keep away from my father, you bastard." Matthew spat. "He's been suspended because of you."

"I don't know what you're talking about," Karl said angrily, rising from his chair and walking around to the front of the desk. "Do I know your father?"

"My father is Superintendent Glendenning, as you very well know. He's been coming to this whorehouse for years."

"This isn't a whorehouse, it's a respectable club and you are trespassing. Now piss off."

"You don't scare me, you filthy lowlife pimp," Matthew spat. "You keep away from my father or I swear to God I'll…"

"You'll what?" Karl goaded, standing menacingly in front of the younger man. "I think you'd better leave before Peter here throws you out."

Matthew walked towards the door and then turned sharply round. "You haven't heard the last of me, Maddox. My mother's in bits because of you and your filthy whores."

"Get out," Karl yelled, striding menacingly towards Matthew.

Peter grabbed Matthew's arm and he spun round, crashing into the door jamb. "You've no idea who you're messing with, young man. Now get out of my club and don't come back." Peter pushed Matthew out onto the landing.

"I'm going to finish you, Maddox," Matthew shouted as he was unceremoniously escorted down the stairs by Peter. "You haven't heard the last of me."

Karl was angry with the encounter. He wasn't used to people speaking to him like that. It was then he remembered David.

Walking over to the cupboard, he opened the door but there was no sign of him. Descending the stairs into the passageway, Karl could see David at the far side looking through the fretwork into the club.

"Pretty cool, isn't it?" Karl said.

"All this time I've known you, I never knew this existed. You're a sly bastard, Karl."

"Only a handful of people know about the passage, that's the way I want it to stay. Okay?"

"Oh don't worry about me. Officially I've never been here, remember? By the way, what's with the gun up there on the shelf? I didn't think you were into guns."

"Oh that? I took it off a vicious little thug a few years back. I've never used it but you never know when it might come in useful." Karl turned and climbed the stairs returning to the office, followed closely by David. "That son of yours is a feisty little bastard, isn't he? He's lucky to get out of here in once piece, talking to me like that."

"Sorry, Karl. I'll speak to him," David sighed. "He's very protective towards his mother and right now things are not good between us."

"Make sure he doesn't pay a return visit or next time he won't be so lucky. Do you hear what I'm saying, David?"

"Don't worry, I'll make sure he won't be back, but right now, there are more pressing things to worry about."

"I've told you, just deny everything. Those wankers can't prove a thing."

"It's not just that, Karl. There's something you should know, and you're not going to like it."

FIFTY-FOUR

Cupid's Angels was the most popular escort agency in the city with over forty girls on its books. Shirley worked as night manager. Business was conducted by telephone and computer from a small unit at the edge of an industrial estate. Shirley was chatting to Colin when the telephone rang.

"No peace for the wicked," she grinned, walking through to the desk in reception. She put on her headset and turned on her computer. "Good evening, Cupid's Angels," she cooed. "How may I help you tonight?"

"I, err, I want a girl to come to my hotel," a man's voice said nervously.

"Yes, of course, sir. Have you used Cupid's Angels before?"

"No, no this is the first time. I, err…"

"Could you give me your name please, sir?"

"My name? Oh it's… it's Harry. Harry Smith."

"Well Harry, do you have any particular type of girl in mind, or would you like me to choose one for you?"

"What type of girls have you got?"

"We have blondes, brunettes, redheads. Do you have a preference?"

"Oh redheads, definitely redheads. Can you send me a young redhead, please?"

"Can you give me your hotel and room number Harry?"

"I'm at the Westbrook, room 233. Do you know where that is?"

"Yes Harry, we know where the Westbrook is. Will you be paying by card or cash?"

"By cash, if that's alright."

"Yes, that's fine Harry. I'm sending Bunny over to the hotel. She will be with you in thirty minutes. Bunny's a beautiful girl in her early twenties with long red hair and a fantastic figure. Do you know our charges?"

"Yes, they're on your webpage. Fifty pounds for the agency fee and then whatever price I negotiate with the girl, isn't it?"

"Yes, that's right, dear." As Shirley was speaking to Harry, she was e-mailing Bunny with details of the booking. "I'm sure you'll have a lovely time with Bunny. She's one of our most popular girls."

Taking off her headset, Shirley turned to face Colin.

"Fancy a Chinese? I'm starving."

"Yes, of course, dear," Colin grinned. "What would you like?" Colin took out a menu from the desk drawer and handed it to Shirley.

"The usual, I think. Chicken Chow Mein with fried rice. What about you?"

"I think I'll have the same. Should I get you a bottle of wine?"

"Colin! You know I'm not supposed to drink whilst I'm working," she scolded, wagging her finger playfully. "What would Karl say?"

"Bugger Karl. If my girl wants a bottle of wine, she'll bloody well have one."

"Your girl?" Shirley smiled coyly. "Is that what I am, Colin? Really?"

"If you want to be," Colin grinned, putting his arm affectionately around her shoulders. "I do love you, Shirley." He gently kissed her on the mouth.

"Oh Colin, I..." Before she could respond, the telephone rang. Automatically she picked up the headset. "Good evening, Cupid's Angels. How may I help you tonight?"

Colin gently released his hold and walked to the door.

"Back in fifteen minutes," he mouthed, smiling. "Don't go away."

FIFTY-FIVE

Erica was in her lounge and already on her second gin and tonic when Marion arrived.

"Drink?" she offered.

"No thanks, it's a bit early for me. Is everything alright, Erica? You look upset."

"Upset? Why should I be upset? I'm about to tell Charlotte how her mother died and my part in the cover-up, but that's no reason to be upset, is it, Marion?"

"For goodness sake, Erica, how many have you had?"

"Not enough. Not nearly enough." Erica flung herself onto the couch and began to sob uncontrollably. Marion sat beside her, cradling her in her arms when the doorbell rang.

"That'll be Joe," she said, slightly relieved. "I'll let him in."

There was a muffled conversation in the hallway before Joe came into the room. Erica held out her arms and Joe picked her up off the couch, holding her tightly.

"There," he soothed. "Please don't cry. Everything will be okay, you'll see."

"Joe, before we visit Charlotte, there's something I have to tell you. I should have told you a long time ago but…"

"Does it concern Karl?"

Erica nodded.

"I've always known you were hiding something," Joe said softly, "but you know you can tell me anything, Erica. Anything at all."

"I'll put the kettle on," Marion said walking into Erica's state of the art kitchen, "or at least I will once I figure out which is the kettle. I've never seen so many fancy gadgets."

"There isn't a kettle, Marion," Erica smiled weakly as she

pulled away from Joe and joined Marion in the kitchen. "There's a boiling water dispenser on the wall. You just press the button."

"Bloody hell, whatever next?"

Erica went back into the lounge and sat on the couch next to Joe. Marion joined them with the tea a couple of minutes later.

"What's that bastard done to you?" Joe asked, stroking Erica's hair gently.

Erica took a deep breath, put her cup down on the table and turned to face Joe and Marion. "I'm going to tell you something that I've never told anyone before except Karl." Joe could feel her body trembling as he held her.

"What is it?" he whispered. "Darling, you can tell me anything, you know that."

"The thing is, there was an accident... a terrible accident, and..."

"What sort of accident?" Joe and Marion said in unison.

"When I was fourteen, I... I killed my father." Both her companions stared at her in disbelief.

"You did what? I don't believe you," Marion said sharply. "You wouldn't kill anyone Erica, you couldn't."

"Believe me, I did. I didn't mean to, I just wanted to make him go away but..."

"Why?" Joe asked. "Why would you kill your own father?"

"Because my father was a paedophile. He had abused Mary for years and when she left, he tried turning to me."

"Why the hell didn't you tell anyone?" Joe said angrily.

"I did tell someone. I told Karl."

"What exactly happened?" Marion asked softly. "From the beginning, love."

Erica's eyes brimmed with tears and she held Joe's hand tightly. "Mary had already gone off to Ireland with Liam. I knew my father had been abusing her, I actually witnessed it once." She began to tremble and Joe kissed her lightly on the cheek.

"Go on," he encouraged. "What happened?"

"One night my father came into my bedroom. It was late and he'd been drinking. He leaned over my bed and tried to kiss me.

I was terrified. I suppose I always knew he might try to hurt me one day like he had Mary. I panicked. I reached for the glass paperweight I kept under the bed and I hit him over the head. I only hit him the once."

"Serves the bastard right," Marion sneered.

"I'd been seeing Karl for a few weeks by this time. After I attacked my father, I was hysterical. He was lying on the floor, his head covered in blood. I didn't know what to do so I rang Karl to help me." Tears began to run down her cheeks as she spoke, and her body trembled. Joe put a comforting arm around her.

"Go on, Erica," he encouraged softly, "what happened next?"

"Karl came to the house straight away. He said the best thing to do was make it look like my father had been mugged so he put his body into his car boot and drove away. He told me later he had dumped him in an alleyway in town."

"Karl told me your father had been murdered," Joe said quietly, "but he never mentioned his part in it."

"So, that's how you came to be in care?" Marion said sympathetically. "You poor love." She gave Erica an affectionate hug. "Paula used to write to me and she told me you two had become friends."

"We became best friends. In fact, apart from Karl, she was the only one who knew what I had done to my father. It had been a terrible secret to keep and Paula helped me to cope with the guilt."

"She never breathed a word about it to me," Marion sighed. "I just thought your father had been attacked and robbed."

"There's something else, isn't there? What else aren't you telling us, Erica?" Joe asked softly.

Erica pulled away from Joe, her posture stiffened slightly.

"You've got this far," Marion coaxed. "You might as well tell us the rest."

"When I went into care, I still saw Karl regularly. We would meet up after school and at weekends. Nobody at the home seemed concerned about where I went or who I saw."

"The man's a bastard," Marion hissed. "Always was."

"I was naïve back then, Marion. I was fourteen and I thought he was wonderful. When I turned sixteen, he asked me to marry him." Marion looked at her disapprovingly. "You've got to remember, I had no one. I'd lost touch with Mary and I had no other family. Karl was kind to me and getting married to him seemed the perfect solution."

"You're not in love with him now though, are you?" Joe asked. "Anyone can see that. Why do you stay with him? Why don't you just walk away?"

"I can't, Joe. Believe me, if I could I would, but it's impossible."

"Why can't you? I don't understand."

"Karl and I had been married about three months when we had a fight. I don't remember what it was about, but I tried to leave the flat. He grabbed me and pinned me against the wall. That was the first time he threatened to reveal to the police what I had done to my father."

"After all this time he can't prove it," Marion hissed. "Nobody's going to take his word against yours."

"You don't understand. Karl said he still had the paperweight I had hit my father with. It has my fingerprints all over it. He said if I ever try to leave him he'll…"

"You mean that bastard's been blackmailing you to stay with him all this time?"

Erica lowered her head. "I daren't leave him, Joe. You know what Karl's capable of. He doesn't make idle threats."

"You leave Karl to me," Joe said firmly. "I'll deal with him. Now we'd better get over to the hotel. We were supposed to meet Charlotte there ten minutes ago."

FIFTY-SIX

It was almost eight-thirty when Joe, Erica and Marion arrived at the Westbrook.

"Does anyone want a drink before we go up?" Joe enquired.

"No thanks, let's just get this over with," Erica answered. All three got into the lift and Joe pressed the button causing it to make its silent ascent. As they stepped out on the second floor, a young woman with striking red hair and wearing a short dark blue dress came towards them.

"Bunny!" Marion cried sharply. "What are you doing here?"

"I've been visiting a client," Bunny replied, looking quizzically at the trio as she stepped into the waiting lift. "Shirley arranged it. Is everything alright, Marion?"

"Yes, of course it is, I was just surprised to see you, that's all."

Bunny shrugged. "Alright, I'll see you tomorrow. Goodnight."

"She's the last person I wanted to see," Marion said irritably as the lift doors closed.

"How long has she been with the agency?" Joe asked. "I haven't seen her before."

"Not long. She came up from London a couple of months ago."

"I hope she doesn't tell Karl she saw us in the hotel," Erica said anxiously. "He thinks I'm here to have dinner in the bar with you."

"Don't worry. Bunny doesn't work in the club so there's no reason for her to come into contact with Karl."

"Let's hope so," Erica sighed as she knocked on the door of room 231.

It was a few minutes before the door was opened by Charlotte. Erica could see at once that she had been crying.

"Charlotte, darling, what's happened? Are you alright?" She pushed her way into the room followed closely by Marion and Joe.

"Erica, you were right," Charlotte sobbed. "I shouldn't have said anything about what you told me the other day."

"Why, what's happened?"

"It's Rory. We were going to get married and… and he's broken off our engagement. Rory said he didn't want the daughter of a common prostitute to be the mother of his children." Tears began to run down her cheeks and she gratefully accepted the handkerchief offered to her by Joe. "He was so angry, Erica."

"It's not your fault, darling," Erica soothed. "None of this is your fault. You must never think that."

"Erica, I have to know what happened to my mother. I have a right to know."

An uneasy silence fell upon the group.

"Alright," Erica said at last. "I'll tell you everything that happened." Erica took Charlotte's hand and gently led her to the couch. "You know your mother was a sex worker?"

Charlotte nodded.

"She actually worked for Karl. He ran the working girls in the city back then."

"She did what?"

"It seems that Paula had something on Karl and tried to blackmail him. I don't know what about, none of us do. That's why he attacked her with a knife."

"Karl killed my mother? You mean you knew what he had done and you did nothing?"

"There were reasons why I couldn't say anything," Erica said softly.

"What reasons? I don't understand."

Without faltering Erica told Charlotte of her father's abuse towards Mary and herself and how she came to accidentally kill him. She explained Karl's involvement in disposing of the body, and later how he had threatened to tell the police if she tried to leave him.

"One word from Karl and I'd be sent to prison, he'd make sure of that. He still has the paperweight I hit my father with. I'm terrified of him, Charlotte. You have no idea what he's capable of."

Charlotte pulled away from Erica. "What happened next?"

"Joe rang me that night and told me what had happened. He said he had buried your mother's body."

"He buried her?"

"Yes. I telephoned Marion straight away and told her that Paula had been killed. We knew we couldn't do anything to help Paula but we could help you. You were only a few months old at the time. Marion and I decided to take you over to Ireland to my sister. She and Liam were desperate for a child, and I knew you would be safe with them."

"My mother knew what Karl had done? She knew?"

"No, Mary didn't know anything about Karl's involvement. We just told her Paula had been murdered whilst working on the streets. Mary agreed at once to take care of you. It was easy for Liam to get the necessary paperwork."

"I took Erica over to Liverpool to catch the ferry the next morning," Joe explained. "We collected you on the way. Within a few hours you were safe with Mary and Liam."

"We did what we thought was for the best," Erica spoke almost in a whisper as tears ran down her face. "I begged Joe and Marion not to tell the police what Karl had done. I knew he would tell them about me killing my father and…" Erica began sobbing uncontrollably and Joe held her tightly in his arms, kissing her lightly on the cheek.

"Your welfare was the most important thing," Marion said. "If the police knew what had happened to Paula they would have put you into care and your mother wouldn't have wanted that. I agreed to keep quiet about Karl's involvement because Erica begged me to. She promised she would always take care of you, and she's kept that promise."

"That's why you've been sending me money every month?"

Erica nodded.

"Joe, you said you buried my mother? Where?"

"I'd seen an open grave at the cemetery. The funeral was scheduled for the following day. I had a spade in the back of the car. I dug an extra foot down and placed Paula's body in the grave covering her with a layer of soil."

"So she's actually buried in a graveyard? In consecrated ground?"

Joe nodded.

"Well, that's something I suppose."

"I know it's no consolation," Joe said trying to lighten the mood, "but Paula put up one hell of a fight. Karl still has the scar on his cheek from where she cut him."

"And nobody has any idea what she had on him? He must have been desperate to keep her quiet, whatever it was."

"We'll probably never know," Erica said quietly.

"You haven't told me about my father. He's still alive, isn't he?"

"Yes he is, but Charlotte, believe me, your father is no good. Please trust me and keep away from him."

Charlotte remained silent, her hands tightly clasped on her lap.

"Now that you know everything that happened, what are you going to do?" Joe asked.

"What do you mean?"

"I mean, are you going to the police and tell them what we've told you?"

"I should. We can't let Karl get away with what he's done."

"We can if it means Erica isn't harmed. She was just a kid when she killed her father, and from what I've heard he deserved everything he got."

Charlotte walked over to Erica and put her arms around her neck, kissing her lightly on the cheek. "Don't worry," she whispered softly. "I won't let Karl hurt you, I promise."

"Well, I don't know about the rest of you, but I could do with a drink," Marion said cheerfully.

"Good idea," Joe grinned. "Are you coming down to the bar, Charlotte?"

Charlotte nodded.

They made their way to the lift and down into the hotel bar in silence. A hen party was in full swing that night and the atmosphere was boisterous as they made their way to a small table at the far end of the room.

"Oh look, there's Bunny," Charlotte cried excitedly, hurrying over to the young woman sat at the bar.

"Hi Bunny, remember me?"

"Of course I do," Bunny smiled. "It's lovely to see you again, Charlotte. I…" Suddenly Bunny became aware of Marion glaring at her. "I'm sorry but I can't stay to chat," she said, hurriedly drinking the remnants of her wine. "I'm meeting a friend in town. See you later."

Charlotte returned to the table smiling. "That was Bunny. Isn't she pretty? I wish I had red hair like her instead of this pale blonde."

"The colour isn't natural," Marion snapped spitefully, "it's out of a bottle. How do you know her anyway?"

"I met her at breakfast the other morning. She was with a client."

"What do you mean a client?"

"I'm not stupid, Marion. I know Bunny's a prostitute."

"An escort," Marion corrected. "She's not a prostitute. she's an escort, and I don't think you should be associating with her."

"I like her."

Marion and Erica exchanged worried looks.

"Charlotte, I've been thinking. Why don't I speak with Rory and try and smooth things out between you two? When I met him at the funeral he seemed like a very kind man. I'm sure I can make him understand that…"

"No, Erica. Rory and I are done. Anyway, I don't think I'd make a very good farmer's wife, do you?"

Erica shrugged but couldn't help smiling. "Well, maybe not dear," she conceded. "Have you decided what you do want to do?"

Before Charlotte could respond, the waitress came to the table to take their order.

"Gin and tonics all round?" Joe asked.

Everyone nodded.

"I think I'll stay in England," Charlotte said once the waitress had left the table. "I have a dual passport, what with my mother being English. I'm a qualified teaching assistant so I'm sure I could get a job quite easily."

"That sounds a good idea, but won't you miss your family in Ireland? When I was there I got the impression you were very close to Liam's relatives."

"We are close, but I can still visit them, or they could come over and visit me, as long as they don't all come at once. There are dozens of them."

"Well, we'll have to see about getting you a job if you're sure you want to live in England."

"Erica, I've been thinking. Would you mind if I stay with you and Karl?"

"Stay with us? But I thought you…"

"Karl doesn't know I'm Paula's daughter, does he?"

"No, of course he doesn't. He knows Mary and Liam adopted you but…"

"Well then, what would be more natural than your grieving niece coming to stay for a while? He wouldn't mind, would he?"

"I suppose not. He's rarely at home these days."

"Too busy running his seedy little empire, eh? I promise you won't know I'm there. Can we arrange it for tomorrow night?"

"Why do you want to stay with us?"

"I just want to see what sort of a person Karl is. I promise I won't make a scene."

Erica glanced at Joe and Marion for support. "Well, alright, I suppose," she said reluctantly, "but you must be careful, Charlotte. Karl is a very dangerous man."

FIFTY-SEVEN

Paul Borowicz was in his late twenties. His dark brown hair was styled by a leading salon and his clothes were from one of the swankiest boutiques. Paul's handsome face was lightly tanned and thick black lashes complimented his dark grey eyes. At six foot four, his muscular frame bore testimony to his four visits to the gym each week.

Paul stood in the shadowy doorway of the jeweller's shop watching the foyer of the hospital. He didn't have long to wait before Rachel came through the revolving door and out onto the street. Paul watched as she crossed the road and hurried along Charlton Street. It was eight o'clock but already the nights were drawing in, heralding the end of summer. Rachel turned down Charlton Street and into Jessop Road. Paul smiled as he realised she was going to the Red Lion pub, just like she had done the previous night.

Rachel Baxter was in her early forties and at least three stone heavier than her five foot three frame should carry. She was a plain woman with thick mousey hair falling onto her broad shoulders with a heavy fringe resting just above her plastic-rimmed glasses. Rachel was single with no children, very few relatives and even fewer friends. Spending an hour in the pub after work each night had become a regular habit, better than spending time alone in her small flat she had reasoned. After ordering her usual pint of lager from the bar, Rachel spun round in search of an empty table. On turning, she bumped into Paul, causing her lager to splash onto the floor.

"Oh, I'm so sorry," she spluttered. "I didn't see you there, I…"

"It's alright," Paul grinned. "It was my fault not yours. Please, let me get you another drink."

Rachel felt the colour rising in her plump cheeks. She always blushed when she was embarrassed and this handsome stranger made her feel very embarrassed, but in a good way.

"There's a table over there," Paul smiled, leading her away from the bar towards the back of the pub. "What is it you're drinking? Lager? Perhaps you'd let me get you something a little stronger? It's the least I can do."

"Well, I..." she spluttered, "if you're sure, maybe a vodka and tonic?"

Soon Paul was back at the table with two drinks. "My name's Paul," he said.

"I'm Rachel."

"Well it's very nice to meet you, Rachel," Paul smiled raising his glass. "So Rachel, what's a nice girl like you...?"

"Please stop," Rachel chuckled. "That's so corny."

"Corny?" Paul said, feigning indignance. "That's my best line."

"What do you do, Paul? I haven't seen you around here before?"

"I'm here for a business meeting. I've just come into town for a couple of drinks."

"What sort of business are you in?"

"Knickers," Paul answered, grinning. "Knickers and bras and all other types of ladies' intimate apparel," he winked mischievously. "I believe it's referred to in polite circles as ladies' lingerie. I'm looking for new outlets."

"Oh Paul, you are funny," Rachel chuckled. "I've never met anyone like you before."

"Another drink?" he offered, rising from the table. "Then you can tell me all about yourself."

Soon Paul was back at the table with two more drinks. "So?" he began, "what do you do Rachel? Or would you like me to guess?"

"Go on then," she encouraged. "What do you think I do?"

"Well, I don't see you as a shop worker or a bank clerk. A teacher perhaps? No, not a teacher, and I don't think you're a policewoman either. Maybe a nurse?"

"That's right," Rachel chortled. "I work at the City General."

"I knew it," Paul cried triumphantly. "I knew it would be something noble and worthwhile. You just have that caring aura about you."

Rachel felt herself blushing as Paul reached for her hand. "How long have you been a nurse?"

"Just over twenty years."

"Twenty years? Christ, you must have started nursing in junior school."

"Stop it," Rachel chastised playfully. "You really are too bad, Paul."

"I want to hear all about being a nurse." Paul suddenly became serious. "What it's like having people around you that are only alive because of your skill."

"Oh it's not like that, really it isn't," Rachel protested. "I'm only a humble nurse. It's the doctors who save lives, not me."

"Nonsense," Paul contradicted. "It's nurses that do the real work, everyone knows that. Nurses might not make the diagnosis but they're the ones that make the difference."

"It's kind of you to say so but..."

"Tell me about the doctors you work with. A load of egotistical wankers, I bet."

Rachel giggled at Paul's comment as she drained her glass. "You really don't understand about doctors. They're not egotists, they're just..."

"Wankers?" Paul suggested, smiling. "I'll get us another drink, Rachel, and you can tell me all about them."

Fifteen minutes later, Rachel was relaying to Paul the shortcomings of her medical colleagues. From Marie, the midwife who was about to marry for the fourth time at the tender age of thirty-two, to Abigail, the sixty-two year old receptionist who had recently declared she was a lesbian and had been living with another woman for the past twenty years.

"I suspect the doctors aren't much better. They probably behave even worse. I bet you know plenty about them, eh?"

The drink was taking its toll on Rachel as her speech became slurred. "Doctors behaving badly?" she grinned. "That will be Doctor Sutton. He's a very bad boy."

"What's Dr Sutton been up to? Why is he a bad boy?"

Rachel began to giggle. "Drugs," she whispered. "There are rumours going round that the hospital board suspect him of stealing drugs."

"What sort of drugs?"

Rachel closed her eyes and her head lolled forward. Paul grabbed her shoulders and gently shook her. Slowly she opened her eyes.

"Rachel, tell me about Dr Sutton and the drugs."

"Under investigation," she mumbled,

"Dr Sutton's under investigation for stealing drugs? Is that what you're saying, Rachel?"

"Yes, but I like him. He's very good looking, just like you." She put her hand up to Paul's face. "Alex Sutton is very sexy," she purred. "All the nurses think so. He's a twin you know."

"A twin? Alex has a twin? Are you sure?"

"Of course I'm sure. I met his twin at the staff Christmas party about three years ago." Rachel closed her eyes once more and her head began to loll forward.

"Wake up, Rachel," Paul said sternly as he shook her more violently. "Wake up, that's a good girl. Tell me about Alex's twin. What's his name?"

"It's not a he, silly," Rachel slurred. "Alex's twin is a girl. Her name is Christina."

FIFTY-EIGHT

It was almost eight o'clock when Alex Sutton parked his Audi in front of the double garage of his home. His wife, Sarah was in the hallway as he entered the house.

"For Christ's sake, Alex, what's going on?" she said angrily.

"What's up?" he asked, taking off his coat and hanging it on the coat stand.

"The card was rejected at the supermarket this afternoon. I had to use my personal account to pay for the groceries."

"Don't worry, I'll sort it. It's just a temporary cash flow, that's all. Now, what's for dinner? I'm starving." He walked through into the lounge, poured himself a large whisky and turned on the television.

Sarah followed him. "Alex, we've got to talk. This can't go on. The two credit cards are both maxed out and now the current account is empty. What the hell's happening? Where's the money going?"

"I said I'll sort it," Alex hissed, grabbing Sarah's upper arm and guiding her towards the kitchen. "Now do as I say and get me my dinner, alright?"

Sarah glared at her husband but said nothing. She knew it was futile arguing with him.

She busied herself preparing the salad to go with the lasagne when the telephone rang in the hall.

"Get that," Alex shouted from the lounge.

A few seconds later, Sarah came into the room.

"That was your mother. She says she needs to speak to you urgently. She'll be round in half an hour."

"What the hell does she want?"

"She didn't say, just that it was important."

"You'd better hurry up with dinner then."

Half an hour later, Lisa drove her Ford Fiesta onto the drive. Sarah was standing by the front door.

"Hello, Lisa," she greeted. "It's lovely to see you."

Lisa smiled and lightly kissed Sarah's cheek.

"I have to speak to Alex alone. It's very important."

"Of course," Sarah replied looking slightly puzzled. "He's in the lounge. Can I get you a coffee?"

"No thank you, darling. I'm not staying long." Lisa walked into the house and through into the lounge, closing the door behind her.

"Mother," Alex smiled weakly, not bothering to get out of his chair. "This is an unexpected surprise. Is everything alright?"

"Alex, I have something to tell you," Lisa began slightly breathlessly. "I think I can get hold of the fifty thousand pounds you need for the partnership in Canada."

"Partnership in…? Sit down, mother," he invited, unable to contain his excitement. "You say you can get me fifty thousand pounds? But how can you do that? When I asked you… no, when I begged you for the money, you said you hadn't got it."

"I haven't, Alex, but your father has."

"My father? What the hell are you talking about? You told me he was dead."

"Yes, I know I did, darling, but I lied. Believe me, I had very good reasons for lying to you, but your father is very much alive. I lied about him to protect you. He's a vicious and cruel man, a gangster."

"My father's a gangster? I don't believe you."

"Darling, it's true. He's worked in the sex industry for years. He owns nightclubs all over the north of England and he runs escort agencies and…"

"Sounds an interesting character," Alex said. "What's his name, this gangster?"

"Karl. Karl Maddox."

"Karl Maddox? I've heard of him. I visited one of his pole dancing clubs on a stag night once, the Topaz I think it was called. And you're saying this Karl Maddox is actually my father?"

Lisa nodded. "We were married when I was sixteen. I left him two years later when I found I was pregnant."

"Did he know about me?"

"No, not until I told him a couple of days ago. When he got sent to prison, I left him and got as far away as I could. I never wanted him to know he had children."

"You had no right to keep all this from me," Alex hissed, "I had a right to know the truth. How did react when you told him he had a son?"

"He was shocked at first, but that's understandable."

"So he just accepted that I'm his son?"

"He insists on meeting you," Lisa sighed. "He refuses to hand over any money unless you and he meet."

Alex walked over to the cabinet and poured himself another drink. "When does he want to meet? Did you arrange anything?"

"I said I would ring him. If you don't want to meet him, darling, you don't have to. We can find another way to get you the money."

"Don't be ridiculous, there is no other way. Arrange the meeting for the weekend." Alex strode to the window and was silent for a moment. He turned to face his mother, a look of faint amusement on his face. "Fifty thousand pounds isn't really much to pay for a son, is it, mother? I'm sure Karl Maddox can afford a lot more than that."

"Alex, don't get any silly ideas. Believe me, Karl's a very dangerous man. Fifty thousand is what you said you needed to join the partnership in Canada and that's what he has agreed to give you."

"Don't be so bloody naïve," Alex spat. "There is no fucking partnership. I need the money to pay off debts."

"Debts? What debts? I don't understand. You told me you had a job offer and..." Lisa rushed over to her son and placed her hand on his arm. "Alex, please tell me what's going on. You earn good money. Why are you in debt?"

"It's nothing to do with you," he snapped, pulling away from her. "Just ring Karl and arrange a meeting. I'm not working this weekend so arrange the meeting for then. I'll take it from there, and make sure don't tell him the real reason I need the cash."

"Alright, but be careful, darling," Lisa sighed as she prepared to leave. When she reached the door she hesitated and turned to face her son. "Alex, when you meet Karl, please don't mention your sister. I don't want him to know anything about her."

"Why would I want to mention your precious Christina? It's not like she's part of our lives anymore, is it?"

"She'll come back one day, when she's ready. I'm sure of it."

"She's been gone nearly two years. I don't think we'll see her again."

"Alex, don't say that. Christina is…"

"Goodnight mother," Alex said dismissively.

Lisa left the room and quietly closed the door behind her.

FIFTY-NINE

Smiling to herself, Bunny walked through the hotel foyer and out into the street. She couldn't quite believe that she had seen Charlotte in the company of Marion. Surely Charlotte wasn't considering becoming a working girl? Marion certainly hadn't seemed happy to see her at the hotel. She was about to hail a taxi when her blue mobile started to ring. This was the phone she kept for private clients.

"Hello Clive," she greeted. "I thought you were still in America."

"Flew in this afternoon," the man answered in a strong American accent. "As soon as the plane touched down, I thought of you, Bunny. Can you come over to my hotel tonight, babe? Say, about eleven?"

Bunny glanced at her watch. It was nine-thirty.

"Yes, of course. Are you staying at the Grand Hotel, same as last time?"

"Sure am. It's the best hotel in town. I'm in room 306. I don't suppose you can get out of working tomorrow and spend the day with me instead? I'll make it worth your while, babe."

"I'm sure that can be arranged," she giggled. "See you at eleven."

"I'll have the champagne chilling," Clive laughed as he hung up the receiver.

Bunny took her pink phone out of her bag, the one she used for working with Cupid's Angels, and dialled a familiar number.

"Shirley, it's Bunny. I'm sorry but I'm not feeling well, a bit of a tummy bug. Can you take me off the rota for the rest of the night and tomorrow?"

"Oh, I'm sorry to hear that, Bunny," Shirley said sympathetically. "You get yourself off to bed and give me a ring when you're feeling better. Alright, love?"

"Thanks, Shirley. I'll be in touch soon." As she was speaking, Bunny hailed a taxi and directed it to her flat. A quick shower, pack a couple of outfits and she could easily be at the Grand for eleven.

She had met Clive a couple of months earlier through the agency, and they had soon come to a private arrangement. Of course Bunny knew she would be in serious trouble with Karl if she got caught doing private work, but she was always careful and besides, she needed the money. Once she had saved enough, she would be leaving escorting behind her and starting a new life.

Shirley put down the receiver and expertly adjusted the spreadsheet on the computer, taking Bunny off the availability list.

"There's something about that girl I don't quite trust," she said to Colin who was busying himself tucking into the box of milk chocolates he had brought for her. "That's three times in the last two months she's taken herself off the rota."

"She probably just wants a night off," Colin suggested as he attempted to take the last coffee crème out of the box.

"That's mine," she snapped, playfully pushing his hand away. "Coffee crème is my favourite."

"I don't suppose there's any chance you'd share it with me?"

"None," Shirley grinned as she popped the chocolate into her mouth. "Here, you can have the nutty fudge."

"I don't like nutty fudge," he complained. "The nuts get in between my teeth and…"

"Then have the strawberry crème instead," she giggled as she placed the chocolate into his mouth. "Do you think I should ring Karl and let him know? I'm convinced Bunny's moonlighting."

"You trust your instincts, love," Colin answered, turning his attention to the tangerine fondant. "She wouldn't dare moonlight, would she? Surely she knows what the consequences would be if she got caught."

"We'll soon find out," Shirley said as she dialled Karl's number. When Shirley had finished the call, she turned to Colin, a worried look on her face.

"What's the matter, love?" he asked with concern.

"Karl was in a foul mood. He's getting one of the drivers to follow her. I just hope I've got it wrong for Bunny's sake."

"Don't worry about it, Shirley. You're just doing your job," Colin said comfortingly. "If Bunny's breaking the rules, she must pay the price. Anyway, changing the subject, you've got some time off soon, haven't you?"

"Yes, I've got three days to come. Why?"

"Well, how do you fancy a couple of days away? We could go to the Dales or the seaside perhaps. You decide."

"Oh, that would be lovely," Shirley beamed. "The seaside, I think. I haven't been for a paddle in years."

"What about Blackpool?"

"Yes, I love Blackpool," she giggled excitedly.

"Good. I'll get it sorted then. It'll do you good to get away from all this shit for a while."

"I think it'll do us both good, Colin," Shirley sighed. "It's just a pity we have to come back to it."

SIXTY

Karl slept well, despite the recent traumas. The pills he'd been given by the hospital seemed to be working and he felt more relaxed than he had done in a long while. Erica was in the kitchen making breakfast. The enticing aroma of fried bacon and freshly brewed coffee filled the air.

"Good morning," Erica greeted, not turning from the cooker. "Sleep well?"

"Very well," Karl grinned, sitting at the breakfast bar. "Have the papers come yet?"

"No, it's still a bit early. How many eggs do you want with your bacon?"

"Just the one thanks. I could do with losing a few pounds."

"Karl, there's something I need to ask you."

"What is it? Is something the matter?"

"It's Charlotte."

"Charlotte? Charlotte who? Oh, you mean Mary's girl Charlotte?"

"Yes. She's asked if she can come and stay with us. You don't mind, do you, darling? It would only be for a few days and..."

"I've never met her. What kind of a girl is she?"

"She's very sweet," Erica said fondly. "She's heartbroken about losing her parents of course. I think it will do her good staying with me for a while."

"Has she made any plans for the future?"

"She wants to stay in England, I think, and try to get a job in a school. She's a teaching assistant."

"A teacher, eh? I don't trust brainy women. Doesn't she have a boyfriend or something? How old will she be now? Nineteen?"

"Eighteen," Erica corrected. "And no, she doesn't have a boyfriend, not any more. So can she stay here for a while, just until she gets herself sorted?"

"I suppose so, but make sure she knows it isn't a permanent arrangement."

"I'll put her in the back bedroom," Erica said excitedly as she placed the plate of food in front of Karl.

"Will you be bringing her down to the club?"

"No, I will not," Erica answered sharply. "Charlotte's been brought up very strict."

Karl laughed crudely. "Maybe it's time she learned what life is really about. When does she want to come?"

"Today," Erica smiled as she poured Karl his coffee. "I'm expecting her here this afternoon."

"As soon as that? It's a good job I said yes then, isn't it?"

"I knew you would," Erica grinned, kissing him lightly on the cheek.

"I have to go to the club this morning, so I won't be here to meet her. Just make sure she doesn't go snooping about the place. I don't want some stranger knowing our business."

"Charlotte's not a stranger and she's not a snoop," Erica said indignantly. "She's a sweet, respectable girl who's had a good upbringing. I don't..."

"Alright, keep your hair on. I was only joking. I don't know what's the matter with you lately, Erica. You seem to have lost your sense of humour."

"I'm sorry," Erica almost whispered. "It's just been a shock losing Mary and Liam like that. I feel responsible for Charlotte, that's all. She has no one else to look out for her but me."

"Okay, I get it," Karl said as he drained his coffee cup and pushed his empty plate away. "Anyway, I must go, I've got a lot on today. I'll try and get home early to meet the girl. Don't worry, I promise I'll be on my best behaviour."

SIXTY-ONE

When Karl arrived at the club, Paul Borowicz was already there. He was carrying a brown A4 envelope.

"Is that what I think it is?" Karl asked, taking the envelope from Paul.

"Yes, boss. I've written down everything I found out about Alex Sutton. It makes interesting reading."

"Thanks. Give Colin a note of your expenses."

"Sure thing," Paul grinned. "If there's anything else I can do for you…"

"I'll let you know," Karl said as he made his way to his office. Karl admired Paul's efficiency. He had given him a couple of jobs to undertake in the past and he had responded well. Karl had a feeling he would be using Paul's services again very soon.

Half an hour later the telephone rang. It was Lisa.

"Alex is free this weekend," she said. "What time would you like to meet him?"

"Sunday would be best, say, midday? Could he manage that?"

"Yes, of course. Do you want me to come along too? It might make things easier."

"Of course I want you to come. I'll see you on Sunday." Abruptly he hung up the receiver.

As he read and re-read Paul's report, Karl could feel his hands shaking and the sweat trickling down the back of his neck. He reached for his pills and took two, washing them down with whisky. Taking a piece of notepaper from his desk drawer, Karl picked up a pen and began to write. Half an hour later the letter was completed and sealed in an envelope. He pressed the internal buzzer on his desk. It was answered immediately by Peter.

"Peter, come up to the office now," he instructed, taking out a cigar from his desk drawer. Peter Borowicz knocked politely on the door and walked into the office.

"Something I can do for you, boss?" he asked smiling.

Peter was big and bulky with a round chubby face that always seemed to be smiling, just like his father Victor. Unlike his brother Paul, Peter's assets were his brawn not his brain.

"Peter, I was wondering about your dad. What's he up to these days? Is his business doing well?"

"He's doing great. I don't see him as much as I should," Peter frowned. "Dad's either working or I am."

"I'm glad it's going well for him. Victor worked for me for a long time before he decided to go into the security business with his brothers."

"They're talking of expanding into Birmingham next year."

"What about you and Paul? Are either of you thinking of joining them?"

"You must be joking," Peter grinned, shaking his head. "Work with dad and my uncles? Don't get me wrong, I love them all to bits, but I could never work with them."

"That's good to know, Peter, because I'm thinking of giving you a lot more responsibility here. Do you think you could handle that?"

"Of course I can," Peter said eagerly. "You know you can depend on me. What is it you want me to do?"

"Do you know the Lucky Ace Casino in Manchester?"

"I've heard of it, but I've never been. Dad taught us never to gamble."

"Victor is a very wise man," Karl grinned. "I want you to go there for me and deliver a letter to Jonny Dalton. He runs the place. Do you think you could do that?"

"Sure. When do you want me to go?"

"I want you to go now," Karl said handing him the envelope. "Ask to speak to Jonny Dalton and hand him the letter personally. Don't give it to anyone else, only to Jonny. Understand?"

Peter nodded and placed the envelope in his inside jacket pocket.

"Do I wait for a reply?"

"No, there's no need. Jonny will contact me direct. Once you've delivered the letter, you come straight back here."

"Alright, boss. I'll go now."

"Good man," Karl smiled. "I'll see you this afternoon."

SIXTY-TWO

Karl's good humour didn't last long. At three o'clock he took a call from Jimmy, the driver he had assigned to check up on Bunny.

"Well?" he growled. "Is she moonlighting?"

"Afraid so, boss," Jimmy sighed. "You remember that American bloke I told you about a couple of months ago, the black guy who wore the white Stetson?"

"Yeah, I remember. What about him?"

"Well, that's the guy she met last night. I followed her from her flat to the Grand Hotel. By the time I'd got parked and made my way into the hotel, she was already inside the lift. She went up to the third floor."

"And?"

"This morning, at half-past ten, Bunny came out of the hotel arm in arm with him. They got into a taxi and headed into town."

"You're sure she spent the night with him?"

"No doubt about it, she never left the hotel. I followed them into town. They went shoe shopping. He bought her three pairs of fancy shoes from that boutique in Frenchgate."

"Go on," Karl encouraged. "What happened next?"

"They had lunch in that posh French place at the top of Briggate. He was splashing the cash on champagne."

"I assume you got photographs?"

"Yes, I got plenty. When they had finished their meal, they went back to the hotel and a couple of hours later she came out and got into a taxi. I followed her back to her flat."

"Thanks, Jimmy, you did a great job. I'll see you back at the club tomorrow. Make sure you bring the pictures with you, okay?"

"Sure, Karl," Jimmy yawned. "I need to go home now and get some shuteye. I'm shattered."

Karl had just replaced the receiver on its cradle when the telephone rang again.

"Yeah," he grunted. "Who's that?"

"Karl, this is Jonny Dalton. I got your note."

"Jonny, thanks for getting back to me so quickly. I…"

"How dare you send me a note like that?" Jonny hissed unpleasantly. "Who the fuck do you think you are?"

"Calm down," Karl soothed. "I'm sure we can sort this out amicably."

"There's nothing to sort out. You keep your fucking nose out of my business or you might get it cut off."

Karl laughed. "I don't think so, mate. Now stop pissing about and let's talk business."

"Fuck off, you nonce," Jonny spat. "You're not dealing with your whores now. I don't take orders from a piece of shit like you."

Karl was silent for a few seconds. When he spoke his voice was calm but stern. "I've told you what I want. I want Alex Sutton's IOUs. I'm prepared to pay the going rate. It's not open to negotiation, Jonny. Understand?"

"Screw you. You can't talk to me like that. Do you know who I am?"

"Of course I know who you are. You're Jonny Dalton, small time dealer, small time gambler and small time dickhead. More to the point, Jonny, do you know who I am? Do you know what I'm capable of?"

There was an uneasy silence. The tone of Karl's voice had the desired effect on Jonny.

"Karl, mate," he said at last. "I think we maybe got off on the wrong foot. Let's start again, shall we? Why don't you come over to the casino as my guest? We can talk privately there."

"There's nothing to talk about. How much does Alex owe? The exact amount, mind, don't try adding extra interest."

"I wouldn't do that," Jonny grinned, trying to lighten the mood. "Alex Sutton owes close to forty thousand pounds."

"Forty grand? As much as that?"

"He's in the casino three or four times a week. A very unlucky gambler is young Alex."

"Send me his IOU's over and I'll give you a cheque."

"I don't think so. I prefer things the way they are."

"Oh you mean the drugs he's been supplying to pay off his debt?"

"Drugs? I don't know what you're talking about," Jonny spluttered.

"I think you do. Now listen to me, Jonny, Alex won't be supplying any more drugs so I'd advise you to accept my offer. Like I said before, send me his IOU's and I'll give you a cheque."

Jonny was silent for a moment. "Alright," he said sulkily, "but if it's all the same to you, I prefer cash."

"No problem. I'll get it to you first thing tomorrow."

"Tell me, Karl, who is Alex Sutton to you? He must be one hell of a good mate for you to pay out forty grand."

"That's none of your business," Karl said sternly, "and, one more thing Jonny."

"Yeah, what's that?"

"If I ever hear you call me a nonce again, I'll personally come over there and rip your fucking head off."

SIXTY-THREE

Erica arrived at the hotel at midday to find Charlotte already packed and in the foyer.

"Are you sure you want to do this?" Erica asked as they made their way to the waiting taxi. "Karl can be difficult. I really think…"

"Erica, stop fussing. I'm not going to create a scene or anything like that. I just want to observe him. I want to see what sort of man he is."

Erica gave a deep sigh as they both got into the taxi. "I think you're making a mistake, Charlotte," she said softly. "Do be careful dear, for everybody's sake."

"I will, I promise. Now stop worrying."

It took the taxi twenty minutes to reach Maddox Mansion, a five bedroomed detached house overlooking the park. Throughout the journey, both women remained silent.

"What a beautiful house," Charlotte said excitedly as the taxi pulled up on the impressive herringbone drive. "Have you lived here long?"

"Nearly ten years," Erica answered, opening the large front door and walking into the hallway. "I'll show you up to your room, then I'll make lunch, you must be hungry."

Charlotte followed Erica up the wide staircase and along the corridor to the bedroom at the rear of the house.

"I hope you'll find this comfortable," Erica said as she placed Charlotte's suitcase on the king-sized bed. "There's an en suite through there," indicating a door at the far side of the room.

"Erica, it's perfect," Charlotte smiled, glancing at her reflection in the ornate mirror above the dressing table. "It's a beautiful room."

"I'm sure you'll be very comfortable here, dear. I'll leave you to unpack. Lunch will be about half an hour."

Twenty minutes later Charlotte joined Erica in the kitchen.

"I've made a pasta bake with a side salad," Erica said as she removed the dish from the oven. "I hope that's alright?"

"Perfect," Charlotte smiled. "I love pasta."

"Would you like a drink? I usually have a glass of wine with my lunch."

"Yes, that would be nice. I've picked up some really bad habits since I came to England. I never used to drink alcohol, but I must admit, I do rather enjoy it."

"Tell me about your life in Ireland. I'm afraid I didn't keep in touch with Mary as much as I should."

"I was very lucky. I had a wonderful childhood," Charlotte beamed. "We lived close to the sea. My dad had so many relatives, travellers most of them, that I had lots of cousins to play with."

"I'm glad," Erica said softly, her eyes brimming with tears. "Paula would have been happy things turned out so well for you."

"You haven't said much about my mother. I know you were best friends when you were in care, but I want to know…"

"Not now, Charlotte," Erica said abruptly. "Please darling, not now."

There was an uneasy silence.

"What time are you expecting Karl home?" Charlotte asked as she ate the last of the pasta on her plate.

"Your guess is as good as mine. He promised he wouldn't be late tonight."

"It must get lonely being on your own such a lot."

"Sometimes, but I've got used to it. I did work at the Emerald when it first opened, but I didn't like it much. I'm much happier staying at home."

"Doesn't it make you uncomfortable, knowing how Karl earns his money?"

"I don't ask how he earns the money," Erica answered defensively, "and he doesn't ask how I spend it. Somehow it seems to work."

"I know I'd go stir-crazy not going to work. How do you fill your days?"

There was no mistaking the annoyance in Erica's manner. "I take care of Karl," she said sharply. "I take care of the house and there's the garden and I… "

"But who takes care of you, Erica?"

"I don't know what you mean. Karl takes care of me of course. He is good to me in his own way."

"Mother always said Karl was a bully. I know you're frightened of him."

"Charlotte, I've explained the situation. I daren't leave Karl. I just can't."

"But you want to, don't you?"

Erica remained silent.

"What about Joe?"

"What about Joe? Joe's a friend, a good friend."

"I think it's obvious that Joe's in love with you."

Erica turned angrily to face Charlotte. "Do you have any idea what Karl would do to Joe if he heard you say that? What he'd do to both of us if he even thought it?"

"Erica, I'm so sorry. I didn't mean to upset you." Charlotte reached across the table and took Erica's hand. "I just want you to be happy and I want Karl to be punished."

"I thought I'd explained the situation to you last night. I can't hurt Karl without hurting myself. He can be very cruel, you have no idea."

There was an uneasy silence between the two women. Charlotte was the first to speak.

"Karl has three clubs now, doesn't he?"

Erica nodded. "Yes, there's the Emerald here in Leeds, the Topaz in Bradford and the Sapphire in Sheffield."

"Joe runs the Topaz?"

"Yes. He's managed the club ever since it opened."

"I'd like to see the clubs. Do you think Karl would agree?"

"Why on earth do you want to do that? You must realise what goes on there."

"Of course I do, but I'd still like to see for myself. Will you ask Karl if I can? Please, Erica."

Erica frowned as she began to clear the table. "If you take my advice, you'll stay away from Karl and the clubs. They're no place for you."

Charlotte remained silent as she helped Erica fill the dishwasher.

"What are you going to do this afternoon? Do you want to go shopping?"

"No, I thought I might have a look through the suitcase Marion gave me. Talking of Marion, I suppose I ought to arrange to meet up with her soon, after all she is my grandmother."

"For goodness sake, don't let Marion hear you call her that. She'd throw a fit."

"I'll ring her and arrange to meet for lunch tomorrow. Do you want to join us?"

"No, dear. I think Marion would like you to herself for a while. I have an appointment at the hairdressers at twelve and I might treat myself to a manicure."

"I'll go up to my room then, if you don't mind. See if I can find any precious stones amongst Paula's things."

"Good luck with that," Erica grinned. "I'm going to do some pruning in the garden. The roses are in a sorry state. I'll see you in a couple of hours."

SIXTY-FOUR

Erica was busy in the garden when Charlotte came rushing out of the house.

"Erica, look at this," she cried excitedly. "I found it inside the case."

Charlotte opened her hand revealing a heart-shaped locket on a delicate gold chain with a broken clasp. "This was my mother's, wasn't it?"

Before Erica could reply, Charlotte opened the locket. On one side was a picture of a very young baby. On the other side of the locket was a photograph of a young couple.

"That's me with my parents, isn't it, Erica? That's Paula and my father." Charlotte thrust the locket towards Erica. "Who's the man? You must have seen him with my mother. Who is he?"

Erica stared at the faded photograph inside the locket. Paula had indeed been a beautiful woman with her deep grey eyes and auburn hair. She was smiling and looked happy and relaxed. The man next to her was strikingly handsome with pale blue eyes and blonde hair. It had been almost twenty years since the photograph had been taken but David Glendenning hadn't changed very much in that time.

"Well?" Charlotte asked impatiently. "Do you know who he is?"

"I'm afraid not," Erica lied. "I've never seen him before."

"Are you sure? Please take a good look. He's very distinctive."

"I'm sorry, I don't know him," Erica said dismissively, picking up the pruning shears. "Now I really must get on."

Charlotte looked at Erica suspiciously. "I think you do know him, Erica. You admitted you knew who my father was, remember? You said he was no good and that I should stay away from him." She began walking towards the house. "I'll show Marion the locket tomorrow. I'm sure she'll tell me his name."

"Charlotte, if you do manage to trace this man, what do you think will happen?"

"Happen? What do you mean?"

"Well, do you think he will welcome you into his life? Introduce you to his family as his long-lost daughter?"

"I don't know, but that's something I have to find out for myself. Surely you can see that?"

"Charlotte, I'm begging you. Please forget about this man."

"I can't. He's my father and I have to meet him."

"You really are very headstrong, aren't you? Why won't you trust what I'm saying and stay away from him? It's for your own good."

Charlotte turned angrily to face Erica. "I've been lied to by you and my parents all my life. Do you have any idea how that feels, to know that your whole life has been one big lie on top of another? I don't trust you, Erica. I don't trust Marion. In fact, I don't trust anyone." Tears began to run down her cheeks.

"Well, I'm sorry you feel that way. Marion and I did what we thought was for the best. I hoped you'd realise that."

"Erica, I'm grateful for what you did. I'm grateful for Mary and Liam taking care of me, but they should have told me I was adopted earlier. To find out only after they were dead is hard. There are so many questions I need to ask them. So many things I need to ask you and Marion."

"I told you all I know about what happened to Paula. What else do you want to know?"

"I want to know about Paula, the person. What sort of woman she was. What she liked to wear, what she liked to eat. I want to know what sort of music she liked, what her favourite colour was. But most of all, Erica, I want to know who she fell in love with. Surely you can understand that?"

Erica put her arm around Charlotte's shoulder and guided her towards the house. "Why don't we have a nice cup of tea and I'll tell you all about her," she said kindly.

"I don't drink tea, remember? But I wouldn't mind a gin and tonic."

Erica smiled. "What a good idea. I think I'll join you."

SIXTY-FIVE

Karl poured himself a whisky with soda and took his usual walk around the club. It was almost ten o'clock and the Emerald was beginning to reach capacity. The Lounge Bar was full of would-be celebrities and middle-aged businessmen, most of whom were regular visitors to the club. They were accompanied by some of the prettiest girls in the area, all elegantly dressed and perfectly groomed. Soft music was playing as the girls chatted and flirted with the men, always with a glass of champagne in their hand. A couple of girls were entertaining discreetly in the booths at the back of the room.

Karl descended the staircase and went into the main part of the club. The music here was much louder. Strobe lights danced around the room as scantily clad girls wound themselves artistically around the poles to the rhythm of the music. There were several minders scattered around the club. Their job was to ensure none of the men touched the girls inappropriately. The club was more boisterous than usual with two stag parties and a group soldiers from the nearby barracks in York.

"Everybody behaving themselves?" Karl asked Peter, who joined him as soon as he entered the room.

"Nothing we can't handle," Peter said reassuringly.

"Just make sure it stays that way. I'm leaving early tonight. If anything kicks off you know where to find me."

"Don't worry, boss, we've plenty of staff if any of the punters gets too frisky."

Karl took a last look round the club before he walked through to the foyer. "By the way, Peter, I want you to do me another errand tomorrow."

"Yes, boss," Peter said attentively.

"I need you to deliver a package to Jonny Dalton at the casino. Be in my office at twelve o'clock sharp."

"Sure thing," Peter grinned, opening the main door for Karl. "See you tomorrow."

Karl drove his Mercedes out of the car park. It was a fifteen minute drive to his home and as usual, he used the time to reflect on the day's business. The most pressing matter was meeting Lisa and Alex on Sunday. He was excited and worried at the same time. The report Paul had supplied regarding his son did not make good reading. At least once he had settled the gambling debt, Alex would be out of Jonny Dalton's grasp.

The meeting he had had with David Glendenning the day before had been worrying him. David had been a useful ally over the years but now he was losing his influence and there was little he could do to help him. If David did get prosecuted for misconduct who knows what dirty little secrets he would tell to save his own skin?

But it was what David had told him at their last meeting that had made Karl feel more uneasy. Proposals were being considered by the council to operate a zero tolerance throughout the city towards the sex industry. This would mean closing down all strip clubs, pole dancing clubs and brothels. Although he hadn't received any official notification as yet, David had warned him to expect a letter outlying the proposals very soon. Karl had already arranged clandestine meetings with several members on the council who were visitors to the club or were regular clients of the girls. He was prepared to use whatever means he could to influence their decision.

He turned on the car radio and turned his thoughts to Bunny, the girl who had been moonlighting. Bunny had been working for Cupid's Angels for the past two months. He'd never actually met her but from what he'd heard from Marion she was a high earner for the agency. Shirley had assigned her the more affluent clients and Bunny had received lots of repeat bookings. Usually when girls had been found to be taking on private clients they would be made to pay a heavy fine and taken off the agency's books. Karl decided he would continue to let her work but would impose a heavy fine, and he would warn her personally of the consequences if she ever moonlighted again.

As Karl pulled the car into the drive of his home, his mind turned to another matter, one that had been niggling away at him all day. If it was true what Paul had said in his report, he not only had a son but a daughter, Christina. Why hadn't Lisa mentioned her to him? Where was Christina living? What was she doing? He needed answers and on Sunday when he met Lisa and Alex, he was determined to get them.

SIXTY-SIX

Karl arrived home just before ten thirty. He parked his car in the garage and made his way into the house.

"Erica, I'm home," he called from the kitchen.

"We're through here," she answered.

Karl walked into the lounge. Charlotte's heart began to race as he came towards her. A tall, well-dressed middle aged man with closely cropped hair, she noted. He had an aura of authority which she found slightly alarming. She noted the scar which ran down his left cheek. My mother did that, you bastard, she thought. Good for her.

"This is Charlotte, darling," Erica said as she walked towards her husband and kissed him lightly on the cheek. "Charlotte, this is my husband, Karl."

Charlotte held out her hand which was shaking slightly.

"It's nice to meet you at last. Erica's told me all about you."

"Not everything, I hope," Karl smirked, winking as he leaned over to kiss her on the cheek. "It's very nice to meet you, Charlotte."

"Have you eaten, darling? There's some casserole in the oven I can heat up."

"I'm fine, thanks, I ate at the club earlier." Karl walked over to the drinks cabinet and poured himself a whisky. "Would anyone care to join me?" he asked jovially.

Both women asked for gin and tonic.

"So tell me, Charlotte," Karl asked when they were all seated comfortably with their drinks, "what do you think of England? Erica says it's your first visit."

"Oh it's grand. I love all the shops you have over here."

"You'll have a lot in common with Erica then. She loves the shops too, don't you, darling?"

Erica smiled but remained silent.

"I hear you're looking for work in England."

"Yes, that's right. I'm a teaching assistant so I should be able to get a job soon."

"Are you staying in this area, or are you looking further afield?"

"I haven't decided anything yet. For the moment I just want to enjoy what England has to offer."

"Well, as long as you don't get bored."

"I'm sure I won't. Actually, I was wondering if you would let me come and look round the clubs sometime. I've never seen the inside of a pole dancing club before."

"I'm sure that can be arranged," Karl grinned, ignoring the hostile look given by Erica. "I'm busy over the weekend, but Monday night should be okay, it's not usually busy on a Monday. Will you be coming too, Erica?"

Erica glared at her husband. "Of course," she said sharply. "I'll need to keep an eye on Charlotte. Goodness knows who'll be hanging around."

"The club lounge has a very upmarket clientele, you know that. You will be my guest in the VIP lounge. I hope you like champagne."

Charlotte nodded and gave Karl her broadest smile. "Well, I think I'll go up now if you don't mind," she said. "I'll see you both tomorrow."

"She seems a nice kid," Karl said when Charlotte had left the room. "Pretty little thing, isn't she?"

"She's very sweet and very innocent. I don't think it's a good idea encouraging her to visit the club. Please tell her you've changed your mind."

"Nonsense. I've told you before, Erica, you can't sugar-coat life. It's time little Charlotte came out from under her bushel and experienced life's realities."

"She's little more than a child. She shouldn't…"

"Enough," Karl snapped getting up from his chair and striding towards his wife. "Don't ever tell me what I should and shouldn't do, Erica. Understand?"

He roughly grabbed her shoulders, pulling her to her feet.

"Now, I think I will have some supper after all."

SIXTY-SEVEN

It was after eight before Charlotte woke. Usually she was awake before seven. Quickly she got out of bed and showered before pulling on blue jeans and a cream top. She brushed her hair and tied it back before leaving her room and making her way to the kitchen. Erica was already busy at the stove.

"Good morning," she greeted. "No need to ask if you slept well."

"Like a log," Charlotte smiled. "It's a very comfy bed."

"Would you like some breakfast?"

"Just juice, please. I'm not really hungry."

"You should eat breakfast," Erica scolded. "What about a buttery croissant?"

"Alright, if you insist. Where's Karl this morning? Surely he's not still sleeping?"

"No, Karl left about an hour ago. He said he had some urgent business at the club today."

"On a Saturday? Doesn't he ever take time off?"

"Hardly ever," Erica shrugged. "What time have you arranged to meet Marion?"

"I said I'd meet her outside McDonalds at ten o'clock."

"You sure you know where to find it? I can take you if you wish."

"Don't worry, Erica. Marion gave me directions yesterday."

Both women ate their breakfast. Erica, scrambled egg on toast with a steaming cup of coffee and Charlotte, a croissant with a glass of fresh orange juice. When they had finished, Erica put the crockery into the dishwasher.

"I suppose I'd better wear something a bit dressier than jeans to meet Marion. I've brought a couple of outfits with me. I'll get changed now." She turned to go upstairs when her mobile phone rang.

"Hello," she answered almost immediately. "Patrick? Oh Patrick, how lovely to hear from you." Charlotte smiled at Erica and hurried up the stairs to her room.

When she came downstairs twenty minutes later, she was wearing the pretty blue floral dress and a white cotton jacket. Her blonde hair was loose, falling over her shoulders.

"You look nice, dear, that's a very pretty dress."

"Thank you," Charlotte blushed slightly. "I bought it the other day in town."

"Charlotte, I know it's none of my business but who's Patrick? Do I know him?"

"I met him in Dublin. His name is Patrick Flynn. He's a solicitor."

"A solicitor?"

"Yes. His father is Shamus Flynn, the solicitor you sent my money to all those years."

"Why was he ringing you? What does he want?" Erica asked with concern.

"He wants to come over to England to see me."

"Why on earth would he want to do that?"

"Because he likes me, I suppose, and I rather like him. He's very good looking, Erica, you'd like him."

"Charlotte, this can be dangerous. If Karl finds out that I…"

"Erica, don't worry, Patrick won't be staying here. He's booked into a hotel in town. Now I really have to go. I don't want to be late meeting Marion."

SIXTY-EIGHT

Charlotte was elated after Patrick's call. She could barely believe that he was actually coming to England to be with her. Every night since she had left Ireland, Patrick had telephoned. There had been no mistaking the tenderness in his voice as they had chatted endlessly about everything but nothing in particular. Charlotte had wanted to confide in him about the situation, but decided to wait. She didn't want a repetition of what had happened when she had confided in Rory. She had made a reservation at the Westbrook Hotel in the centre of Leeds, the hotel she had stayed at when she had first come to England.

Charlotte hurried along the busy street. She was due to meet up with Marion, her only known living relative. There were still questions she needed to ask about her mother. As she rounded the corner of Turner Street onto the Headrow, she caught sight of Marion outside the Regent Cinema.

She was about to wave when she felt herself being pushed violently from behind. At the same time, she became aware that her bag was being wrenched from her hands. Frantically Charlotte tried to hold on to her bag, but the assailant, a lad no more than twenty and wearing a green hoody, pulled it from her grasp, pushing her hard against the wall, causing her to fall heavily to the ground.

Charlotte screamed as the thief raced up the Headrow, pursued by two young men who had witnessed the assault. They both returned after a few minutes triumphantly clutching the stolen handbag.

"The little runt legged it," said the first young man. "We got the bag back though. I don't think he's nicked from it." He handed the bag to Marion who was cradling Charlotte, on the ground.

"Thanks, lads," she said. "The police are on their way and… oh here's the ambulance."

"I don't need an ambulance," Charlotte protested weakly. "I'll be fine, I just want…"

Less than ten minutes later, Charlotte was in the A&E Department of St James Hospital with an anxious Marion and Erica by her bedside.

"Don't try to talk," Erica said soothingly as she gently stroked Charlotte's cheek pushing her long hair out of her eyes. "Marion rang me and told me what happened. You're alright, darling," she soothed, "the doctor doesn't think it's anything serious."

The cubicle curtain was pulled back and an elderly Asian doctor, accompanied by a stern looking young nurse came in and stood alongside the bed.

"Hello, young lady," he greeted jovially. "I'm Doctor Ali and this is Nurse Lowe. I hear you've been mugged. I bet you're feeling a bit sore, eh?"

"A bit," Charlotte said softly. "He just came out of nowhere and pushed me into the wall and…"

"Quite so, quite so," the doctor nodded. "The streets can be a dangerous place these days, you must always take care. The good news young lady is that there doesn't seem to be any bones broken." He watched as Nurse Low began taking Charlotte's pulse. "Now if you don't mind, ladies," he said, addressing Erica and Marion, "I need to examine my patient. You can get a coffee from the machine down the corridor."

Erica and Marion got up to leave.

"We won't be long, darling," Erica said. "We're just outside if you need us."

After they left, Doctor Ali began his examination. When he had finished, he smiled at Charlotte. "Well, young lady, you've been very lucky. No broken bones, just bruising. I'll give you some painkillers but I prescribe you rest up for a few days."

"Thank you, doctor," Charlotte smiled weakly. "Can I go home now?"

"Go home? Why does everyone want to go home? Don't you like it here?" he chortled. "Yes, young lady, you can go home if you must. I promise I won't be offended."

Still grinning, he made to leave her bedside as a second nurse put her head round the curtained screen. "There's a police officer here, doctor. He wants to speak to the patient."

"Show him through, I'm sure you're able to tell the policeman what happened, aren't you, dear? Do you want me to get your companions?"

"No, I'll be fine," Charlotte answered propping herself up on the pillows.

Charlotte was still feeling a little woozy as the young policeman came through the curtained cubicle and sat on the chair at the side of her bed.

"Good afternoon," he said politely. "I'm Police Constable Matthew Glendenning and I need to take a statement from you about the incident earlier today."

SIXTY-NINE

Sunday morning was bright and sunny. Karl was up early, dressed and ready to leave when Erica came into the lounge.

"Is that a new suit?" she asked. "I haven't seen you wearing that before."

"I've had it at least a month," he lied. "Perhaps you don't notice any more."

Erica, wearing her nightdress and dressing gown, shrugged in response and went into the kitchen. "What do you want for breakfast?"

"Not hungry," came the response. "I'll get something later at the club."

"Will you be home for dinner tonight?"

"Probably, I'll give you a ring later and let you know. By the way, how's young Charlotte this morning? Has she recovered from her brush with death?"

"She's fine, just a little shaken, that's all. I thought I might take her breakfast in bed."

"You're spoiling her. Let her come downstairs and eat properly."

Before Erica could respond, Karl was through the door, slamming it behind him.

The Emerald Club was deserted when he arrived. He made his way up to his office, softly whistling to himself. It felt strangely quiet at this time in the morning. He felt both excited and apprehensive knowing that in just a few hours he would meet the son he hadn't known existed until a couple of days ago.

He paced nervously up and down the office. He opened the safe and removed the IOUs which Peter had brought from Jonny

Dalton the day before. Forty thousand pounds worth of IOUs. He frowned as he checked the dates. Some of them went back almost a year. Karl heard a noise and pushed the documents quickly into the desk drawer just as Peter walked into the office.

"Oh sorry, boss, I didn't know you were in already. Fancy a coffee?"

"Yeah, that would be nice, and a couple of bacon butties would be even better."

"Sure thing," Peter grinned. "The café down the street should be open by now. I'll be ten minutes."

When Peter returned, he was carrying two small paper carrier bags. For the next half hour, both men ate their food and drank coffee whilst making small talk.

"I'm expecting visitors at lunchtime," Karl said as he placed the empty paper bag into the waste bin. "See to it I'm not disturbed."

"Okay," Peter said cheerily. "I'd better get downstairs. The cleaners should be here any time."

Left alone, Karl turned his attention to the computer printouts for the previous night. He frowned as he studied the recorded takings. "These figures seem low," he thought. "Peter said it was busy here last night." He checked the returns from the Topaz and the Sapphire clubs. They too were not as high as he had expected. "What the hell's going on?" he muttered, dialling Joe's number.

"'Morning, Karl," Joe said after his phone had rang half a dozen times. "You're early this morning. Is everything okay?"

"No, it bloody well isn't. Have you seen the takings from last night? They're way down on what they should be."

"I wasn't working last night, Karl. I'll look into it when I get to the club and ring you back."

"Do it now. I want to know what the hell's going on." He slammed down the receiver and rang Colin's number. It was a few minutes before he answered the phone.

"Calm down," Colin soothed in response to Karl's angry tone. "I think I know what's happened. It's young Barry, the lad who's been helping me that's made the cock-up. He's a nice lad, but not very bright. I put him in charge of recording the figures on the computer whilst I went away for a few days break. It looks like he's sent you the figures meant for the tax man by mistake. Don't worry, Karl, I'll get the proper accounts over to you tomorrow when I'm back at my desk."

"Are you sure that's all it is?" Karl asked suspiciously. "You haven't been up to your old tricks again, have you?"

"Karl, what do you take me for?" Colin said indignantly. "I've told you what's happened. I'll get it sorted tomorrow."

"Make sure you do, and get rid of that stupid little bastard. I don't know why you need an assistant for in the first place."

"To cover for me when I need time off, that's why I'll speak to Barry tomorrow. It won't happen again, I promise."

"It better not," Karl snapped as he angrily put down the receiver.

He began to drum his fingers on the desk glancing over at the drinks table. "No," he told himself firmly, "not this early in the morning." He quickly picked up the internal phone. "Peter, bring me another coffee, mate, and put plenty of sugar in it."

A few minutes later Peter put the steaming mug of coffee on Karl's desk. Karl sipped at the sweet liquid and grimaced.

"Bloody hell, how much sugar did you put in here? It tastes foul."

"Sorry, Karl, I'll make you another."

"Oh don't bother," Karl said sulkily, pushing the mug away.

"Anything else you want, boss?"

"No, I don't think so. Oh, you could get some posh biscuits for my visitors."

"Posh biscuits?"

"Yeah, that's right," Karl said irritably, "and whilst you're about it, get some decent mugs."

"I'll see what I can do." Peter shrugged as he headed towards the office door, a broad smile on his chubby face.

Karl looked anxiously at his watch. Half past ten. Just ninety minutes to wait. He began to drum his fingers impatiently on the desk once more. There was something else he had to do today, but what was it? "Ah yes, Bunny," he said triumphantly. He dialled her number and it was answered almost immediately.

"This is Karl," he said sharply. "I think you and I need to talk, young lady."

"What's the matter?" Bunny asked nervously.

"Did you really think I wouldn't get to hear about you moonlighting, you silly bitch?"

"Karl, I don't know what you're talking about. I've never…"

"Don't you dare lie to me, Bunny. I have photos of you and the yank at the Grand Hotel. Ring any bells?"

"Karl, I can explain," Bunny spluttered. "Clive is a family friend, he…"

"You're lying. He's a punter and you cheated my agency out of the fee. I figure you must have made a fair bit on that booking."

"Karl, I've told you, Clive is a friend. We never…"

"Bunny, if you lie to me one more time I'll make sure you'll never be able to pull another punter again, do you understand?"

"Please Karl, I…"

"Three grand, that's what you owe me," Karl said menacingly. "Make sure you bring me three thousand pounds to my office first thing on Monday morning. Oh, and by the way Bunny, that's not a request."

"Karl, I swear he didn't pay me anything like that," Bunny protested. "I've told you, Clive is just…"

"Bunny, just bring the cash. Don't make me come looking for you or I promise you'll regret it." Before she could respond, Karl had replaced the receiver.

He glared at the lukewarm coffee on his desk with distaste. "Oh fuck it," he hissed, as he purposely strode over to the drinks table and poured himself a whisky, adding just a splash of soda. "Life's too short."

SEVENTY

Bunny was trembling as she placed her phone back into her bag. She always knew it was risky seeing clients privately, but she had always been careful. Clive understood the danger she faced if she got caught moonlighting, that's why he was overly generous when paying for her services. Her booking with him had netted her five thousand pounds. There was no way she was going to give Karl three thousand of that money.

Bunny went into the bedroom and took down a suitcase from the top of the wardrobe. She had almost twenty-four hours to get away, she reasoned. You could go a long way in twenty-four hours. It was then she noticed the car parked across from her apartment. A familiar red Ford Mondeo. The car that Cupid's Angels sometimes provided to transport girls to their bookings. Inside was Jimmy, one of Karl's drivers.

Frantically she began to fill her case with clothes, tears streaming down her face. Just a few more weeks and she would have had enough money to leave escorting behind and start a new life. Bunny had longed for that day but now it looked like her plans were ruined. She felt angry. Angry with herself for getting caught, but angrier with Karl. How dare he dictate who she could and couldn't meet?

Nervously Bunny peeped through the window blinds. The Mondeo was still there, parked just across from the only entrance to the flats. Nervously she began to pace the room. Perhaps, she wondered, if she gave Clive a ring he would be able to convince Karl they were just friends, but she knew this was hopeless. Clive was back in the States. He had a family. There was no way he would want to become embroiled in this. No, she decided resolutely, the only way to deal with this was to face Karl head on. She would try and reason with him, pointing out how much she had made for the agency in the past through other clients. The more she dwelt on this course of action, the more she convinced herself it was the only thing to do. However, she wasn't going to wait until tomorrow. No, this had to be dealt with now.

Bunny picked up her phone and dialled for a taxi. She was annoyed that it would be almost an hour before one was available. Walking into the kitchen, she made herself a coffee and sat at the table to wait.

SEVENTY-ONE

Just before twelve, Peter knocked on Karl's office door and announced that Dr and Mrs Sutton were in Reception.

"Show them up," Karl ordered, straightening his tie in the wall mirror.

A few seconds later Lisa came into the room followed by a young man.

"Glad you could make it, Lisa," Karl smiled, kissing her lightly on the cheek. "And this must be Alex? It's very nice to meet you at last."

Alex Sutton was in his late twenties, tall and slim with thick black hair and dark brown eyes. He was dressed immaculately in grey slacks and a pale lemon shirt. A dark grey jacket was worn elegantly over his shoulders. A handsome face, Karl thought, but an arrogant one.

"Hello, Karl," Alex said cordially, holding out his hand. "Lisa tells me you're my father."

"So it would seem. It came as much a surprise to me as it must have done to you."

Alex shrugged and sat on the leather couch. Lisa sat next to her son.

"Your mother tells me you're a doctor. That's very impressive."

"Being a doctor was Lisa's idea, not mine," he replied coldly.

"Alex, that's not true. You love being a doctor, you know you do."

"Love it? You must be joking. Having to listen to stupid people moaning about their aches and pains all day, what is there to love about that?"

"You don't mean that. There's a lot more to being a doctor than that, you know there is."

Alex laughed harshly and placed his arm around his mother's shoulders. "Of course I don't mean it, Lisa. I love being a doctor. You know that."

Karl had been watching Alex closely. There was something about his manner that he didn't like, son or no son.

There was a rap on the door and Peter came into the room carrying a tray with three china mugs and a plate of chocolate biscuits. He placed the tray on the corner of the desk.

"Thanks, Peter," Karl said, trying hard to stifle a laugh at seeing this hard man acting as waitress. "Please see to it that I'm not disturbed." Peter nodded and closed the office door. Karl turned to his guests. "Lisa, would you like a coffee? What about you, Alex?"

Lisa smiled and took the mug from Karl. Alex declined the drink.

"Your mother tells me you're looking at joining a medical practice in Canada. That sounds exciting."

"I am if I can get the money together. It's going to cost fifty thousand pounds to join the partnership. Lisa thought you might be able to help out."

"Fifty thousand pounds is a lot of money," Karl said sternly.

Alex glared at Karl. "I would have thought it was peanuts to you."

"I wouldn't say peanuts exactly," Karl frowned.

"That money can change my life. Surely you can see that?"

"I'm sure it can, but it's still a lot of money."

"Don't you think you have a responsibility towards me?" Alex's manner suddenly became aggressive. "After all you're my father but you haven't paid a single penny towards my upkeep. I would have thought it's the least you could do to put things right."

"Oh, do you now?"

"Let's face it, Karl, you must be worth at least a couple of million. I know all about the clubs that you run and your other businesses and…"

"Alex, that's enough," Lisa snapped. "It's unfair to blame Karl.

He didn't know anything about you until a few days ago. That was entirely down to me."

"Yes it was, you stupid bitch," Alex spat, turning angrily to face his mother. "You deprived me of a father and Karl of a son all these years. That was unforgiveable."

"There were reasons why your mother did what she did," Karl responded defensively. "Reasons you don't understand."

"Don't make excuses for her," Alex hissed. "What Lisa did was wrong. You and I should have met years ago."

Karl rose slowly from his chair. "Lisa, would you mind leaving Alex and I alone for a few minutes? I need to speak to him privately." He guided her by the arm through the door leading into the lounge bar. "Peter, can you take care of Mrs Sutton? See to it she has everything she needs."

"Sure, boss," Peter grinned, glad of any distraction from polishing the glasses behind the bar. Karl walked back into his office, firmly closing the door behind him.

"Good. Now we've got Lisa out of the way, perhaps we can get down to business," Alex smirked, removing the jacket from his shoulders. "I need…" Alex didn't see the punch but he felt it, as he fell to the floor clutching at his jaw. "What the hell was that for?" he yelled.

Karl grabbed Alex roughly by his shoulders and pulled him to his feet.

"If I ever hear you disrespect your mother like that again, I swear I'll kill you," he hissed, his face close up to Alex. "And in future, you show respect to your mother. You will refer to her as mother, not Lisa. Understand?"

"Alright, whatever you say," Alex said, struggling to regain his composure.

"Good. Now we understand each other, perhaps you can start speaking the truth."

"Truth? I don't know what you mean, Karl. I…"

"This money you're wanting. You say it's to buy into a partnership in Canada?"

"Yes, that's right. I…"

"Alex, you don't seriously think I would pay out fifty grand without checking, do you? I know exactly what you want the money for."

Alex stared down at the floor but remained silent.

"I've heard you have serious gambling debts. Is that right?"

"No, I wouldn't say serious exactly. It's true I enjoy a little flutter at the casinos now and again but so what?"

"It's not just a little flutter though, is it, Alex? I know you owe forty thousand pounds to Jonny Dalton at the Lucky Ace. I know that you've been stealing drugs from the hospital's pharmacy to help pay off your debt, and I know that you'll shortly be under investigation about the thefts."

"How did you…? Look Karl, I can explain. I…"

"I also know you're up to your eyes in debt through your gambling. I don't think Sarah's going to want to stay married to you when she realises how much debt you have brought to her door, do you?"

"Sarah? What's she got to do with anything? For fuck's sake, Karl, are you going to help me with the money, or not?"

"I'm not a fucking bank."

"I know exactly what you are," Alex spat. "This club is just a fancy knocking shop, isn't it? You can pretend to be as respectable as you want but in the end, we both know what goes on here."

"It's adult entertainment. It's all perfectly legal. I don't need to explain to you about how I make my money."

Alex walked towards the door leading into the lounge. "If you're not going to help me, I don't see the point of my being here. I'll get Lisa, or should I say mother, and we'll be off."

"Not so fast. I think you should know that I've picked up your IOU's from Jonny."

"You've done what? You mean I don't owe that bastard any more money?"

"That's right, you don't. You owe me the money instead."

"Karl, I don't know what to say. I was out of my mind with worry."

"Don't think the debt's written off, Alex, because it isn't. You still owe the money, and one way or another, I will get it back, believe me."

"I'm sure we can sort something out, Karl. This calls for a celebration, don't you think?" He walked over to the drinks table. "Do you mind?"

"Help yourself." Karl said, opening the door to the lounge. "Mine's a whisky and soda."

Lisa came back into the office, an anxious look on her face. "Is everything alright?" she asked nervously.

"Of course it is, mother. Karl and I have sorted a few things out. Would you like a drink to celebrate?"

Lisa shook her head. Alex sat on the couch next to his mother. Karl sat on the chair opposite.

"Does this mean you'll be able to take up the partnership in Canada?"

"No, mother, that won't be happening now. I've decided to stay in England after all."

"Oh darling, I'm so glad. I didn't like to say anything, but I would have missed you if you had gone all that way."

"Well, don't worry, I'm not going anywhere. I'm going to stay around and get to know my father. Isn't that right, Karl?"

Suddenly there was the sound of raised voices from the lounge and the office door burst open. Peter was holding Bunny by the shoulders.

"You can't go in there," he growled at her. "Karl has guests."

"I need to speak with Karl now," Bunny screeched as she freed herself from Peter's grasp and ran into the room. "Karl, I…" Bunny stopped mid-sentence and stared open mouthed at the two visitors in the room.

"Christina," Lisa cried, rising from her seat. "Christina, is it really you?"

SEVENTY-TWO

"Christina!" Lisa cried hysterically as the girl turned and ran back down the stairs. "Christina, please come back!"

Karl quickly picked up the internal phone. "Peter, Bunny's coming down the stairs. Get Jimmy to take her back to the flat and stay with her. I'll be there shortly."

"Okay, boss," Peter answered as he grabbed the fleeing girl by the arm.

"Bunny? Why are you calling my daughter Bunny?" Lisa yelled as she frantically attempted to push past Karl, tears streaming down her face. "Her name is Christina."

"Don't worry about her, she's quite safe," Karl said as he held Lisa's wrists tightly. "Now suppose you tell me about Christina. I take it she's my daughter?"

Lisa pulled away from Karl, glaring defiantly at him, but she remained silent.

It was Alex who broke the silence. "Christina is my twin. This is the first time we've seen her in over two years."

"Why's that?"

"She ran away. She wanted to be with some man."

"He was a married man," Lisa sighed. "I begged her not to go but she wouldn't listen."

"Who was this man? Does he have a name?"

"Rosso," Alex volunteered. "His name is Guido Rosso."

"Where is he now?"

"He lives in London somewhere. He owns a couple of restaurants down there. I contacted him at the restaurant a few months ago but he said he hadn't seen Christina in nearly a year."

"I thought she must be dead." Lisa began to cry softly. "No one knew where she was."

"Here, drink this," Karl said, handing her a whisky and soda. "You look like you could use it."

Lisa took the glass without protest and sipped at the contents. "Karl, what was Christina doing here? She doesn't work here in the club, does she?"

"Would it be such a bad thing if she did?"

"Karl, she's your daughter. Of course it would matter."

"When were you going to tell me I had a daughter, Lisa?"

Lisa stared at her husband and he could see the defiance in her eyes. "I wasn't," she said at last. "I didn't want you anywhere near her."

"Do you really hate me that much?"

"What mother means, Karl, is that…"

"I'm sure your mother can speak for herself," Karl interrupted. "Well, Lisa, do you?"

"I don't hate you, not anymore," Lisa said softly. "I just don't think you'd make a good father, that's all."

"You didn't exactly give me a chance to find out, did you?"

"Well, that's in the past. What's important now is finding Christina."

"You leave her to me. I'll go to her flat and speak with her."

"I want to come with you, I need to see her."

"No Lisa. You and Alex book into a hotel and I'll be round later tonight."

"But Karl, I…"

"Do as I say. Alex, take your mother to the Marriott, it's the nearest hotel."

Alex nodded. "Come on, mother," he coaxed. "Let's do what Karl says. Christina will be okay, won't she, Karl?"

"Of course she will, now hurry up. I'll come over to the hotel as soon as I can."

All three went down the private staircase and out into the rear car park.

"I'll see you in a couple of hours," Karl waved, getting into his Mercedes. It roared into life and joined the busy stream of traffic.

SEVENTY-THREE

Bluebell Tower Apartments was a smart, ten-storey building on the outskirts of the city. The tinted windows and stainless steel balconies made it one of the more desirable places to live. Karl parked his car and hurried towards the entrance. Taking out his phone he rang Jimmy. "What number?" he asked.

"201," Jimmy answered. "Hurry up, Karl, for Christ's sake. The silly bitch is going crazy up here."

Karl entered the foyer and got in the glass and chrome lift to the right. Within seconds he was on the second floor facing room 201. Before he could ring the bell, Jimmy opened the door. His face had deep scratches down both cheeks and blood was trickling down his face onto his shirt collar.

"Have you seen what the crazy bitch did?" he snarled. "I thought she was going to kill me."

"It's okay, Jimmy, I'll take it from here. You get back to the club. Peter could do with a hand."

"That's fine with me," Jimmy said as he rushed out onto the landing and headed towards the lift. "Watch out for her nails, they're like talons."

Karl entered the apartment and closed the door behind him. Christina was standing by the window, staring out into the street below. Before Karl could speak, she spun round and rushed towards him.

"You have no right to keep me here," she hissed. "I want to leave now." She attempted to push past Karl, but he grabbed her shoulders and forced her down onto the couch.

"Calm down," he soothed. "I just need to talk to you, Christina. That is your proper name, isn't it?"

The girl glared at him.

"What were my mother and brother doing at the club? Did you tell them where I was?"

"I didn't tell them anything. They came to see me."

"Why? What would my mother want with you?" Christina was almost hysterical.

"I want you to calm down. You and I have got things to sort out."

"Is it the money you say I owe you? I'll get it for you first thing tomorrow and…"

"No, it's not about the money, Christina. It's about you and me."

"I don't understand. What about you and me? There is no you and me." She tried to get off the couch, but Karl's grip remained firm.

"Christina, just a couple of days ago I learnt something from your mother that came as a shock." Karl's tone became softer. "I was married to Lisa a long time ago, in fact, technically, I suppose I still am."

"You were married to my mother? I… I…"

"When I got sent to prison, she left me. I didn't know where she went, she just disappeared, but I had no idea that when she left she had been pregnant with you and Alex."

Christina sat motionless, staring at the floor.

"Do you understand what I'm saying, Christina? You're my daughter."

Christina remained silent. It was several minutes before she spoke. "Lisa said my father was dead," she whispered. "Why would she lie? I don't understand."

"She had her reasons, I'm sure."

"But why would she tell you about us now after all this time? I don't understand."

"Oh, that's down to Alex getting into a mess over money."

"Alex is always in a mess with money. He gambles, you know."

"Yes, I know, but I'm not here about Alex. I want to talk about you."

"Me? What is there to talk about? You know how I earn my living. I'm very good at it too as you can see."

"Your mother said you left home to be with a man. What happened?" Karl could sense the tension in Christina's body as she glared at him.

"I don't want to talk about it," she said angrily. "It's over, I just want to forget."

"Tell me," Karl insisted. "Tell me everything that happened to you, Christina. I have to know."

Christina was silent for a moment but when she spoke her voice was quiet and calm.

"His name was Guido. Guido was the love of my life. I adored him."

"So what went wrong?"

"Karl, I really don't want to discuss it. It was a mistake and…" Christina lowered her head into her hands.

Suddenly, Karl's tone changed. "I don't care what you want to do. From now on you'll do as I say. Now, tell me what happened?"

Defiantly, Christina raised her head and looked Karl in the eye. "I loved him, that's what happened," she said quietly. "When he suggested I move into his swanky apartment by the Thames, I didn't hesitate."

"You knew he was married?"

"Yes, of course I knew, but I didn't care. I loved him."

"Did he love you?"

"I thought he did. His wife was called Bella. She spent most of her time in Naples looking after her mother. Guido told me as far as he was concerned the marriage was over. He said he was going to divorce her and I believed him."

"Go on," Karl encouraged. "What happened?"

Christina got up from the couch and walked over to the drinks cabinet. "Want one?" she asked, pouring herself a vodka.

"Whisky," Karl answered.

Christina walked over to him and handed him the glass.

"You were telling me about Guido," Karl said sternly.

"Everything was wonderful for the first few months. Guido

was so kind, he treated me like a princess." Christina lifted her glass and swallowed its contents in one gulp. "We'd been together for a couple of months and then one day he brought a friend to the apartment, a man called Louigi." Christina walked over to the cabinet and poured herself another vodka before continuing. "We all had a meal and Guido and Louigi were speaking in Italian. Suddenly Guido grabbed my arm and pushed me into the bedroom and onto the bed. Louigi followed us."

Karl could see that Christina was becoming agitated. He walked over to her and gently placed his arm around her shoulder.

"Go on, Christina," he said gently. "Tell me everything. No one can hurt you now."

Christina began to cry softly. "Suddenly Louigi began pulling at my clothes. I screamed for him to stop. Guido was standing in the doorway. He watched as Louigi raped me." Tears began to cascade down her cheeks and her body trembled uncontrollably.

Karl held her close, kissing her lightly on her forehead.

"Guido had sold me to Louigi," she gulped through her tears. "Guido said that from now on Louigi would be taking care of me and I was to do what he said."

"He said what?" There was no disguising the anger in Karl's voice.

"Louigi was a lot older that Guido. He was cruel. He would tie me up and beat me and sometimes he would lock me inside the apartment for days at a time. He would bring men back and I was made to have sex with them. It was horrible."

"How long were you with the bastard?"

"About three months. One night, after Louigi had been drinking heavily, I managed to escape. It was impossible to take much with me, but I did manage to steal a couple of hundred pounds from his wallet. I got the first train north. That night I said goodbye to Christina and hello to Bunny. I think you know the rest."

Karl was standing by the window staring out into the street. His eyes were stinging with unshed tears and he wiped them away with the back of his hand.

He turned to face Christina. "This Guido Rosso, Alex said he has a restaurant in London, is that right?"

"He has two, one in Chelsea and one in Mayfair."

"And Louigi? Where do I find him?"

"Louigi's dead. I heard he had a heart attack soon after I left."

Karl walked over to the couch and sat next to his daughter. Gently he took her hands in his. "What is it you want to do with your life, Christina? You're a very beautiful young woman. You could be anything you want. Surely you don't want this work to be your life?"

"Of course I don't," Christina said sharply. "I'm saving up to buy my own salon. I'm a qualified hairdresser and beautician."

"A hairdresser? That's good, very good."

"I've almost got enough saved. Just a few more wealthy clients and I should…"

"No more clients," Karl snapped. "I can help with the money you need. I don't want you working like this again, ever."

"Karl, I want to do this on my own. I'm never going to depend on a man for anything again."

"I'm not just a man. I'm your father and I'm going to help you."

"No strings?"

"No strings, I promise."

Christina smiled at Karl and gently kissed him on the cheek.

"I suppose we'll have to think of something to tell your mother," Karl said at last. "I could say you were working as a hostess at one of the clubs."

Christina began to giggle. "She'll throw a fit, but I suppose it's better than telling her the truth. That would really finish her off."

"I'd better go and tell Lisa the good news," he smiled. "Perhaps we can all meet up for dinner this evening? Lisa and Alex are at the Marriot. They have a pretty decent restaurant. I'll make reservations."

"Alright," Christina said slightly hesitantly, "but please tell her not to ask too many questions."

"Don't worry, I'll be there to look out for you," he winked mischievously. "Oh, there is one more thing Christina."

"What's that?"

"The phone. I want you to give me the phone."

"What phone?"

"The one you use for your private clients. We don't want temptation, do we?"

Christina picked up her handbag and removed the blue phone. "Goodbye, Bunny," she whispered as she handed it to Karl.

"I'll see you at the Marriot at eight," Karl grinned, kissing her lightly on the cheek.

Christina walked with Karl to the door. "See you at eight o'clock, dad," she smiled, throwing her arms around his neck affectionately.

Karl waited until he was inside his car before he picked up his phone and dialled a number.

"Paul? Paul, I have a job for you. Meet me at the club in twenty minutes, oh and you'd better pack an overnight bag. You're going to the big smoke."

SEVENTY-FOUR

Erica and Charlotte were finishing their breakfast when Karl came into the kitchen whistling.

"Somebody's happy this morning," Erica grinned.

"It's a beautiful day, why shouldn't I be happy?"

"Do you want breakfast, or is it just coffee?"

"I'm starving, full English this morning, I think. Good morning, Charlotte. How are you feeling today?"

"Oh I'm alright, thanks. I really should be more careful crossing the road."

"Do you still want to come and have a look round the club today?"

"No, sorry, Karl, I've got other plans. Perhaps another time?"

"Suit yourself," Karl shrugged sulkily, picking up the newspaper.

Charlotte hurriedly put her breakfast bowl and glass into the dishwasher.

"What are you up to today, dear?" Erica asked lightly.

"I'm going shopping. I thought I might buy some jeans."

"Girls shouldn't wear jeans," Karl grunted from behind his newspaper. "Jeans are for boys."

Both women stifled a laugh.

"Will you be back for lunch?" Erica asked.

"No, I promised Marion I'd meet her for lunch. I should be back about four."

"Alright, dear, I'll see you then. Have a nice time."

"See you later," Charlotte smiled, as she went through the front door.

"Did she say she was meeting Marion for lunch? What the hell is she meeting her for?"

"I think they get on well. Charlotte really is a lovely girl."

"Has she said anything about moving out yet?" Karl grunted putting down his newspaper. "She does know staying here was only a temporary arrangement, doesn't she?"

"Charlotte's no trouble. In fact, she's good company for me. It gets lonely here on my own."

"Then come back to work in the club. There's always plenty to do."

"You know I don't want to do that, I hate working there."

Karl glared at Erica. "You never used to hate it. I always thought you liked poncing round the lounge bar, dressed up to the nines."

"No, Karl, I didn't. Anyway you have all the staff you need now. I only went to help out."

He shrugged and picked up his newspaper once again. "I meant what I said about Charlotte. I want her gone by the end of the week."

"Why? She's only just got here. Please let her stay a little longer. She needs us."

"One week," Karl snapped. "We'll need her room for another guest."

"What guest?"

"Never mind, just make sure she knows she has to go. I won't repeat myself again, Erica."

Erica sighed heavily as she busied herself making Karl's breakfast. "She's meeting a young man tomorrow," she said lightly. "He's a friend of hers from Ireland."

"Good, then he can take her back with him. The girl doesn't belong here. Now, where's my breakfast?"

SEVENTY-FIVE

It was half past eleven when Charlotte arrived at the Elkin Arcade. She'd visited several times before and was familiar with its layout. Barlow's Coffee Lounge was tucked away at the back of the building, quiet and discreet. It was here that Charlotte headed. Matthew was already there. He rose from his seat as she approached.

"I wasn't sure you'd come," she grinned as she took her seat at the table.

"Who wouldn't come at the invitation of such a pretty girl?" Matthew smiled. "Especially when the invitation was laced with intrigue."

"Matthew, I…"

"I take it you have no after effects after the incident? You were very lucky not to have been seriously hurt."

"Yes, I know. It was a silly thing to do. I was in a hurry to meet someone and…"

"What can I get you?" the chubby waitress wearing a lilac and white uniform asked as she pushed plastic menus in front of them both.

"A cappuccino, please," Matthew answered. "What about you, Charlotte?"

"Orange juice, please."

"Anything to eat?"

"No, thank you," they both chorused.

The waitress waddled over to the counter with their order. She returned a couple of minutes later carrying the drinks. When she left, Charlotte turned to face her companion.

"Matthew, I had to meet with you. There's something I think you should see."

"This is all very mysterious."

Charlotte opened her bag and took out the gold locket, opened it and handed it to Matthew.

"Tell me I'm not going mad, but that man in the photograph, he looks just like you."

Perplexed, Matthew took the locket and stared hard at the picture.

"That's my dad," he said at last. "What are you doing with a photograph of my dad? And who are these people with him?"

Charlotte took a sip of juice before she answered. "The baby is me," she said softly. "The woman is my mother. Her name is Paula. I believe the man is my father."

Matthew's hands began to tremble slightly as he picked up the locket once more and stared intently at the photograph. "He can't be. That's ridiculous," he spluttered. He turned to face Charlotte. "What makes you think he's your father? He could just be a friend of your mother or…"

"Look at me, Matthew," Charlotte said gently. "Can't you see the similarity between us? Our skin tone, our hair colour, even our eyes are the same pale shade of blue. I don't think there's any doubt that I'm your sister."

Matthew began to slowly shake his head. "That can't be right, Charlotte. I always knew my father played around with other women, but to father a child by one? Even he wouldn't be that bloody stupid." Angrily he thrust the locket across the table towards her. "We can have a DNA test. That will prove if we are related."

"Of course we can, and we must," Charlotte sighed, "but from what I've been told, Paula and your father had an affair and were very much in love. She told her friends that he was leaving his wife so they could be together."

"The bastard," Matthew hissed, bringing his fist crashing down onto the table. "The cheating little bastard."

"Where's your father now? Is he still around?"

"Oh yes, he's still around alright. He's a senior policeman. Can you believe that?"

"I don't really know very much about him," Charlotte sighed. "I found the locket in my mother's effects and then when I saw you at the hospital and realised how much you resembled the photograph, I just knew…"

Matthew turned to face Charlotte. "I take it your mother is dead?" She nodded.

"She died when I was a baby. I was adopted and brought up in Ireland."

"I'm so sorry, Charlotte, I really am."

"Will you tell me about my father?"

"What is there to tell? He's a lying scumbag. He's made my mother's life hell over the years with a string of affairs."

"This must be difficult for you, meeting me and seeing the proof of your father's infidelity," Charlotte said softly, "but I had to tell you. You have a right to know the truth."

"It is a shock, but you did right telling me. My mother and I knew he saw other women, but they were usually prostitutes. He still does see them as a matter of fact. He's never away from that whorehouse run by Karl Maddox."

"You mean the Emerald Club?"

"You've heard of it?"

"Who hasn't? Tell me, do you think I should confront your father, let him know he has a daughter?"

"What on earth for? If you take my advice you'll stay as far away from that bastard as you can."

"But he's my father too. He…"

"Charlotte, trust me, the man's toxic. You need to stay away from him."

They both lapsed into silence for a few moments. It was Charlotte who spoke first.

"There's something else you should know,"

"Oh God, not more surprises?" He lowered his head and cupped it in both hands. "What is it?"

"My mother was a sex worker when she met your father."

Matthew sat bolt upright and stared hard at Charlotte. "A prostitute? Your mother was a prostitute? This just gets better."

"I was a baby when she died. I was adopted by Karl Maddox's sister-in-law and her husband. I was brought up by them in Ireland." Charlotte took a sip of juice before continuing. "They were both killed in a car crash a couple of months ago. That's why I came to England to be with Aunt Erica. I'm staying with Karl and Erica at the moment."

"You're doing what? Are you mad? Don't you know that man's reputation?"

"Of course I know, but I have my reasons to be there. Aunt Erica has been very good to me."

"As far as I'm concerned, Karl Maddox is just as responsible as my father for breaking my mother's heart. She's in pieces because of the mess dad's got himself into. I don't know how she's going to react when she finds out about you."

Charlotte looked concerned as she took Matthew's hand in hers. "Do you really think telling her about me is a good idea?"

"I think she has a right to know," he said determinedly. "She's away on a spa break at the moment, but she'll be back in a couple of days. I'll tell her then. Perhaps this will finally convince her to divorce him. She should have got rid of him years ago."

The waitress came back to the table and picked up the two empty containers. "Do you want anything else?" she asked as she briskly ran a damp cloth over the plastic table top.

"No thanks," Matthew said putting on his leather jacket which had been hanging on the back of his chair. He turned to face Charlotte. "I don't know about you but I could do with a proper drink."

"What a good idea," Charlotte grinned. "I should just have enough time before I meet my grandmother for lunch."

"Your grandmother? Is that Paula's mother?"

"Yes. Her name's Marion. She's nice, you'd like her. Now, what about that drink?"

SEVENTY-SIX

"Thank you for the lunch, Marion," Charlotte said as she ate the last of the carbonara on her plate. "I didn't realise I was so hungry."

"Glad you enjoyed it, dear. Would you like more wine?"

Without waiting for a response, Marion refilled her glass.

"So tell me, what have you been doing with yourself this week?"

"Oh nothing much, just shopping. But I did meet someone earlier today."

"It all sounds very mysterious. Who did you meet?"

"Marion, if I tell you, you must promise not to tell Erica or Karl."

"Charlotte, you're not making sense. Who did you meet?"

"You remember the locket, the one in my mother's case?"

"What about it?"

"There was a photograph of my father inside. I've found out who he is. His name is David Glendenning. He's a policeman, and this morning I met my brother, Matthew."

"Your brother? Charlotte, I don't understand."

"Matthew's a policeman too. Marion, you wouldn't believe how much I look like him, it's uncanny. When I saw Matthew at the hospital the other day I just knew…"

For the next ten minutes Charlotte relayed to Marion her encounter with Matthew at the hospital and their subsequent meeting.

"You must stop this now," Marion said sternly once Charlotte had finished speaking. "You're opening up a very dangerous can of worms. No good will come of it, believe me."

"But he's my father. He has a right to know he has a daughter, surely you can see that? I need to meet him, to talk to him."

"David thinks Paula had you adopted straight after you were born. He has a family of his own. He won't want you spoiling all that. Please darling, for everyone's sake, keep away from him."

"It's too late for that. Matthew's going to confront him today and then tell his mother about me."

"Oh Charlotte, what have you done? You don't understand how dangerous this can be."

Charlotte sipped the last of her wine.

"Matthew said he has treated his mother abominably over the years cheating on her with a string of other women. He thinks once she finds about me, she'll divorce him."

Charlotte stood up and began to put on her coat.

"Oh, I almost forgot," she said picking up her handbag and removing a large brown envelope. "I've been through the suitcase you gave me. I've kept a couple of photographs and a bit of costume jewellery. These are photographs of you with Paula when she was young. I thought you might like to keep them." She handed the envelope to Marion. "There are some old insurance documents and a few legal papers in there as well. They probably need to be thrown away."

"Thank you, dear," Marion said as she took the envelope from Charlotte and placed it in her own bag. "I'll look through them and throw out anything I don't want."

"Well, I must be going. Erica will think I've left home."

"Are you enjoying staying with her?"

"Erica's lovely but I can barely look at Karl without wanting to scream abuse at him. Knowing what he did to my mother and how he is abusing Erica makes my blood boil. If there was a way to hurt him, Marion, I swear I would do it."

"I really think you'd be better moving out of Karl's house. He's not a fool. If he suspects for one second who you really are…"

"Don't worry, I'll be careful," she grinned. "I might be moving soon anyway."

"Moving?"

"Yes, back to Ireland."

"Are you going to stay with Liam's family?"

"I've not decided anything definite yet Marion, but I might have a new boyfriend."

"Not Rory?"

"No, definitely not Rory. I don't ever want to see that man again."

"Then who is he?"

"His name is Patrick Flynn and he's a solicitor from Dublin."

"Erica mentioned him. I didn't realise you were together though."

"We're not together exactly. Well, not yet. We've been speaking on the phone every night and he's coming over to England tomorrow. He's staying at the Westbrook. That's the hotel I stayed at before."

"Well, I hope everything goes well," Marion smiled. "But please remember what I said about your father. Stay away, Charlotte, for your own sake. Please stay away."

SEVENTY-SEVEN

"No Charlotte this morning?" Karl enquired as he drank his coffee. "Don't tell me she's actually left already?"

"She's gone to meet her friend," Erica answered as she attempted to retrieve the poached haddock from the pan. "His name is Patrick and he's come all the way from Dublin to see her."

"I hope he's not expecting a bed here."

"Of course he isn't. He's booked into a hotel."

"Is Charlotte staying with him tonight?"

"I wouldn't think so, but that's none of our business. Charlotte's eighteen so she can do what she wants."

"She's pretty enough but, I don't know what it is, there's something about her that's not quite right. I can't put my finger on it but there is something."

"I don't know what you're talking about. Charlotte's a lovely girl. She's had a good upbringing. Mary saw to that."

Karl merely shrugged. "Haven't you caught that damned fish yet? I've got to leave soon. I've got a busy day."

"There you are," Erica smiled as she handed Karl the plate containing the elusive haddock. "Will you be home for dinner tonight?"

"No, in fact it might be the early hours before I get back so don't wait up."

"What's happening? The club is usually quiet on a Tuesday."

"I won't be at the club. I'm looking at a new business venture."

"Not another club?"

Karl tapped the side of his nose. "You'll find out," he grinned as he busied himself with his breakfast. "Now pour me another coffee, this one's gone cold."

When Karl arrived at the Emerald he was surprised to see Colin waiting for him in the office.

"Good morning, Karl," Colin greeted nervously.

"You're early. Is anything the matter?"

"I need to speak to you urgently."

"You'd better sit down," Karl invited. "Now what the hell's wrong?"

"Nothing's wrong exactly," Colin spluttered nervously. "Well, not really wrong. It's just that I, well, Shirley and I to be exact, we're... well we're both thinking of retiring."

"Retiring? What the fuck do you mean, retiring?"

"I'm turned sixty, Karl, and I want to retire. Me and Shirley were thinking of moving up to Scotland and setting up house there."

"Scotland? Are you mad? Why Scotland?"

"It's Shirley's idea. She likes Scotland."

"When has Shirley ever been to Scotland?"

"When she was a child she visited her grandma up there. She said it was wonderful and she always wanted to go back."

"Take her on holiday for a week."

"No, we've decided it's time to retire. Shirley quite fancies getting a little flat in Edinburgh."

"Who's going to look after the books if you go swanning around in Scotland? That twerp Barry that you've got working for you is bloody useless."

"Barry's not so bad. He just made a silly error the other night but I've shown him where he went wrong and..."

"No, you can't retire, Colin, it's out of the question. I need you here."

"I'm sorry, Karl," Colin said sharply as he removed his glasses and began polishing them furiously with the edge of his jumper, "but I've decided I'm leaving and you can't stop me."

"You ungrateful little bastard," Karl screeched. "After all I've done for you. I was the one that gave you a job when nobody else would, remember? And this is how you repay me?"

"I'll always be grateful for what you did for me, but that was twenty years ago. I've earned my keep over the years. You're only paying a quarter of the tax that you should be paying. I think that makes us even, don't you?"

Karl was silent for a moment, his anger steadily rising. "Alright," he said at last. "I can't make you stay but I want you off the premises right now. Get out and take that slapper Shirley with you."

Before Colin could respond, the telephone rang.

"Yeah?" he growled. "Oh Paul, it's you. Just hold on a sec…"

He turned to face Colin. "Are you still here? I said get out and don't come back."

Hastily Colin went out of the office, banging the door noisily behind him.

"Sorry about that, Paul. What have you got for me?"

SEVENTY-EIGHT

Charlotte was in the foyer of the Westbrook Hotel scanning through a fashion magazine she had bought at the nearby kiosk. She checked her watch just as the familiar figure of Patrick Flynn came through the hotel's revolving door.

"Patrick," she squealed excitedly, rushing towards him with arms outstretched.

Patrick put down the suitcase he was carrying and picked her up in his arms, spinning her round. "Hello, Charlotte," he grinned. "That was a grand welcome, so it was."

"Oh, it's lovely to see you."

"Well, that's good to hear," he grinned. "I'll just get checked in and then we can go for a coffee and a catch-up. Oh I forgot, you don't drink coffee, do you?"

"Never mind that," Charlotte said impatiently. "Hurry up, Patrick. I've got lots to tell you."

Twenty minutes later they were sat in the hotel's dining room, Patrick drinking a milky coffee and Charlotte her usual orange juice.

"So tell me," he grinned, "how are you enjoying England?"

"It's alright," she said thoughtfully. "Erica's been wonderful. I'm staying with her at the moment."

"I thought you didn't like her husband. Don't tell me you've had a change of mind?"

"Karl is an evil man, believe me. I hate him for how he treats Erica and for other things he's done, things you wouldn't believe."

"I'm sure Erica can stand up for herself," he said lightly. "Father always spoke very highly of her."

"No, you don't understand. Erica can't stand up to him at all. She's terrified of him. He..."

"Slow down," Patrick said gently. "Why don't you start at the beginning and tell me exactly what's been going on? Do you think you can do that?"

"I can't tell you. If I do, you'll hate me, just like Rory did."

"Of course I won't hate you. I could never hate you. Now, take a deep breath and start at the beginning, that's a good girl." Patrick reached out and took her hands in his. "Go on, Charlotte," he encouraged. "I'm here now. There's nothing to be afraid of."

Charlotte's heart was pounding so fast she thought it might explode. Faltering at first, she told Patrick about what she had learnt about her mother, how Karl had killed her and why Erica had felt a responsibility towards her. She told him how Erica had accidentally killed her own abusive father when she was a child, and how Karl had blackmailed her into staying with him. She took the locket out of her bag and handed it to Patrick, explaining about her meeting with Matthew and what she had learnt about her father, David. When she finished, she looked at Patrick defiantly.

"Well," she said at last, "that's what I've discovered. It's not a pretty story, is it, Patrick? I wouldn't blame you if you…"

"Charlotte, Charlotte," he said softly, gathering her in his arms and kissing her lightly on the cheek. "You poor girl. The sooner I get you away from these people the better."

"I can't leave, Patrick. Not until I settle the score with Karl Maddox."

"Settle the score? What exactly do you propose to do?"

"I'd like to kill him. Shoot him or stab him or…"

"And end up spending the rest of your life in prison? Take my advice and walk away. It's not worth it, believe me."

"I can't let him get away with what he's done. I just can't."

Patrick was silent for a moment. "In my opinion," he said, his tone suddenly becoming stern, "the only way you can hurt Maddox is through his business interests."

"You mean through the clubs?"

"Yes, that seems to be where most of his money comes from. You damage those and you damage him."

"What are you suggesting? He's very clever, you know. All of the clubs are legal, at least on the surface."

"Yes, but they are vulnerable."

"I don't understand what you mean."

"You have family in Ireland, don't you, on your father's side?"

"I've got loads."

"Then why don't you ask for their help? Get a few of your uncles or cousins to come over to England on the ferry and burn down all three clubs. They could be on their way back to Ireland on the morning ferry."

"Patrick, that's a wonderful idea," she said excitedly. "Actually, three of my cousins are working on the fairgrounds in Sheffield. I could give them a ring and ask for their help."

"No, Charlotte, you can't do that. You do know I was joking, don't you?" Patrick sounded alarmed. "Arson is a serious offence. You can get sent to prison for a long time."

"Only if you get caught, and my cousins have never been caught causing mischief. Anyway, nobody actually lives on the premises so if fires were set late at night the clubs would be empty. The only thing to get hurt would be Karl's pockets."

Patrick was silent for a moment. "You're determined to go through with this, aren't you?"

"Yes. Karl deserves it, after all the bad things he's done. I'll give my cousins a ring right now."

"You'll have to be far away from here when it happens. Why not come back to Ireland with me?"

"Ireland? I don't know, Patrick. It's a big step and…"

Suddenly Patrick was holding her in his arms and kissing her gently on the lips. "I've wanted to do that since the first time I saw you," he whispered. "Come back with me, Charlotte. Let me take care of you, darling. Oh and I think I should warn you, I don't believe in long engagements."

SEVENTY-NINE

Guido Rosso was a handsome man of Mediterranean appearance. In his late thirties he could easily be taken for ten years younger. Guido was just short of six foot with a lean but muscular physique. He spoke perfect English, slightly laced with an Italian accent, which he knew women found sexy.

Guido gave a contented sigh as he nibbled on the black olives and sipped the last of the Nero d' Avola from his glass. Life was good, he contemplated, not for the first time that evening. With two successful restaurants and a beautiful, attentive mistress waiting at his apartment life indeed was very good.

It was just after midnight. He regarded this as the best part of the day. Guido's Italian Ristorante had closed at eleven o'clock with customers having left happy and satisfied. The staff had cleared away and gone home, leaving him alone to enjoy a glass of his favourite wine in the quiet stillness.

He was deciding whether to have a second glass of wine when he heard a faint humming noise coming from the direction of the kitchen. He listened intently, trying to identify what it could be. Getting up from his chair, he walked over to the doors leading into the kitchen.

The kitchen was illuminated by night lights. They emitted a dull glow, enough to find your way around but not bright enough to work by. Frowning, Guido stood at the door and surveyed the room. It was the light at the far side of the kitchen that caught his attention. Yes, it was definitely the deep fat fryer that was still operating he realised. Angrily, he strode down the line of kitchen appliances until he reached the large fryer. "That bloody Mario," he spat as he reached for the switch to turn off the machine.

Without warning, he felt a heavy blow to the side of his head and he instantly fell to the ground. Dizzy and disorientated, he attempted to get to his feet. There was a punch to his ribs, no, not a punch he realised, it was a kick. This was followed by another and another.

"Please," he pleaded, attempting to get to his knees. "I have money. I give you money."

There was another kick, this time to his head. Still his assailant remained silent. Semiconscious now, Guido was pulled to his feet. Blood trickled down his face and into his eyes.

He was being forced over the fryer. He could feel the heat on his face and hear the oil sizzling in the pan below. He tried in vain to struggle free. Suddenly there was a searing pain to both hands as they were thrust into the oil. He gave out a deafening scream. It was several seconds before his attacker released his grip. Barely conscious, he fell to the floor, whimpering like an injured animal. His skin felt like it was on fire. The pain was unbearable.

"Why?" he muttered pitifully. "Why me?"

But the room was empty. The only noise was the banging of the door leading out into the alley as it swung in the night breeze.

EIGHTY

The Sapphire Club in Sheffield was the smallest of the three clubs owned by Karl Maddox. On weekends, the club was always full to capacity but quieter during the week. Like the Emerald and the Topaz, the Sapphire had a private member's lounge where between six to twelve girls would work. The club consisted of five podiums with half a dozen private booths. There was always a minimum of eight dancers, but during the weekend this would rise to around fifteen. The club's clientele were mostly young men out on the town. There were a number of regulars who Simon knew lived locally. In the five years he had been managing the Sapphire, there had never been any serious incidents.

Tuesday was Simon's night off. He was at home enjoying a pizza whilst watching a box set when his phone rang. It was Freddie, his deputy.

"Si, I think you should come down to the club. There's something not right."

"What sort of something?" Simon asked irritably.

"Three Irish blokes, I don't like the look of them. I think you should come down."

"Can't you handle it, Freddie? Throw them out if they're causing trouble."

"They're not causing trouble exactly but…"

"What are they doing then?"

"One of the minders overheard them talking. He's sure they're planning to do the club over. I think you should come down, Si. See what you think."

Reluctantly, Simon turned off the television, picked up the last of the pizza and headed out of the flat. He arrived at the club in less than ten minutes.

"That's them," Freddie said as soon as Simon joined him at the bar. "They're sat over there by the booths."

Simon glanced casually over at the three men, noting two were in their mid-thirties and one in his early twenties. All three were dressed in jeans and trainers and were wearing casual hooded tops.

"What exactly did they say?"

"Martin, come here a minute," Freddie said, addressing a young man employed as a minder. "Tell Si what you told me."

Martin was in his early twenties. He was well over six foot tall and a stocky build with sandy collar-length hair, a ruddy complexion and pale blue eyes. At being summoned by the boss, the colour in Martin's cheeks began to rise and he fidgeted nervously with his uniform tie.

"Well?" demanded Simon. "What is it that's made you suspicious?"

"I was … I was in the toilets," Martin stammered nervously. "I'd had an upset stomach, I think it was a dodgy kebab I'd eaten earlier and…"

"For fuck's sake, I'm not interested in your bowel movements. What did you hear, man?"

"Well, like I said, I was in the loo, the one round the corner reserved for staff only. The three blokes over there came in to use the urinals. The toilets were empty apart from them." Martin began to sweat and his breathing became erratic.

"Calm down, man," Simon snapped irritably. "You'll give yourself a heart attack."

Martin took a deep breath before continuing. "The one in the blue top seems to be in charge. I heard him say they would do the job tonight. Burn this place to the ground."

"You sure he was talking about the Sapphire?"

"Oh yes, boss, there's no doubt about it. I heard them discussing where they were going to set the fire. Then one of them, the younger one with the long hair, said they would do the other two clubs tomorrow night. I assume he meant the Topaz and the Emerald."

"Right," Simon said thoughtfully. "You go about your business but stay close in case you're needed. Freddie, you come with me."

Both men walked over to the three Irishmen who were now standing at the bar drinking.

"Good evening, gentlemen," Simon said politely. "I'm afraid I'm going to have to ask you all to leave the premises."

"Leave? Why in heaven would you be asking us to leave?" said the man in the blue top.

"We have a strict dress code, sir, no jeans or trainers allowed in the club, and certainly no hoodies."

"Well, that's easily sorted," the man in the blue top grinned, putting down his beer glass. "We'll take them off. What do you say, fellas? Should we get naked?"

All three men laughed heartily at this suggestion.

"I don't want any trouble," Simon said sternly. "Please leave the club now."

"Do you know how much we've spent tonight in this poxy club? Nobody objected to our clothes when they were taking our money," he growled.

"Well, I'm objecting now. I want you all off the premises."

"Fuck this," hissed the younger man. "Do you know how much cash I've put down that bird's knickers tonight?" He indicated a pretty brunette dancing on one of the podiums. "I want a private dance in the booth before I leave." He walked towards the girl and tried to grab her wrist. Within seconds, Freddie and Simon pulled him away and frogmarched him to the exit. They were joined immediately by Martin.

"I want all of you out now," Simon ordered.

"Come on, let's go, boys," said the man in the blue top. "It's a dive here anyway. Let's go and find some real action."

All three men left the club and went out into the car park. Simon watched as they got into a white transit van and pulled away. Carefully he made a note of the number.

Back in the club, Simon made his way to the small office and picked up the telephone. He rang Karl's number but there was no reply.

"Fuck," he hissed. "Where the hell are you?" He dialled a second number. This was answered almost immediately. "Joe, it's Simon. We've got some trouble, mate. I can't get hold of Karl but I need help here at the Sapphire." He quickly relayed to Joe what had happened.

"I'll be there as soon as I can," Joe said, putting on his coat. "Sorry, love," he said softly, turning to his companion who was laying on the couch, "It's business. I have to go over to Bradford. I don't know how long I'm going to be."

"Don't worry, Joe, it's time I was leaving anyway," Erica smiled. "I don't want Karl getting home before me, do I?"

He kissed her gently on the mouth. "I'll ring for a taxi before I go."

EIGHTY-ONE

It was three o'clock in the morning. The Sapphire Club was in darkness. Simon, Freddy and three of the minders were inside the club whilst Joe and Peter were outside in the shadows.

"Someone's coming," Peter whispered as a white transit van slowly snaked its way into the car park, its headlights dimmed. Three men climbed out of the vehicle and made their way to the van's rear doors. Each one picked up a two gallon drum of petrol and headed towards the club's rear exit.

"Now!" Joe shouted as he and Peter ran towards the men. "Get the bastards!"

Suddenly the club doors burst open and Simon and the three minders ran out into the car park. The three Irishmen dropped the petrol drums and attempted to get back into the van but were dragged out by Joe and Peter.

"What the fuck do you think you're doing?" Joe yelled as he punched one of the men in the face. All three men tried to fight but they had been drinking heavily all night and their reactions were slow. Peter grabbed the youngest of the three and head-butted him, causing him to fall to the ground screaming in pain as blood poured out of his nose.

"Who are you?" Joe demanded, addressing the man in the blue top who Martin had identified as the ringleader. "Who sent you?"

The Irishman merely spat in Joe's face by way of reply.

"Fuck you," he screamed in defiance.

The man Peter had grabbed attempted to run away but one of the minders grabbed him by the hair, punching him hard before dragging him back.

"Please," he pleaded. "No harm done. We're out of here, okay? We were just drunk and…"

"Bollocks!" Simon yelled. "You weren't drunk when you were planning this earlier tonight. Now, last chance, mate, who sent you?"

The young man trembled in terror as Simon pinned him against the side of the van and brought his fist back menacingly. "Well?"

"It was Charlotte," he whimpered. "Charlotte told us to burn Karl's clubs down."

"Who the fuck's Charlotte?"

"She's a cousin. She was mad at him and asked us to help her get even with him. That's all I know." He began to shake uncontrollably and tears of pain ran down his face. "Please, can we go now? We'll go back to Ireland and you'll never see or hear from us again. Isn't that right, lads?"

His two companions, who had each received a kicking off the two minders, were heaped on the floor groaning.

"Get the bastards out of here," Joe ordered.

"Not yet," insisted Simon. "We can't just let them go. We have to find out who Charlotte is and what's going on here."

"I said let them go," Joe said angrily. "I'll deal with Charlotte, don't worry about her."

"You know her?"

"No more questions, Simon. Just let them go. They'll not give us any more trouble. Isn't that right, lads?" All three nodded.

Joe walked over to the van and opened the rear doors. Inside were half a dozen more drums of petrol. "Get these out," he ordered two of the minders. "We don't want them getting any ideas about coming back, do we?" He watched as Martin and another minder removed the drums from the vehicle.

"Now piss off back where you came from before I change my mind," he growled addressing the three men. "If I ever see you around here again, you'll regret it. Believe me."

All three men climbed into the van. Simon stood back as it roared into life and made its way onto the road.

"Follow them," he ordered Freddy, throwing him his car keys.

"Take a couple of lads with you and make sure they head for home."

"Sure thing, Si," Freddy said. "Martin, Steve, I want you to come with me."

When the vehicles had left the car park, Simon turned to face Joe.

"I hope you know what you're doing, letting them leave like that. Karl won't like it."

"Don't worry, Si. I'll deal with it."

"Who is this Charlotte they were talking about? Is she one of Karl's girls?"

"No, not exactly."

"For fuck's sake, Joe, don't be so evasive. That fucking bitch tried to have the Sapphire burnt to the ground. I have a right to know what's going on."

"Simon, for the last time, let it be. I'll speak to you tomorrow, okay?"

"I suppose so," Simon said sulkily as he headed towards the club.

Joe's car had just pulled out of the car park when Simon's phone rang.

"Karl, thank goodness you rang. I've been trying to get hold of you all night…"

EIGHTY-TWO

Karl enjoyed the drive up the M1. The road was almost deserted and he was able to think clearly without the distraction of driving through traffic. He felt a glow of satisfaction at his encounter with Guido Rosso. Guido had inflicted pain and humiliation on his beloved daughter Christina. That was enough reason for him to seek revenge. He smiled as he thought of Christina, the daughter up to a few days ago he hadn't known existed. He had such plans for her future. She would share his house and he would provide her with the business she had always dreamt of.

He turned his attention to Alex. Of course he would have to keep Alex on a tight leash for the time being where money was concerned. Karl grinned as he remembered the look on his son's face when he told him he had picked up the forty thousand pounds of debt from Jonny Dalton. Yes, Alex was a smart boy. He would do exactly as he was told, Karl was sure of that.

It was a pity Alex turned his back on the medical profession though. He quite liked the idea of having a doctor for a son. On the other hand, he was looking for a successor to take over the business one day and who better than his own son? He would discuss that with Alex later.

The main problem facing him was what to tell Erica. He couldn't exactly tell her he was still married to Lisa and that he had two children to her. Meek and mild as she was, even Erica wouldn't stand for that. Perhaps if he let Erica think the kids were from a relationship, not from a marriage, he might just about get away with it. After all, Erica had done exactly what she had been told for almost twenty-five years. There was no reason to suppose she would find the courage to cause him any trouble.

That just left Lisa. Lisa was a problem. Karl wasn't sure about his feelings for her. She had been the love of his life when he was young. He adored her in his own way but Lisa was much more headstrong than Erica. He smiled as he put his hand up to his right ear and felt the scar where she had hit him with a dinner plate after he had complained about her cooking. Yes, Lisa always did have a fiery temper.

Lisa had built a new life for herself in London, but would she want to stay there when both her children were in Leeds with him, he wondered? He had been reminded of Lisa the very first time he saw Erica. She was the same slim build, the same golden blonde hair, even her eyes the same shade of blue. Erica had only been fourteen at the time, but Karl knew if he couldn't have Lisa, then Erica would be a very good substitute. The incident with her father had made sure she would never be able to leave him, not like Lisa had done.

Karl suppressed a yawn and rubbed at his eyes with his left fist. He looked at the clock on the dashboard and saw it was almost four o'clock. It was then he realised that he had turned off his mobile phone. He quickly switched it on and glanced at the screen. There were three missed calls from Simon at the Sapphire, the last one only thirty minutes ago. Karl quickly dialled Simon's number.

"Karl, thank goodness you rang. I've been trying to get hold of you all night..."

EIGHTY-THREE

Karl's car screeched to a halt as he pulled onto his drive. Opening the front door of his house, he ascended the stairs two at a time. Once he reached the landing, he went straight to the bedroom at the back where Charlotte was sleeping. Without knocking, he flung the door open and switched on the light.

"Charlotte, what the hell...?" he shouted. It took a few seconds for him to realise that the bed was empty. He quickly turned and ran towards his own bedroom, just as Erica came out of the room and onto the landing.

"Karl, what on earth's the matter?" she asked sleepily, rubbing her eyes. "Is everything alright?"

"No, it fucking isn't alright. Where is she?" he yelled, shaking Erica violently by the shoulders. "Where the fuck is that little bitch?"

"If you mean Charlotte, she's gone. She left yesterday." Erica struggled to free herself from Karl's iron grip but he held firm.

"Where has she gone? You'd better tell me the truth or I swear to God, I'll..."

"Let go of me," Erica whimpered, "you're hurting me."

Karl released his grip and pushed her into the bedroom and onto the bed. "Well?" he demanded, standing menacingly over her. "I won't ask you again."

"Charlotte came here yesterday afternoon with Patrick," she faltered. "She packed her case and left. She said they were going touring around England for a few days before going back to Ireland."

Karl sat on the side of the bed, his breathing heavy and erratic. "Get my pills out of the drawer," he demanded.

Obediently Erica handed Karl his pills and got a glass of water from the bathroom.

"What has she done, Karl?" she asked timidly. "You shouldn't get yourself worked up like this, it's not good for you. You know what the doctor said."

"Fuck the doctor," he spat. "That little bitch tried to get the Sapphire burnt down."

"No, that can't be right," Erica protested. "Charlotte's a good girl. She wouldn't do anything like that."

"Wouldn't she? I told you from day one there was something wrong about her. Did she say anything to you about wanting to destroy the clubs?"

"No, not a word."

"Are you absolutely sure?" Karl snarled. "You and Marion seemed to spend a lot of time with her. She must have said something. Think, woman."

"Karl, I promise you she didn't. What makes you think it was Charlotte?"

"The three Irish thugs that tried to burn me down said so. One of them said he was her cousin. What I don't understand is why she would want to destroy the clubs."

"Couldn't you get the men to tell you more?"

"If I'd been at the Sapphire, believe me, they wouldn't have got off so lightly, but I was dealing with another matter. Joe and Simon were at the club when it all kicked off. I think Joe's going soft. He just gave them all a good kicking and put them back on the ferry. I'll be having words with him later."

"Well, it's over now," Erica said softly. "Come to bed, Karl, you need your rest."

"Rest? I won't rest until I've got my hands round Charlotte's scrawny little neck. Anyway, who's this bloke she's with?"

"His name's Patrick. I don't really know much about him but he seems very nice."

"Do you think he's behind it? A rival wanting to muscle in on my business?"

"I wouldn't think so, Karl. Patrick is a solicitor. Solicitors don't go around burning down clubs, do they?"

"Well, somebody wanted my clubs gone and I won't rest until I know who and why."

Erica climbed under the duvet. "I'm tired," she yawned. "Are you coming to bed?"

"No, I need a drink," Karl grunted, slamming the bedroom door and making his way down the stairs.

EIGHTY-FOUR

Joe was woken early the next morning by the sound of banging on the door of his flat. The bedside clock showed seven fifteen.

"Who the bloody hell's that?" he muttered to himself as he climbed out of bed and walked over to the door.

"Marion? What on earth's the matter? Do you know what time it is?" he grumbled, releasing the chain from the door.

"Never mind that," Marion cried breathlessly, "I have something to show you."

Marion pushed past Joe and went into the lounge. "Look," she said, retrieving an A4 piece of paper from her bag. "Look at this, Joe."

Joe walked over to the table and picked up the document.

"It was amongst some old papers of Paula's," Marion said excitedly. "I hadn't paid much attention to them before. In fact, I'd offered everything belonging to Paula to young Charlotte, but look here. You know what this means?"

Joe was silent as he stared at the document, a death certificate, in the name of Thomas Edward Meadows. Thomas Edward Meadows was the name of Erica's father, the paedophile who Erica believed she had bludgeoned to death when she was fourteen years old.

"It says he was stabbed," Marion cried excitedly, pointing to the entry stating the cause of death. "Look, '*multiple stab wounds*', that's what killed him. Erica has been innocent all this time. It must have been that bloody Karl that killed him and let poor Erica take the blame."

Joe stared at the document for several seconds.

"The bastard," he hissed. "I'll kill him. I swear to God, I'll kill the lowlife bastard!"

Marion reached over to Joe and held his arm. "Calm down, love," she said softly. "There's time for revenge when we get Erica safely away from him." She guided Joe to the couch and they sat down.

"I bet that's what Paula was blackmailing him with," she said thoughtfully.

"I know Erica confided in Paula about what she had done to her father when they were in care," Joe said quietly.

"We can't let him get away with this," Marion said determinedly. "That's two people Karl's killed. He's got to be stopped."

"Don't worry," Joe spoke almost in a whisper. "Karl's going to get what's coming to him. I can promise you that."

"You need to take Erica as far away from that evil bastard as you can get."

"That's just what I'm planning to do."

"You'll have to be careful though. You know what he's like. He will come after you."

"Don't worry about him. Karl won't be making trouble for either of us. I think it's about time I cashed in my insurance."

"What do you mean? Cashed in your insurance?"

"Never mind. Just a little something I've been saving up."

Joe went into his bedroom and returned a few minutes later dressed.

"Be careful, Joe. Karl can be…"

"Don't worry, Marion. I can handle Karl. He's probably on his way to the club now. I'll ring Erica on my way there."

"Joe, don't you think we should call the police? Let them handle it?"

"No, not the police. This is something I have to deal with. I should have dealt with it a long time ago. Oh, by the way, before I forget, I have some news about your granddaughter."

"Charlotte? What's she been up to?"

Joe outlined what had occurred the previous evening at the Sapphire Club.

"Oh, the silly girl, she'll be getting herself killed. She's not still at Erica's, is she?"

"No, Erica rang me yesterday. Charlotte left with that guy from Ireland. Patrick, I think he's called."

"If Karl finds her he'll…"

"Don't worry, he won't find her. She's quite safe. Charlotte asked me to give you this." He handed Marion a piece of paper. "It's her new mobile number. She wants you to give her a ring as soon as you can."

"Oh, the poor kid, she must be terrified."

"Charlotte is a very capable young woman, believe me," Joe said, walking purposefully towards the door.

"Be careful, Joe," Marion said but he was already out on the street, heading towards his car.

Left alone, Marion picked up the phone and dialled the number Joe had given her.

EIGHTY-FIVE

It was just before eight when Lydia arrived home. Worried by the text she had received from Matthew late the previous evening, she had driven the three hour journey home at speed. As she entered her lounge, Matthew was standing by the window staring out into the garden, his hands thrust deep in his trouser pockets. David was sitting in the armchair smoking.

"Had a good time, dear?" David asked in a tone laced with sarcasm.

Lydia stared at her husband in disgust. He looked different, she thought. He seemed to have aged twenty years in the short time she had been away. His hair was untidy and his clothes dishevelled. She noticed he held a glass of whisky in his hand.

"Welcome home, mother," Matthew said quietly as he walked over to his mother and gently kissed her on the cheek.

"What's happened? Your text said it was urgent. Has he lost his job? I thought the hearing wasn't until next week."

David gave a harsh laugh. "Go on, Matthew. Tell your mother. I know you're dying to." He gulped down the remains of the whisky and reached over to the table to pour another.

"Isn't it a bit early to get pissed?" Lydia spat. "Even for you?"

"If I want a fucking drink in my own house, I'll fucking well have one, you stony faced bitch," he slurred.

Lydia sat down heavily on the couch and turned to her son. "Matthew, what the hell's going on?"

Matthew sat beside his mother and put his arm around her shoulders. "Mother," he said softly, "I thought it only right that you should know. Father has a daughter."

"A daughter? I don't understand."

"He has a daughter to a prostitute. Isn't that right, father?"

"So it would seem. She must be almost twenty now by my reckoning."

"I met her the other day," Matthew continued. "Her name is Charlotte and she's living in Karl Maddox's house."

"She's what? Oh no, I don't believe this. Tell me it's not true, David."

"Matthew seems to think it is. I've never met her so I wouldn't know."

"Who's the mother?" Lydia asked, turning to her son. "You say she's a prostitute? Are you sure?"

"Charlotte told me so herself. She said her mother died when she was a baby. She got adopted by Erica Maddox's sister who lived in Ireland."

"David, please tell me this isn't true. It can't be true. Even you couldn't be so cruel."

"I hope it is true," David said angrily as he got up from the chair and walked unsteadily over to his wife. "I hope I do have a daughter. A sweet, beautiful girl just like her mother was."

Lydia rose from the couch and raised her hand to slap David's face. He grabbed it and roughly pushed her back onto the couch. Matthew bolted forward to shield his mother.

"That's enough, you leave her alone, you bastard," he yelled. "Are you alright, mother?"

Tears streamed down Lydia's face. "Just get that bastard out of my house."

"Don't worry, I'm going," David sneered. "I don't want to spend another minute in this fucking mausoleum."

"Get back to your whores where you belong," Lydia screamed at him. "I'm going to divorce you, David. By the time I've finished with you, you'll have nothing. Nothing, do you understand?"

David staggered out into the hallway and unsteadily made his way upstairs. A few minutes later he came down carrying a holdall.

"I'll collect the rest of my things later," he hissed as he opened the front door. "I'm going to find my daughter."

He slammed the door loudly behind him to the sound of Lydia sobbing uncontrollably.

EIGHTY-SIX

It was just after eight when Erica heard Karl shut the front door noisily and rev up the car's engine. She waited until he was gone before she dared to venture downstairs. Picking up the telephone, she rang Charlotte's number but the phone rang unobtainable. Panicking, she rang Joe's mobile and it was answered almost immediately.

"Erica, I was just about to ring you. Is everything alright over there?"

"No," Erica sobbed. "Karl's gone crazy. He's accusing Charlotte of trying to have the Sapphire burnt down last night. That can't be true, can it?"

"I'm afraid it is, but don't worry about Charlotte, she's quite safe. It's you I'm concerned about."

"What do you mean? Please tell me what's going on, you're scaring me."

"Erica, I need you to trust me," Joe said sternly. "You do trust me, don't you, darling?"

"Of course I do, you don't need to ask that."

"Then please, do exactly as I tell you. I want you to pack a few clothes and your passport. I'm taking you away from Karl forever."

"Joe, you know I can't leave him. He'll…"

"Erica, please just do as I say. Everything will be alright, I promise. Now hurry up, we don't have much time."

"Well, alright," Erica faltered, "if you're sure, but…"

"When you're packed, get a taxi to the Belmont Café on Richmond Street, you know the one. I want you to wait for me there, okay?"

"Where are you going? Why don't you come here and collect me?"

"There's something I have to deal with first, but I should be with you before ten. Now hurry up and get out of that house as soon as you can."

"Alright," Erica said hesitantly. "I'll see you at ten, and Joe…"

"Yes?"

"I do love you."

Erica ran upstairs and quickly got showered and dressed before piling clothes into a suitcase. He heart was racing. She couldn't believe that she was actually going to be leaving Karl after all this time. Walking over to the safe concealed behind a wall mirror, Erica tapped out the combination and its door flung open. She grinned as she remembered how she had watched Karl open it one night when he had been drunk. He thought she had been asleep but she had managed to memorise the numbers. She had been into the safe a few times over the years hoping to find the paperweight Karl had been blackmailing her with, but without success.

Erica had only intended to take her passport and jewellery but she was astounded to see several large bundles of twenty pound notes inside plastic bags. For a few seconds she stared at the money. Grinning, she reached out and placed the bundles into her bag. "You owe me this, you bastard," she hissed. Removing her wedding ring, she placed it on the bedside table before going downstairs to order a taxi.

EIGHTY-SEVEN

Joe had almost reached the club when his phone rang. It was Karl.

"I'll be there in ten minutes," Joe spoke into the receiver.

"Make it five," Karl snapped. "You and I have things to discuss."

Karl was in the main club when Joe arrived. He looked angry as he strode menacingly towards him.

"What the fuck were you playing at last night, letting those wankers off scot free? Are you going soft?"

"They didn't get off scot free. The lads gave them a good kicking. They've learnt their lesson, they won't be back."

"You shouldn't have let them go until I'd spoken to them," Karl screamed almost hysterically. "I need to know why they were targeting my clubs. I need to know exactly what that little bitch Charlotte's involvement was in it, and I need…"

"What you need to do, Karl, is answer your bloody phone. Si tried to get hold of you half a dozen times last night."

"I was busy," Karl answered sulkily. "It's up to you and Si to take care of things when I'm not around."

"And that's exactly what we did, for all the thanks we get. Anyway, I haven't come here to talk about your poxy clubs." Joe took out the death certificate from his coat pocket and held it up in front of Karl. "I came here to discuss this."

Karl stared at the document. Joe could see the colour drain from his cheeks, leaving him looking pale and ashen.

"Where the fuck did you get that?" he demanded, attempting to snatch the paper from Joe's grasp.

"That doesn't matter. It says here that Thomas Edward Meadows, that's Erica's father, died from multiple stab wounds."

"So?"

"So, you've been bullying Erica all these years by saying that she killed him with a blow to the head."

Karl stared at Joe, a look of anger and suspicion on his face. "How did you know about that?"

"Erica told me."

"Did she tell you that her father was a bastard paedophile?" Karl spluttered. "He ruined his first girl and was planning to do the same to her. He had to be stopped."

"So tell me, what really happened that night Erica asked for your help?"

"It's got nothing to do with you. That's between me and Erica."

"Not any more it isn't," Joe said defiantly.

"What do you mean? What has Erica been saying?"

"She said you told her that her father was dead, that she had killed him. But he wasn't dead, was he, Karl? He was still alive when you dumped him in Coopers Alley. It's time you started telling the truth about what really happened that night."

"What does it matter now? The bastard's dead. He can't hurt any kid again."

"Erica thinks she's responsible. You've got to tell her the truth."

"I don't have to do anything," Karl said menacingly. "He's dead and as far as I'm concerned, that's an end to it." He retrieved a cigar from his jacket pocket and lit it. "Has Erica seen that?" he asked, nodding towards the certificate. "Does she know how that bastard died?"

"Not yet, but she will, I promise you that."

"What's in this for you anyway? I never had you down as a good Samaritan."

"Erica has to know the truth. You can't keep lying to her."

Karl drew heavily on his cigar and slowly walked over to one of the tables at the far side of the room. He sat down and indicated for Joe to join him.

Joe declined, choosing to stand. "Well? I'm waiting."

"Alright," Karl said at last. "I'll tell you if it'll shut you up." He drew heavily on the cigar once more before continuing.

"When I went over to the house, Erica was hysterical. She told me what he tried to do to her, and that she had hit him with a paperweight. He was lying on the floor, his head covered in blood. I really did think he was dead. I put him in the boot of my car and drove over to Coopers Alley. I thought if I made it look like a mugging…"

"Yes, I know all this. But what happened next?"

"When I pulled the bastard out of the boot, he started to come round. He began grunting like the pig that he was and managed to stumble to his feet." Karl put the glass to his lips and drank the contents in one gulp. "Before I realised it, I had the knife in my hand. I don't know how many times I stabbed him. All I could think about was what he had been planning to do to Erica." Karl's breathing became laboured and he was trembling slightly as he continued. "He deserved it, Joe. The bastard deserved to die. You'd have done exactly the same in the circumstances, you know you would."

"Who knows? Perhaps I would," Joe said, almost in a whisper. "Maybe he did deserve to die, but I would never let a fourteen year old girl believe she was responsible. I'd never have done that. That was a wicked thing to do."

Karl leant forward putting his head between his hands. "Yes, I felt bad about that," he sighed, "but you have to understand I was head over heels in love with Erica. I couldn't bear it if she left me, and she'd never leave me, not when she thought I knew her dark secret." He got up from the chair and walked over to the bar, poured himself another drink and returned to the table. "I've looked after her over the years. She can have anything she wants, money, clothes, anything."

"She doesn't love you," Joe said sternly. "The poor girl's terrified of you."

"Rubbish. You don't know what you're talking about. Anyway, what business is it of yours? You're just the hired help."

"Erica's leaving you."

"Leaving me? What are you talking about? Erica would never leave me."

"She's coming with me."

"Are you out of your fucking mind?"

"Karl, Erica and I have been lovers for years. Once she knows the truth, you'll have no hold on her anymore."

Karl sprang to his feet, screaming profanities as he hurled himself at Joe. Both men went crashing to the floor. Joe managed to free himself from Karl's grip and get to his feet.

"That's enough," he yelled. "Erica's leaving with me and there's nothing you can do about it."

"You try and take my wife and I'll come after you. I'll find you and I'll kill you, I'll kill both of you."

"I don't think so," Joe hissed. "I have a little insurance of my own. Remember Paula?"

"Paula? Who the fuck's Paula?"

"Surely you haven't forgotten? Paula's the girl you stabbed to death in Canal Street."

"Oh, her? That stupid little bitch tried blackmailing me. She tried to take me for ten grand."

"That's a lot of money. What had she got on you?"

"Somehow she'd found out about how Erica's father had died. She rang me and demanded the money or she would tell Erica and the police."

"So that's why you went looking for her that night? To kill her?"

"I had no choice, surely you can see that? Even if I'd paid her the money, there would have been no guarantee she'd keep her mouth shut. Anyway, what's that little scrubber got to do with anything after all these years? That's all in the past."

"The knife you used to kill her isn't in the past. That's very much in the present."

"What do you mean, in the present? You got rid of the knife that night."

"No, Karl, I kept it. In fact the knife is with my solicitor right now, along with a letter to the police telling them where to find Paula's body. If you try to harm either me or Erica, it gets posted."

"You bastard," Karl spat. "You fucking bastard. After all I've done for you." A cold anger swept through his body and he could feel the sweat trickling down the back of his neck. His hands began to tremble. "So tell me, what are you planning? To disappear into the sunset with the beautiful Erica by your side? It'll never work. She's too good for you. You'll never make her happy."

"Shut the fuck up," Joe yelled. "You don't know what you're talking about." He walked towards the door leading to the foyer. "Oh, there's something else you might want to know."

"What's that?"

"Charlotte is Paula's daughter."

"What? Paula's daughter? I... I don't understand. How...? When...?"

But the room was empty. Joe was already in his car heading towards the Belmont Cafe.

EIGHTY-EIGHT

Erica sat nervously at the table in the Belmont Café. It was a popular venue for office workers who popped in each morning for their fancy caffeine fix. Erica had just finished her cappuccino and croissant when she saw two familiar faces coming towards her.

"Shirley," she greeted as Shirley and Colin approached.

"I thought it was you," Shirley grinned drawing up a chair to the table. "I'm so glad to see you, Erica, I'd have hated leaving and not saying goodbye."

"Karl did mention you were retiring," Erica lied. What Karl had actually said was that he had sacked both her and Colin.

Colin gave a roguish grin as he joined the two women. "Good morning, Erica, I want you to be one of the first to know." He reached over and held up Shirley's left hand showing a shiny gold band.

"You've got married? Oh that's wonderful," Erica smiled.

"This morning," he beamed. "Leeds Register Office at eight forty-five." He leant down and kissed Shirley's hand affectionately.

"Congratulations. I hope you'll both be very happy." Erica put her arm around Shirley, giving her a hug. "So, you'll be off to start your new life in Scotland?"

"Well, no, not exactly," Colin said slightly embarrassed. "That's what we want people to think, what we want Karl to think really."

"We're going to live in Spain," Shirley blurted excitedly. "We go there next week. Colin's bought a villa by the sea. It's wonderful, Erica, you'd love it. Four bedrooms, two balconies and…"

"We'd prefer it if you kept that to yourself," Colin suddenly became serious. "Things could become… well, a little awkward

I suppose when Karl finds out I… err … well, let's just say…"
He removed his glasses and began polishing them furiously with
a paper napkin.

"Don't worry, Colin, your secret's safe with me," Erica smiled
reassuringly.

"Let's all have a nice cappuccino to celebrate," Colin suggested.
Replacing his glasses, he walked over to the counter.

It was then that Shirley noticed the luggage down the side
of the table. "Going anywhere nice, Erica?" she asked, nodding
towards the cases.

Erica looked at her friend, tears stinging her eyes. "I've left
him, Shirley," she whispered, her body trembling slightly. "I've
left Karl and I'm going away with Joe. He should be here soon."

"About bloody time," Shirley grinned. "I don't know what
you saw in that bully. I hated him, I don't mind telling you."
Colin joined them at the table. "Did you hear that, love? Erica
has left that bastard Karl and is running off with Joe. Isn't that
wonderful?"

Colin took Erica's hand and gently squeezed it. "I think you've
done the right thing," he said with sincerity. "The things I know
about that man, you wouldn't believe. You'll be so much happier
with Joe. I've always thought so."

"What do you mean?" Shirley said indignantly. "You knew
about Joe and Erica and never said anything to me?"

"Of course I knew, dear," he said as he patted Shirley's hand
kindly. "A blind man could see they were in love."

"Oh dear, I thought we were being discreet," Erica blushed.

"Nothing much gets past me, isn't that right, Shirley?"

Shirley nodded in agreement. "That's right, very astute is
Colin."

Erica checked her watch looked anxiously out of the window.

"Don't worry, he'll be here," Shirley said reassuringly. "We'll
wait with you until he gets here."

"Thanks," Erica smiled appreciatively. "He shouldn't be long.
He said he'd be here by ten and it's only a quarter to."

The waitress came over to the table carrying a tray with the three drinks. Colin nodded and smiled his appreciation. Shirley stared out of the window and for a few minutes there was silence.

"Cedar Road's just down there," Shirley said wistfully, pointing down the street opposite. "That was my beat when I first started working for Karl."

"Yes, I remember. Karl gave up the street girls when he opened the clubs and the agency. He said it made him a lot more money with half the hassle."

"That's right. It's been taken over by foreigners now. Nasty, vicious little bastards most of them from what I've heard." Shirley sipped her coffee. "I have some very happy memories working in Cedar Road. I made some good mates there. They've all moved on now, of course."

"Don't you see any of the girls?" Erica asked.

"Susie's still knocking around. I bump into her now and again. She's looking rough these days. I think she's on drugs, the silly cow."

"Was Susie the tall thin girl who loved wearing red plastic?"

"Yes, that's Susie. Then there was Lynda. I hear she married a punter and lives the high life now down in London. Always did land on her feet did Lynda."

"I don't remember her."

"You won't do, she wasn't with Karl long. It's young Paula that I miss the most," Shirley sighed. "She just left one night and never came back. She went off with that boyfriend of hers most probably. It would have been nice if she'd said goodbye though. You knew Paula, didn't you, Erica?"

"Yes, we were both in care at the same time."

"I don't suppose she ever got in touch with you after she left?"

Erica shook her head but remained silent.

"There were rumours that she had a kid, but I don't know if that's true. Paula was always talking of running off with this bloke. She said he was the love of her life. He was a policeman, can you believe that? A bloody policeman of all things. The stories Paula would tell about what he got up to, you wouldn't believe." Shirley took out an e-cigarette from her bag and put it to her lips. "You see over there by the side of the pub, that's Coopers Alley. Paula told me her policeman friend found his first dead body in there. A schoolteacher he was. He got mugged, throat cut from ear to ear. I still can't walk past there without getting the shivers."

Erica sat bolt upright and stared attentively at Shirley. "A schoolteacher? Are you sure about that, Shirley?"

"Yes, of course I'm sure. It was in all the papers at the time. They never did catch who did it." Shirley sipped at her coffee and turned to face her friend. "Erica, are you alright, love? You've gone as white as a sheet."

"I'm not surprised she looks faint, all this talk of murder," Colin snapped. "This is meant to be a happy time, Shirley. We should be... Oh look, Erica. It's Joe. Hey, Joe," he shouted. "We're over here."

EIGHTY-NINE

Karl sat motionless for a few minutes after Joe had left. His breathing became laboured. His vision was blurred and a dull pain filled his chest as sweat trickled down the back of his neck. Erica, gone? She couldn't be gone, she belonged to him. Joe and Erica together? This wasn't right. Erica was his wife. They had to be stopped. He must stop them. Karl stumbled unsteadily out into the foyer. His office. He must get to his office. He had to think, to plan.

"Are you okay, boss?" It was Peter. "You don't look well, Karl."

"I'm fine," he replied as he slowly climbed the stairs.

"David Glendenning's here. I told him to wait in your office."

"What the fuck does he want?" Karl muttered, more to himself than to Peter. "I can't see anybody now, I've things to do."

David was standing by the window with his back to the room when Karl entered. He was used to seeing his friend well-groomed and smartly dressed so David's dishevelled appearance surprised him.

"What's up?" he asked abruptly. "I'm too busy for a chat this morning, David. I've got stuff to do and…"

He stopped as David turned round to face him. David's eyes were bloodshot and tears were streaming down his face, a face that hadn't seen a razor in several days.

"Christ, man, what's happened to you? You look bloody awful."

David was sobbing silently but did not speak.

Karl walked over to the cabinet and poured two large whiskies. "Here, drink this," he said, handing him a glass.

David took the glass and drank the contents in one gulp.

"Well, what's happened? Have those bastards given you the

push? Don't worry if they have. I told you there's always a job here for you. I…"

"I heard what you said," David spoke in almost a whisper, his body trembling. "I was down there," he indicated the cupboard leading to the back stairs. "I heard everything you said to Joe. Everything."

Karl was breathless as he reached for his pills from the desk drawer. "David, believe me that bastard Meadows deserved to die. He was a paedophile, a dirty, filthy kiddy fiddler. He tried to seduce my Erica. I had to kill him, he…"

"Meadows? I don't give a fuck about Meadows. I'm talking about Paula. You killed my Paula."

"Paula? What the fuck's she got to do with anything? Paula was nothing but a cheap little tart who tried her hand at blackmail. She got what she deserved."

David sat heavily on the couch placing his bowed head in his hands. "I killed a girl once," he said shakily. "That skinny little thing who worked here. The one that was raped by Victor."

"Lindsay? You killed Lindsay? What the fuck did you do that for?"

"I was at the station the night she reported the rape. Lindsay recognised me when I came to the club's opening. She threatened to tell my wife and my boss that I was a member at the Emerald." Tears began to roll down his cheeks and he wiped them away with his coat sleeve. "I did her in her flat a couple of days later. I was so angry. I kept hitting her and hitting her. The ironic thing though is that I was put in charge of the investigation into her death. Can you believe that? Those stupid bastards at the station didn't have a clue." He drained his glass before continuing. "But there isn't a day goes by that I don't think about that poor kid."

"Well, you more than most will understand that sometimes things have to be done for the greater good. Both our lives have been better since these people were eliminated."

"Eliminated? You mean murdered."

"We both did what had to be done. It's over now, let's just forget about it and move on."

"Move on? I can't move on, not without Paula. I loved her, don't you understand? We were going to be together and… Where's Charlotte? I have to speak to Charlotte. I have to explain to her about…"

"Don't talk to me about Charlotte. She's in big trouble when I find her."

"What are you planning to do? Kill her like you killed her mother?"

Karl leaned back in his chair, his chest pains were getting stronger. "I need an ambulance," he gasped, reaching for the telephone. He attempted to dial for help but David snatched the phone from his grasp.

"Tell me where she is. Charlotte's my daughter and I have a right to see her." David was yelling now, his face contorted with rage as he grabbed Karl by the shoulders. "What have you done with her? I need to see her."

"She's gone," Karl said in almost a whisper. "I don't know where she is. Now let go of me, you stupid bastard. I need an ambulance."

David released his grip and walked back to the window. "The trouble with us, Karl, is that we both have bad blood. Maybe that's why we remained friends all these years." He laughed, the shrill laugh of a man losing his mind. "I came here to say goodbye. I was going to top myself."

"Don't be bloody stupid," Karl hissed breathlessly as he hurriedly dialled 999. "Nothing can be that bad, mate. Tomorrow things will look different – Ambulance – urgent – Karl Maddox – Emerald Club, Fleming Street – chest pains." He put down the receiver. "Now why don't you get yourself cleaned up and…"

Karl stared at his friend, panic beginning to take over from the pains in his chest. "What the fuck are you doing? Put that gun down, David. Don't point it at me, you stupid bastard."

"I hadn't planned to take you with me," David sobbed, "but you killed my Paula, my beautiful, sweet Paula, and now you're planning to kill my daughter. I can't let you do that."

"No, don't. Put the gun down. I'll leave Charlotte alone, believe me, David. I…"

Peter was in the foyer when he heard the first gunshot. He was halfway up the staircase when the second rang out.

NINETY

Joe and Erica were in the First Class Departure Lounge at Manchester Airport.

"I heard from Charlotte this morning," Erica said excitedly. "She's invited Marion to go to Ireland to live with her and Patrick."

"Good for her," Joe smiled. "I hope everything works out for her. She deserves some happiness."

"Well, I'm going to look round Duty Free for ten minutes," Erica smiled as she kissed Joe lightly on the cheek. "Do you want anything?"

"No, I'm fine. I'll just get a coffee and wait here, but don't be long, darling. The flight will be called in half an hour."

Erica waved as she lightly skipped over to the shops. She had never felt as happy as she did right now. Life with Joe was going to be wonderful, something she had always dreamt of but never thought would happen. Happily she began looking through the perfumes displayed in one of the glass cabinets when she felt someone touch her lightly on the shoulder.

"Erica, it is you, isn't it?" She turned round quickly, her heart racing. Behind her was an attractive black woman in her late thirties looking very stylish in a dark blue tailored trouser suit and pale pink blouse.

"Angela. Oh how lovely to see you after all these years." Both women embraced. "You're looking well. Joe will be so pleased to see you."

"Joe? My brother's here?"

"Yes, Joe and I are together now. He's in the Departure Lounge. We're going to France. Do you want to come and say hello?"

Angela looked anxious.

"Are you sure he still wants to see me after what I did? I really am sorry you know. It was a very bad time for me."

"Of course he wants to see you. He talks about you all the time, wondering what you're up to. Are you still with Ray?"

"Oh, please don't mention that man. I haven't seen him in years. Actually it was rather frightening what happened."

"What was frightening? What do you mean?"

"When we left Leeds after we stole the money, we went to Manchester and stayed in a hotel. We were walking back from a restaurant one night when a van pulled up and three men jumped out. They grabbed Ray and bundled him into the back of the van."

"Who were they?" Erica asked with concern.

"I honestly don't know. I was too frightened to report it to the police. I stayed at the hotel for a few more days but I didn't hear a word from Ray so eventually I left."

"Angie, you must have been terrified."

"Yes I was, but it made me take a long hard look at my life and I decided it had to change. I got a job as a receptionist in a hospital and that's how I met Josh."

"Josh?"

"This is him," she said proudly, taking out a photograph from her bag. "Josh is a doctor and these are our two boys, Nathan and Daniel." She quickly scribbled a telephone number on the back of the photograph before handing it to Erica.

"We're taking the kids to Disneyland," she grinned. "Will you ask Joe to give me a call in a couple of weeks when we get back? I miss him so much."

"Of course I will. He'll be so excited to get in touch."

"Angie, hurry up love, they're calling our flight."

Erica turned to see a handsome black man of about forty with a young boy in his arms and an older boy by his side.

"That's Josh," she beamed. "I must go, but please, give my love to Joe."

Erica waved goodbye and made her way back to the Departure Lounge.

Joe got a coffee and a newspaper from the stand. He felt worried. What if the threat of revealing the knife was not enough to stop Karl perusing them? Deciding to take Erica away had happened so quickly, he hadn't had time to make a proper plan. Joe knew he had to get her away from Karl as quickly as possible. He looked around anxiously, half expecting to see Karl bursting into the Departure Lounge at any moment.

He glanced casually at the newspaper's headlines and his posture stiffened. Joe's hands began to tremble. He read the article through twice. He couldn't believe what he was reading. There had been a fatal shooting at the Emerald Club. Karl had been shot by a policeman and seriously wounded. Chief Superintendent David Glendenning had been named as the suspect and he had then turned the gun on himself with fatal results. Why? Joe wondered. Why would David shoot Karl? They were supposed to be friends.

Slowly the tension that Joe had been feeling since his confrontation with Karl began to drain from his body. Karl being injured meant that he would not be able to follow them, for now at least. It gave him more time to make sure Erica was safe.

He looked up to see Erica coming towards him, a broad smile on her beautiful face. Without hesitation, Joe folded the newspaper and placed it firmly in the litter bin.

Printed in Great Britain
by Amazon